"I'll help free your s

His expression was one of a monumental challenge. But all she felt was disappointment. Tess already agreed to help without demands attached, and the way Louve was looking at her now, she felt that he would attach so many exceptions, her sister would forever be locked behind a door. Forever guarded by men who meant to do her harm. If she could scale towers, if she had coin to bargain. If she had anything else, she wouldn't be standing here with this man, whom...she could stare at the rest of her life and could never trust.

That took her beyond disappointment into irritation. "And I'm to trust you?"

His eyes flashed. "I said I'd do it."

"That's all you've said."

He lowered his chin. "I'll help you escape as well. Both of you."

That went without saying. "Before I tell you anything, give me something of you."

"Something of me," he said slowly as if the words were simple, but the meaning wasn't. "Such as..."

"Something...meaningful."

Author Note

Louve was far too complicated for any one romance, which is why readers have seen him in several books...but that just made him more complicated. Those friendships with Nicholas and Reynold changed him.

Here was this hero who came from a happy home, who cherished his friendships. But the happy home wasn't his own, and the woman he gave his heart to never accepted him. When he becomes a mercenary for the Warstones, he fights battles for their power; he plots intrigues for their wealth.

In all these years, never does he belong to one place...to one woman.

Along comes Biedeluue, who believes everything and everyone is hers. Have burdens? She'll take care of them. Can't till your own field? She'll earn coin for oxen.

But Louve? He has burdens she's not prepared for, and his heart? Well, that remains to be seen...

NICOLE LOCKE

The Maiden and the Mercenary

◆H HARLEQUIN
HISTORICAL

HARLEQUIN®
HISTORICAL™

Recycling programs for this product may not exist in your area.

ISBN-13: 978-1-335-50590-3

The Maiden and the Mercenary

This edition published by arrangement with Harlequin Books S.A.

For questions and comments about the quality of this book, please contact us at CustomerService@Harlequin.com.

Harlequin Enterprises ULC
22 Adelaide St. West, 40th Floor
Toronto, Ontario M5H 4E3, Canada
www.Harlequin.com

Printed in U.S.A.

Nicole Locke discovered her first romance novels in her grandmother's closet, where they were secretly hidden. Convinced that books that were hidden must be better than those that weren't, Nicole greedily read them. It was only natural for her to start writing them— but now not so secretly.

Books by Nicole Locke

Harlequin Historical

The Lochmore Legacy
Secrets of a Highland Warrior

Lovers and Legends
The Knight's Broken Promise
Her Enemy Highlander
The Highland Laird's Bride
In Debt to the Enemy Lord
The Knight's Scarred Maiden
Her Christmas Knight
Reclaimed by the Knight
Her Dark Knight's Redemption
Captured by Her Enemy Knight
The Maiden and the Mercenary

Visit the Author Profile page
at Harlequin.com for more titles.

Some stories can't be written without people who, just by your sitting and sitting...and sitting and sitting near them, eventually, graciously, become your friends.

So to you all at South Seattle Writers Group: Dan, Olin, Scot, Mark, Meg, Kelly, Cheri, Tony, Jamie, Lauren and Joe. Thanks for allowing me to be that strange woman in the corner. You can't possibly know how much it has meant to me.

And thanks to that Denny's on Fourth Avenue. The one that lets me sit at the bar...all day long. Thanks especially to Bobbie, Christina, Clark, Denetta, Kay, Linda, Mario. Oh, and I know I'm missing others! Please know, if I could be there now to pester you all, I would.

Chapter One

France—1297

Biedeluue wiped the back of her hand against her mouth and concentrated on the tower of goblets stacked on the well-worn table before her. The chanting crowd around her and her challenger jostled for a closer position and she shoved back.

'These hips of mine aren't moving for anyone!' She brandished the goblet in her hand and they all stepped merrily aside.

'I'll move your hips!'

Galen winked one eye, then the other much more slowly. Ah, not winking, but trying to focus through the haze of ale, like her.

'Attempting to move my hips when drunken is how you first fell to misfortune, Galen.' She pointed somewhere in the vicinity of his stack. 'Now, let's see how you apply yourself with smaller…goblets.'

'As if he could be so fortunate!' shouted Tess, from the baking ovens.

Someone clapped and everyone from the wafer maker to the cup bearer howled. The kitchens were normally bustling, but now, even the doorways were crammed with field people. The kitchens were as large as kingdoms, but even so, she heard a crash to her right as the crowd moved and several heads whipped around to see the destruction.

She didn't, however—any quick movement was ill-advised. How many gulps of ale had she had? She'd stopped counting after twenty, trusting the betting crowd had their own vested interest to keep track of the game.

It was up to her to stack the goblets for each gulp of ale. She narrowed her eyes at the wavering mound. Ten… twenty? Oh, maybe twenty-five gulps of ale.

Which meant Galen, the challenger, had also had twenty-five… No, he'd just thrown back another and grabbed a goblet to stack on top of the tower he'd made.

Damn him, his height and those arms that were twice as tall and…twice as many as he had before. Four arms? An unfair advantage to be sure!

'No helping!' she called out as Henry sneaked a supporting hand to Galen's back when he staggered backwards.

Henry lifted both his hands and she nodded her head at him in satisfaction. A mistake, which she fixed by widening her stance.

If Galen fell, she won. If Galen toppled his goblets before her, she won. And if she won, she got… She got…

She'd win! She liked that part best. Right now she needed to win. It was important because she wasn't winning at anything else and there was more at stake here.

A roiling wave to her stomach as her thoughts darkened. She blinked hard, peering at the raucous crowd and the goblets she had stupidly assembled entirely too high. She needed to put another on the top.

An easy task. All the tasks were easy. Stack the goblets, drink the drink and beat the brewer Galen, who reportedly hadn't lost a game of drink since he was a babe. That was a bet she could win because she hadn't lost a game of drink since she was a babe and she was older than Galen. In fact, she was older than most of the servants in the Warstone kitchens. The only ones older than her were the ones already with babies and who lived in the village outside the fortress.

She was old enough for a husband and family of her own, too, but had been avoiding any such connections. Entirely because of the village men who'd enjoyed manipulating a girl whose father had abandoned her, her four siblings and their weakened mother.

Though she couldn't imagine a family of her own, the one she had she'd do anything for. By the time she could, Biedeluue, after hours in the fields, helped her mother cook, clean and cuddle away the pain of scrapes and bruises of her siblings. When that wasn't enough, she had left to earn coin and only returned to give her mother and siblings what she could to ease her family's struggles.

All her siblings, save for one, were still in their village outside Lyon. And though she travelled to work, they still never left her in peace. They still needed her and she did what she could for them.

So when she received that scrap of parchment from the youngest, Margery, the one not at home, that she was in danger and to send their brothers immediately, Biedeluue didn't hesitate to rush to her aid, just as she'd always done before.

Because out of all the hardships she'd had to endure to save her family...the fact she couldn't save Margery from a worse fate pained her most of all. Margery, who always had to be protected because, when times became truly hard, the village men didn't stop at just Biedeluue.

What had happened to Margery now? That message. Hastily scrawled so that Biedeluue could barely read it. Not even signed, but she knew who'd written it because of one distinctive loop. Always the beautiful loops in the writing even if the message was terrifying.

However, after asking for work and gaining the trust of the servants, she didn't know how to aid her sister who was trapped here in this Warstone fortress. Bied had now been here for a fortnight and still hadn't seen or spoken to her sister. Wasn't even certain she was held captive because no matter whom she asked, no one knew a woman named Margery. No one…

What if she wasn't here? She must be. This was Ian of Warstone's personal fortress. One Bied recognised from the overt wealth, intimidation and malice in every stone and floorboard. She'd never met that man whom her sister had been overjoyed to have captured the attention of, but everything Margery had told her in that letter gave her goose pimples and not the good kind.

No, regrettably, her sister must be here. The chambermaid let slip that if the mistress kept weeping, no amount of cold water would ever get her swollen lavender eyes lovely again.

Lavender eyes. Margery was the only one of her siblings to have eyes that colour. Her sister. Trapped and fearful. So close and… Mustn't think dark thoughts. Mustn't…

Biedeluue swallowed hard, tasting the ale and her worry.

'If you're wanting to spew,' Henry said, 'there's a goblet right in your hand.'

'Or a…few…in front of you.' Galen belched.

She narrowed her eyes. Galen needed to fall and soon. Except… Swinging her attention back to the tower in front of her, she saw that the goblets hadn't got smaller in her reverie. There was over a…a lot of them…and she still had one in her hand.

Where had that come from?

* * *

'I have been sent on many missions before,' Louve of Mei Solis said, 'but this is by far the most foolish one yet.'

'At least you said foolish and not dangerous,' Balthus of Warstone said. 'That lends hope.'

Louve loosened his hands on the reins, but the horse beneath him pawed the earth. No doubt it felt the unease from him and his men. It was the wait weighing on them. It was the fact that by going forward, some would be killed.

And this was one of the easier of days after hard travel gathering men and supplies, which took far longer than it should, so by the time they investigated the area they were plagued by rain and frost. Now they were supposed to penetrate an impenetrable fortress and either procure information which would end wars or capture the man who held such important secrets.

Given the fortress and a certain man were surrounded by hundreds of well-trained warriors, the task was not a simple one.

'When I said foolish, didn't that imply the mission was dangerous?' Louve said.

Balthus shrugged. 'How am I to interpret your vague and insouciant descriptions? We've known each other less than a month. Even that has been too much.'

Louve ignored the insult. Balthus had made it obvious since the beginning of this journey from Troyes he didn't want Louve's company. In that, he was exactly like the rest of his family. 'I learnt vague from your brother Reynold.'

'Whom, in my entire life, I have spent less time with than you.'

Louve could hear both the accusation and the curiosity in Balthus's voice. Even if he had a lifetime, he couldn't describe Reynold, one of the four brothers of the Warstone family, and the man who'd hired him as a mercenary. Over the years, Reynold had become a friend to Louve, though Reynold continued to deny it.

The fact he could even call such a man friend was an irony, since Reynold of Warstone was an enemy of his only other friend, Nicholas of Mei Solis. Also, the Warstones were secretly undermining the King of England. An act Louve couldn't fathom given he wasn't from nobility or familiar with the intrigues of court.

Intrigues which had led him here on the same mission that Reynold had borne his entire life. To stop the Warstone family from gaining the power they so hungrily garnered. Their wealth, their reach already could cripple monarchs, and still they weren't satisfied. They were also...evil.

Husband against wife. Brothers raised separately. The Warstones only combined against kingdoms. Then Reynold had broken ranks, turned on them all.

Somehow Louve, of no noble blood, whose skills were more with ledgers than daggers, was in the middle of it all. For a man who dreamed of a little land of his own and a gentle wife who accepted him, how did he end up in these conspiracies? Because he wanted to earn enough coin so he could acquire the quiet life he yearned for.

Where did that leave Balthus, brother of Reynold? Was he a friend? No, nor did Balthus desire to be. But the younger man was growing on him and that in itself was a worry.

Because the man they were here to steal from, or torture for information, whichever became necessary first, was the last Warstone brother: Ian. Four brothers, one already dead. All raised to be enemies against each other. Reynold and Balthus finally combined against the last, but Ian was reported to be the most diabolical.

As far as Louve was concerned, that could be applied to any one of them. In the time he'd spent with the two

Warstones, he knew they had much commonality between them: greed, arrogance and an unnerving intelligence. Every bit of it Louve felt penetrating him as Balthus stood at his side.

'Are you watching me?' Louve said.

'You went unnaturally quiet and stared unblinkingly at a barren tree,' Balthus said. 'You do this, and I worry for your reasoning. I worry for mine since I'm trusting you with my life.'

He wondered if he was going mad as well and only more so lately as he debated his choices. First was leaving his home to become a mercenary for Reynold, the next was agreeing to go on a mission with a Warstone he didn't know. Recognizing that he needed coin, and that becoming a mercenary was the more effective way to do it, did little to mitigate the aggravation of the situation.

Mere months ago, Balthus, the youngest, approached Reynold for an alliance against Ian. Louve was there for it all, knew what was at stake and accepted the consequences of which he knew there would be many. Alliances between madmen wasn't a secure beginning.

Still, in the hopes for peace in his own life, Louve humoured the two brothers. Warstones. The name implied it all. 'Your brother is too cunning to hire foolish men.'

'How am I to know of my brother when you tell me nothing?'

'You won't know any more than he tells you himself,' Louve said.

'Years in his employ and you won't share something?'

'Not if I want to keep my head. Your brother wouldn't appreciate it. If you're truly curious, look to yourself for answers,' Louve said. The fact both were curious and refused friendship, but still held some sense of honour and loyalty, fascinated Louve.

'Damn you, you know I would be curious about this,' Balthus said.

'Your thoughts will keep you well occupied, unlike this hope you talk of. Hope, I remind you, we have no use for.'

Balthus shrugged one shoulder. 'Hope is better than this wait. I liked the journey here, for at least then we wagered and raced horses. Now I'm just cold out here.'

'I thought you hated those wagers because you always lost to me,' Louve said.

'Everyone lost to you and I hate this wait more.'

'You simply don't like paying men when there's no profit.'

'Who would? It took us too long to find them all.'

'We couldn't use Reynold's men, and you couldn't entirely trust your own. We needed many new mercenaries.'

'Now my pockets are empty. If we could have travelled farther to that estate—'

'Mei Solis,' Louve offered.

'I'll never remember such an odd name,' Balthus said. 'However, if we could have stopped there first, I'd have some coin.'

Louve had a chest of his own, but Balthus was used to enormous sums. Sums which were in abundance in Mei Solis coffers. An estate that was weeks away and in another country. Balthus would have to get used to being poor, which was almost enjoyable.

'You'll simply have to suffer with the coin given to me,' Louve said. 'We received your brother's message to come here. Plans change.'

'We received that message less than a day after leaving Troyes. I'm still not certain if Reynold already possessed the information and was too cowardly to tell us in person.'

Louve couldn't fault Balthus for trying to get an answer from him, but his tactic was too obvious.

'Not willing to divulge anything more?' Balthus sighed.

'You were different in Troyes. You talked—I think you even smiled.'

He'd been different in Troyes, he'd been different at Mei Solis, but the more risks he took for someone else's games, the less he found humorous. There was nothing light-hearted about his vow to protect Balthus of Warstone. Facing this dark fortress of death could be his doom as well.

'If you're concerned about finances,' Louve said, 'I'm certain some of your own great fortune you left behind is inside the fortress.' Louve indicated with his chin. 'You could walk through the gates and greet your brother. After all, you are a Warstone.'

'One Ian tried to kill, so no thank you to your idea.'

'Ian doesn't know you know of his treachery.'

'Still, why would I show up and remind him I'm alive?'

'Thus, we are left with my original scheme.'

'Which I disagreed with,' Balthus said.

'We are out of any options. The routine of the watch guards is never consistent, and they are frequently rotated. We know they train. Can see their inflicted injuries even from this distance.'

'Ian must leave the fortress at some point. His wife and two sons aren't in residence.'

'Which implies he is a loving father and husband who misses his family. Given your familial history, that's unlikely. Further, he hasn't surfaced since he killed the messenger at Reynold's gates. Reynold is too aware of him now for him to risk exposure. Will you tell me why your brothers are determined to kill each other?'

'Reynold and I are not,' Balthus said.

'You and Reynold aren't trying to kill each other...yet.'

'I'll prove my honesty to him,' Balthus said.

Louve had his doubts, but then he mistrusted many people, including himself because nothing he had done over many years felt true. He wanted coin to earn something of his own and dreamed of finding a woman to accept him, yet here he was, spying over an impenetrable fortress and scheming to destroy its owner.

'I am Reynold's brother in heart and will prove it with my deeds,' Balthus repeated.

Louve pointedly looked at Balthus's wrapped hand. 'Mere words.'

Balthus lifted his left hand. 'This means nothing.'

'If so, why do you keep it wrapped? Why not show what your mother did?'

'The wrapping is a reminder, that is all.'

Another reason why Balthus could only be trusted so far. The pain of the injury should be enough of a reminder. Balthus's mother, a woman bent on defeating her husband and the King, required her sons to repeatedly hold their left hand over a flame to prove their loyalty.

Which begged the question, one that directly affected him. 'Is it healing?'

'If it comes to a battle of swords, it won't matter if my left hand is healing or not.'

'Until your sword arm is rendered useless, then you would be useless to me. I care very much how well you fight.'

'Should we prove ourselves to each other again, Louve? Last time, I was restraining my full skills.'

'Mere posturing. All I know with certainty was that *I* was holding back,' Louve said. 'I have no knowledge of your skills.'

'I told you—'

'It's not only your sword arm I worry about—I'm concerned you won't be able to perform the hand signals,' Louve pointed out.

'Those are useless,' Balthus said.

'Not if we're stuck in the room, but unable to talk. We

may need to divide the room on attack and it's best to know what we're doing without letting the enemy know.'

'The enemy being my family.' Balthus exhaled loudly. 'What makes you think you can get into Ian's fortress?'

'I was something else before your brother hired me.'

'Your estate management,' Balthus scoffed.

Not his estate, but a childhood friend's. For now, though he had much coin, he needed more for the estate he wanted for his lineage.

'Disdain it all you want, but my experience will save this wretched mission,' Louve said. 'I'm approaching the fortress and asking for work. No mercenaries, no reinforcement. Ridiculous though they might be to any of you, my past skills will be useful.'

He might be a mercenary now, but before he'd only managed another's estate. He wanted his own; he wanted land. If he kept to that plan, if he remembered what all this intrigue was for, perhaps he'd keep his head.

'You won't get to use your skills when they gut you.'

'They don't know who I am.'

'They know!' Balthus said. 'They always know.'

Reynold had often argued the same. 'Fair enough. They know, and they'll let me in as some form of amusement, or they gut me. But what other choices do we have? None. You can't go and the rest of the men only know how to swing swords. It will be me who completes the tasks. It always was.'

'If they let you in and you find work, what then?'

'I search all the rooms for this mysterious parchment Reynold insists Ian must have.'

'It won't be merely lying about, and what happens if it doesn't exist?'

'Then we capture Ian and you can torture him for information.'

'Why am I talking to you? You're a dead man...' Balthus exhaled '…who shouldn't be worried about some great treasure no one knows about except Reynold.'

'We don't know if no one knows of it. Ian might have already guessed, given he's got the parchment, and your parents probably know, too.' Louve shrugged. 'If they know of the Jewell of Kings and the parchment and put them together… You appreciate neither Ian nor your family can gain any treasure that can fell countries.'

'It's foolish going after treasures,' Balthus said. 'What will truly tip the balance is to acquire the legend. We should be pursuing the dagger and jewel, not information. Why can't you or my brother understand the Jewell of Kings resurfacing has changed everything with the war against Scotland?'

'Which is why your family wants it and so does the King of England. But the legend only holds if there's something to support it. Hence the treasure. As much as King Edward believes it is, the gem isn't truly magical like Excalibur.'

Louve couldn't believe the weight of the world and his hope of a peaceful life rested on legends, but they did. Over the last years, the Jewell of Kings, a green gem, much compared to Excalibur, resurfaced thanks to the Warstones' intrigues. The legend was that whoever held the gem held Scotland. Whether true or not, the perception of it was enough to sway everything to King Edward's side. Since the Warstones wanted more power than the King, they coveted it as well.

But Reynold had studied the gem, which had been hidden in the hollow handle of a dagger, and was certain it had another meaning. Together they'd point the direction to enough wealth to bring all monarchs to their knees. Reynold didn't want anyone to have any of it. In that, Louve agreed.

'We must obtain the gem, the dagger and any written words leading to the legend or to any treasure. We're here to obtain at least the parchment hidden somewhere in Ian of Warstone's fortress.' Louve loosened his hands on the reins. 'We can't let your family obtain more wealth or power.'

Balthus scoffed. 'Some stupid legend, some gaudy gem and here we are, breaching a fortress for a scrap of paper, and have no strategy to get out.'

'I'm to go in as a humble servant. We're agreed to my plan?' Louve said.

'No,' Balthus said. 'But we are resolved.'

Chapter Two

Biedeluue let out a rough exhale, then another. Over forty goblets now in front of her, over forty gulps of ale.

For the first time in her life, she wasn't happy with her short legs and arms, nor the shelf her breasts made in front of her. Breasts she'd proudly inherited from her grandmother were no good now. She was two heads shorter than Galen, who could dust the ceiling with his head if he wanted. And he was thin like a broomstick, with these unnaturally long arms which meant the ale should have hit him by now.

She narrowed her gaze on him. All five of his legs were as unsteady as the rest of him. It wouldn't be long now. All she had to do was…hmm.

She shoved her breasts to one side, then the other. When they bounced back to the front, she tried moving the left one over the… No, that just hurt. She willed them to suddenly decrease.

'Need some help with those?' Henry shouted in her ear. 'Ow!'

'That's what you get for startling someone,' she said.

Henry rubbed the side of his head. She didn't think she'd hit him that hard with the goblet.

'I was here the entire time, Biedeluue.'

'And standing too close!' If he bumped into her one more time, she was truly going to hurt him.

'Of course I'm standing close. How am I to hold them away for you!'

Someone guffawed.

She elbowed Henry. 'Maybe you should get someone to hold yours first.'

The crowd roared and Henry, who was as round as she, stepped gingerly back. She knew he wouldn't let the insult rest. She hoped he wouldn't make her pay now when she was up against his closest friend and someone she'd only known for a couple of weeks.

All these people she'd only known for a couple of weeks. Hence, she played games like this in the hope of ingratiating herself with people who'd known each other their entire lives. She needed to be their friend, too. Needed them to trust her without question. She needed them to think her honest and fun and all good because she needed to. Because her sister, her sister was...

Goblets! She clenched the one in her hand and eyed the wobbling tower she'd made before her.

She approached the table again as an idea entered her head. If she bent to the right and used her left arm at just the right angle, it was possible. Oh, yes, it was possible. Flashing them all a grin she couldn't contain, she shouted, 'Watch and weep, Galen. Watch and weep.'

The chanting grew to an all out roar.

Louve had never seen such utter chaotic carnage before in his life. This was saying a lot after years on the road, of inns, of mercenaries, of drinking until he woke up with two women the next day, only to discover he'd blacked out before anything had begun.

The mercenaries had told the tale over and over for a year. He'd been grateful when their contract ended and they were dismissed. Most of the mercenaries he knew only a short time. Only he stayed in the employ of Reynold of Warstone, which was like befriending a dagger pointed towards you. One which he parried with jests and a continual meddling that eased the dark nights and even darker deeds they were forced to do.

Humour he knew, but this pandemonium was pure recklessness on a scale that had no known limit. For one moment, only one, he let himself revel in the sheer entertainment. The crooked goblets, the spilled ale. The ruddy faces of those imbibing and those simply filled with laughter at the frivolity.

At one time in his life, this was something he would have encouraged, would have done. But now, with everything at risk, this *enjoyment* could get him killed. He refused for there to be a slip. Not this soon, and fast, not after each step had been carefully cultivated.

It was nothing to gain access into the fortress despite the mesnie surrounding the gates. Not a weapon upon him, hunched shoulders and clothing indicating poverty. He looked no more or less like any other villager or tenant as he approached the five guards.

He told the first watchmen he was looking for work within the household. There was a burst of laughter, but the man on his right who was just out of his direct sight sobered up too quickly, which instantly alerted Louve. As Louve glanced his way, the man forced a chuckle and reported it was their lucky day. He pointed the way to the porter who allowed access through the fortress door.

With a quick glance at the guards, the porter swung the door open and told him to find the Steward. When he approached the Steward, he seemed almost frightened of Louve. So Louve kept his eyes lowered and hunched his shoulders even more.

From his experience, stewards from grand houses were

often more arrogant than the lords. With good reason—their duties were both financial and ministerial. They oversaw everything from deciphering ledgers for the lord's children, down to what the brewer needed from the fields to make more ale.

This Steward's temperament would not ease and Louve couldn't slump any further without stooping, and he couldn't make his voice any less menacing as he answered the typical questions. Even so, through his agitation, the Steward became sycophantic, almost ridiculously grateful.

It was true Louve knew the duties of a steward. He was educated in ledgers as well as the supplies needed for the poulters, but something wasn't right. Still, when he was offered the position of usher, he took it. Everything about this mission was dangerous. If it was a trap, it was too good of a one to ignore.

An usher oversaw the hall, the cook and food supplies. He was denied access to the coffers and spices, but with everything else he had access to most of the house and to Ian of Warstone.

He could poison or capture Ian to bring to his brother Balthus for questioning. Or, if he was fortunate, he could rifle through his private rooms and find the parchment Reynold sought to defeat the Warstones.

Weeks of scheming, of examining this entire mission from every angle, and nothing came close to this opportunity, which meant absolutely nothing could jeopardise it.

When the Steward waved him to the kitchens, saying he'd follow him in shortly, Louve entered the cavernous rooms with a confidence he felt to his bones. This was the mission that would earn him the last bit of coin he needed. Not only the wealth, but the power he needed to protect it.

Which meant the scene before him was insupportable. Over thirty servants in the middle of the morning, drinking, chanting, chairs overturned, the whitest of flours spilled through a doorway, and two tables stacked with what was could only be described as a steward's nightmare: goblets for banquets that could topple, break and the cost lost!

If the Steward saw the debacle in front of him, Louve wouldn't oversee anything on the Warstone estate, he'd be marched right out as easily as he came in.

'Stop this at once!' The voice behind Bied boomed across the kitchens. The resonating authority of it quashed all joviality and startled every party involved, including herself, shattering any bit of concentration Bied had to stay steady with one knee on the table, one leg off. One arm stretched over the stacked goblets, one chest pointed the opposite direction. One sweaty palm on a table ledge, which spasmed and slipped.

She didn't stand a chance then. Though she truly tried, because her first instinct was to fall forward onto the table. Less distance than the floor, and most of her weight was already on it. Self-preservation demanded she fall forward.

But the goblets, the goblets, the goblets. She might as well be falling on priceless daggers. So, swinging her goblet-holding arm over her head, she propelled herself towards the floor.

Sounds began then. Cursing from that cutting voice, shouts she recognised from Tess, the baritone of Henry's. Something wetter, fouler, as Galen heaved whatever he'd eaten.

When had *he* had time to eat? Cheater!

All of it she was aware of, as if it was happening outside herself. Her fingers suddenly releasing the heavy goblet; her horror as she registered its trajectory. Tess appearing on the other side, reaching her arm out like a bread paddle, swatting it away from her tower and towards Galen's. Henry's great arm thrusting forward to block.

His fingertips making contact, sending her goblet so it hit only the side of Galen's goblet tower. One tumbled, two, three… Henry scrambling full into her view to stop the next goblet's fate.

That wasn't right. Her vision changed to the top of the ceiling, the thick oak beams heavy with smoke, and bird droppings that needed to be—

Oh, my. She was falling and it was going to hurt. 'Henry! Henry, you were supposed to remain behind—oomph!'

Her head cracked against the top of a shoulder, two arms snapped around her waist, her body continued to plummet, but didn't fall. Only continued to press, press, press against an unyielding object, who cradled her body until her feet slid to the floor one after the other.

A clumsy safe landing that was part drunkenness, part the fall and entirely the fault of the man who was holding her steady.

She swung around in his arms, stared at a chest that no amount of poorly weaved tunic could disguise as less than absolutely glorious and stabbed her finger right into the middle of it. 'How dare you!'

The arms around her constricted, her breasts pressed tighter, her nose bumping forward, flattening her palm between them. A palm that might have ever so slightly brushed across to feel every ripple. Oh, yes. Glorious.

'Can you even stand?'

She peered upward to an unknown strong jawline. 'Where'd you come from?'

'Bring a chair,' he boomed.

That voice! She shoved against his chest—he didn't move. 'Let me go!'

'Chair, now! Remove that man from the kitchens, clean up the mess he made. You and you, get these goblets back to the pantry, and, you, take care of this ale. You as well.

And all those gawking in the doorways, if you don't clean the floor immediately, and that includes the flour, I'll wipe it up with your carcasses.'

People moved. They moved as if this glorious-chested man with his strong jawline had anything to do with any of them.

'Now, wait! You have no authority here. This is a private…affair. We're conducting important matters for the lord, we are. You can't barge in here.'

'Sit,' he ordered.

Where had the chair come from? 'You sit,' she told the jawline.

'Female.'

Ooh, this was different. Very different. His voice wasn't booming, but the authority was there. Yes, it was, more so, and it caused her eyes to wander a bit higher and then a bit higher yet.

Glorious…everything. Black eyelashes, brows, aquiline nose, a tiny scar under his left eye that begged for a kiss.

Then there was blue. A blue so blue, the sky would be envious. And…so many eyes. Why did he have so many eyes when the rest of them only had two? Unfair!

'You're too far gone for the chair, aren't you?' He'd swung his gaze away from her. 'Who is responsible for this female?'

'Now that you are hired, that would be you.' The Steward's reedy voice slithered into the kitchens.

Steward, who controlled everything, including her employment. A position which was important because she needed it to save her sister.

'I think I'm going to be sick,' she whispered.

Louve had his arms full to brimming around trouble. There was no other word for the woman who'd completely dismantled a kitchen, his authority and who, though her skin was a shade closer to grey than the vibrant rose hue from before, was, none the less, absolutely, breathtakingly riveting.

Anything less and his body would have immediately reacted differently. Caught her. Released her. Not clutched her closer like a boy feeling a woman's breast for the first time. Not gallantly catered to her inebriated state, ordering her a throne to sit upon, like some knight of lore. Not still been holding her close when his superior, who'd hired him on a probationary period, was standing in front of them, his brow arched over a pointed gaze.

A gaze he'd have perfected as his position demanded, but which Louve could belittle and demean with a swift...

He wasn't a warrior. Louve immediately hunched. The woman in his arms slipped and he had one choice. One. To keep supporting her and reveal his true strength that came about after years of sword training, or...

Louve dropped her.

Chapter Three

Biedeluue was going to punch the stranger. Just as soon as her head stopped spinning and her rear stopped stinging. She would get off this floor, grab a goblet and knock it solidly on that jawline.

Shouting. Different voices. One over the other. Steward's, certainly, and Tess's, who was foolishly defending her. Her feet weren't working. Why were her feet going in opposite directions? The stranger's legs were annoyingly steady.

They were also ominously quiet. *He* was silent. That sneaky bastard. Getting her and her friend in trouble. She heard him ordering people about, but now the Steward was in the kitchen he'd gone mute while the rest of them looked contrite. When she finally stood, she would knock him down faster than a drunken Galen.

What she needed was something… A chair! Biedeluue crawled to it.

'Stay down,' the stranger hissed.

Like hell she would.

'Now, see here, Usher.' Steward's voice. 'I won't… Ah!'

A thud of a falling body, the squeaking protest of table legs and the ominous rattle of goblets. Loads and loads of goblets.

The stranger cursed, shoved a hand on her back and hunched over her. Goblets crashed around them. Biedeluue clenched her eyes against the horrific sound they made, the stranger's hand gripping her back with every goblet that hit him.

A shrieking steward and the trampling of legs. Then another kind of silence. The one which didn't bode well for anyone.

The stranger straightened and, before she could sit properly, Steward was right there and she was staring at different kneecaps. If she narrowed her eyes, there were only four kneecaps as a thudding began in her heart and her legs stayed unsteady beneath her.

She couldn't crawl away either; she'd been cut off from the chair. If she moved, she truly would be sick. Especially at the words being said over her.

'Yes, I know I must keep—' Steward began saying, then stopped.

'Must what?' the stranger said. His voice lost that booming quality from before—now it sounded meek. His legs didn't look meek. Was this a game to make her look inferior? Extra-sneaky bastard.

'Wait,' she said. 'He's—'

'Never mind,' Steward interrupted, overly loud. 'I will… Oh, yes, that is perfect. I will remedy this situation.'

'Am I…relieved of my duties, Steward?' The stranger's voice was pacifying. A fraud! Feet like his weren't conciliatory. Legs like that weren't apologetic. They marched across battlefields and stormed towers. She needed to alert someone.

'He's not—' she said.

'On the contrary,' Steward said. 'You… Yes, you will have more domain to roam as freely as you want. I will have to leave to obtain new goblets.'

There was a decided pause. Bied waited as well. Did Steward say he was leaving?

'You do not have potters?' the stranger murmured.

'One,' Steward answered. 'Only one and he cannot make these goblets the lord prefers. No, he can't. These goblets must be procured only after I travel far, which will take a great amount of time.'

The stranger stayed mute.

So did she. Steward was leaving while the lord was in residence and there was a mess on the floor. Steward didn't like it if a grain was left on a table after a feast.

'So perfect timing for your arrival,' Steward said, almost gleefully. Her head was full of knives and tablecloths. The kneecaps surrounding her were making no sense. Steward sounded pleased the goblets had toppled!

'I am to *complete* my employment?'

Hadn't the stranger already asked that question? She'd drunk copious amounts of ale and even she could understand the words floating above her. Although, maybe she couldn't understand the *meaning* of the words floating above her. There seemed to be too many pauses for her to keep any train of thought.

'Most certainly,' Steward said. 'Especially since I am to depart.'

'Sir, don't you wish to instruct me in procedures, introduce me to staff? Perhaps lend me keys to gain access to certain rooms as befitting my station?'

'Oh, no, no, no, Usher. You told me your credentials. You will be most adequate. Immediately, I must leave this situation. I shouldn't be here at all now you are here. And I've been wondering how I would do that once you—' Steward stopped, cleared his throat. 'I meant I shouldn't be here at all with these most important goblets ruined. I'll need to remedy this situation as soon as possible. In the meantime, yes, serve the lord from the remaining goblets, none other, and do something with that!'

A bony finger smacked Biedeluue.

'Ow!' Bied rubbed her nose.

Steward's uneven steps disbanded all the sound and movement in the room. The pause afterwards lasted so long, Bied was certain she'd fallen asleep until she heard the stranger exhale, then whisper, 'This is wrong.'

It was. Steward never walked funny and he was never pleased if something was broken. Even one measly serving bowl which was completely empty and had cracked in two neat pieces and hurt no one whatsoever... He hadn't been pleased about that either. He'd never let her forget about her clumsiness for days afterwards.

Who heard of *special* goblets? Why didn't anyone tell her they were costly and couldn't be made anywhere else and...? Maybe... Had Henry said... Oh, her head hurt! Everything was so terribly wrong. None of it would have happened if Steward hadn't fallen. If the stranger hadn't entered the room!

'You need to get up immediately,' the stranger said. '*Now*. I refuse to be responsible for whatever you are any longer.'

He *refused*! Biedeluue's head throbbed from the drink, a sign she was sobering up too quickly, and her rear still stung from the fall, which made it a certainty that she'd exact some heinous revenge on this man who had come in and ruined everything. Everything.

Finding purchase on the chair with her feet, she rose and dusted her skirts to stand and face whatever fate was about to be thrown her way. Not only would she face it, but she'd destroy it. Her sister's life hung in the balance.

And why not? She'd been in worse predicaments over the years, most she'd caused herself. This was hardly the worst. Even that wouldn't have been terrible if this man had appeared. A few more goblets and another shot of ale, and Galen would have conceded. If not, they would have run out of goblets. A good sweep and a day to sober up while she interrogated very drunken people. She still needed to know when the lord slept, when he visited his mistress, when he usually left the residence.

Questions she hadn't dared ask when she'd first arrived. No, she waited until they were properly inebriated. Until they trusted her with facts.

Everything was in place and well under control until this stranger entered the kitchens. She wouldn't have it. 'Sir, I demand an explanation.'

Maybe other servants would accept punishment, but she was too old and wise for such behaviour. She'd learnt over the years that the way to approach any of these events was to be on the offensive. It was the way she got anywhere in life.

This man would simply…be beautiful. Raven-black hair, summer-sky-blue eyes, lashes that were completely, utterly, unfairly long. And lips…

'You want an explanation?' he said.

The lower lip was full, a dimple just to the side of it… Bied blinked. Another dimple perhaps on the other side, if he didn't clench his jaw so. She would have to—

'*Madame!*'

Blinking, Bied stared into eyes that were losing their blue. Was he *still* glowering? She glowered back. 'You enter here with no announcement, no forewarning. Do you know the chaos you caused?'

'*I* caused?' One raven brow arched, a glare to the blue that made him almost intimidating, which might have worked if he wasn't repeating everything she said. Glorious he might be, but this man was simple.

'Chaos,' she repeated slowly, giving him a chance to

understand her. 'You entered the kitchens and shouted, which startled everyone. That's why the goblets tumbled.'

'My shouting caused the goblets to fall?' he said, his voice rising. 'My. Shouting?'

Repeating again. She held out her hands in appeasement. Simple he might be, but he was larger than her, although…maybe he wasn't larger, he was all…hunched. His shoulders rounded. That did nothing for him. Why, he'd be almost handsome if he… That was unquestionably a dimple on the other side. Two dimples, how could any woman resist?

'Answer me,' he said.

'Answer—' she said.

'*Madame*, I asked if you are the cook?' he said.

He didn't ask her any such thing. He was worse than simple. A liar? Storyteller? She needed to defuse this situation. What if he was violent? He came in ordering and shouting; violence was certain to come next.

'She isn't the cook. Cook is that heap in the corner,' a high-pitched voice squeaked behind her.

That would be the…red-headed boy. She hadn't learnt everyone's name yet. But that wasn't what concerned her. What worried her was there were children present despite the danger. Couldn't people see this man was dangerous? She needed to soothe the stranger and quickly. She wouldn't have violence around them.

'Take whatever you want and go back to wherever you came from,' she said in a rush.

'Go back to where I came from?' The stranger didn't turn his gaze towards the corner where Cook wheezed. 'The children, *madame*, are making more sense than you.'

She hated when people didn't respect children. Hated when they bullied and hurt simply because they were bigger. Simple man he might be, but he needed to learn this and go. 'Of course they're making sense,' she retorted. 'They're called words. In sentences. That do not repeat.'

'Bied!' a harsh whisper broke through. Oh, Tess was here, too, trying to protect her again. Bied's heart warmed at having such a friend in so short of a time. When had that ever happened in her life? Never. She felt almost remorseful that she was deceiving her.

'What is Cook doing in the corner?' The stranger's demeanour changed again. Something darker and far more menacing. His hunched shoulders along with that muscle ticking in his jaw was making every hair on the back of her neck stand up.

'He's always in the corner,' the boy piped up as cheerful as could be. 'For weeks and weeks.'

The stranger's glower darkened. His fingers stretched and clenched at his side. Bied knew what that meant. Spreading her arms wide, she straightened to her full height and shouted, 'Tess, get the children out now! I'll hold him off.'

What had he got himself into? Louve stared at the madwoman. It didn't take long to determine the kitchen's disarray and the cause of it, but this woman elevated everything to something he could not comprehend and he'd seen a lot of bedlam in his life. Drunken she might be, but this...

'*Madame*, what are you doing?' he said.

She was waving her arms, her feet shuffling from one side to the other. Everything about her a distraction. *Everything.*

From her hair that couldn't decide if it was blond or brown. From her eyes that flashed between blue and something else that made no sense in any eye colour. Not brown, not green, not anything except some gem colour, but when added to the blue something happened to that colour... Something indeterminable.

Everything about her was in between. Except her body. That wasn't in between. It was as if God made a woman and then He kept making her. Kept adding to her until any other woman wouldn't ever compare.

Not to those ripe lips or the expanse of her pale throat and neck. Never to the long tapering in her fingers, or the plump lines around each wrist. When she pushed unsteadily to stand, her hands flat on the chair, her legs skittering under her, the rest of her undulated in the most mesmerising of ways. Louve looked away before he lost *his* footing.

And now in front of him she waved that very body about, her feet taking her one way, her hips another, swaying to some dance his eyes powerlessly tracked. Swinging as if...she was blocking him!

'I won't harm the children,' he spat, appalled at the words leaving his lips.

'That's what they all say,' she retorted. 'They always say that.'

'Who says that?' Louve couldn't think. The Steward had left; no steward would do that. He needed to think and he couldn't with this woman and her words, and her everything else.

'As if you don't know,' she said. 'Always with soft false words first before the fists strike. Hence here I am if you want to hit someone so badly. If violence is all you—'

A black rage overtook him and he grabbed a waving wrist, quickly trapping the other. Clenched them both against his heart which thundered at the accusations she flung out. She was unadulterated, ale-addled mayhem. Right this moment, not one breath more, she needed to understand.

She stiffened, but he didn't let go. Just stared into her

eyes which continually blinked as if finding it difficult to focus. He pushed his every thought forward, willing her to understand him very, very clearly. 'I do not harm children.'

She tried to wrench her wrists away, a sound escaping her lips. Her eyes wide in understanding, in defiance, in...fear.

Disturbed, *horrified*, by what he'd done, he released her hands, took a step back. Searched the rest of the kitchen for some orderliness. It was empty, but many curious eyes peeked around corners from the other rooms and stations. Only the heap that was Cook remained in the corner.

After this drunken woman had shouted her warning, the servants scattered from him as though he was some brute. As though he'd come charging in here on his war-horse with sword drawn. Not like a humble broken man who came begging for employment so he could slink around unnoticed into areas where he shouldn't be. This situation was a debacle.

He sunk into himself, lowered his eyes. 'There's been a misunderstanding,' he said.

The woman swayed, swallowed hard, but didn't back down.

'You heard Steward,' he continued, keeping his voice as meek as he could ever make it. 'He hired me to assist with the household. Perhaps he hired me to help you? You seem to have the ear of the kitchens.'

'Steward hired you?' she said slowly, her pallor waning a bit. 'To help me?'

He wondered what'd happened to the Valkyrie. She seemed shocked that he was hired. 'You heard him. He will depart to obtain goblets. I was told to liaise between stations. To be an usher so that—'

'An usher, for the kitchens,' she said.

She was repeating him. Repeating what she'd already

heard from Steward! He held to his patience. This woman was *unhinged*. Steward had fled in the most irregular fashion. Louve knew with certainty he was out of his depth. His safety, and that of Balthus and the men, was completely compromised. And this was before he faced Ian of Warstone. Before he even began his search for papers that could fell countries.

'As well as other parts of the fortress,' he continued.

'You have access to the private chambers?' Her expression was hopeful and decidedly unwell.

He usually wouldn't have access to private chambers, but Steward had left and announced his free rein in front of this woman, who wrecked property with no repercussions, who commanded servants. Perhaps this was the way she could help him in the mission. If she believed he had access to private chambers, he would not correct her.

'Access to all rooms,' he said, in his most agreeable voice. 'Like you do.'

'Access to the private chambers. To the chambers, like I...do,' she said, gulping. 'I'm going to be... I'm going to be—'

Clasping her waist, Louve swung her into the chair and held back her hair as the madwoman heaved all over worn floorboards, broken pottery, and heaved again until she blacked out.

Chapter Four

How did she get here? Bied woke carefully. Opening her eyes in any hurried way wasn't possible. Wasn't—

The light was, however, different. Because it was afternoon or the next day? She listened hard and still couldn't tell.

Her stomach roiled and her mouth was dry, and at the same time she was starving, but couldn't imagine sipping even the weakest of ales. So that was no help to tell the time of day either.

She was, however, grateful she was in bed, but the quilt wasn't hers, she wasn't fully dressed and she stank like—oh. She'd heaved hastily gulped ale from her empty stomach all over the kitchen floors!

Tess's displeasure would know no bounds. The goblets had crashed and the Steward was there. She remembered shouting. She rolled over and groaned as one certainty became clear. Steward would toss her outside and bar her from the fortress. Bied wanted to cry as despair ripped through her. Her sister! What would become of Margery when she was marched—

'Thank goodness you're awake.' Tess strode into their room. Behind her was the red-haired boy who carried in a small tray of food. 'Set the food on that bed there, Thomas.'

Bied covered her exposed ear and watched Thomas dart out the room.

Tess grinned evilly over her and whispered loudly, 'Are you still poorly?'

She couldn't even glare.

Frowning, Tess straightened. 'You never sicken. I'll get Galen for this. I wager he put something in your ale. I've seen you drink twice that amount and never do what you did.'

She was never sick, though Tess couldn't truly know that given their short acquaintance, yet Tess seemed concerned for her health. Most likely it had been she who had taken care of her before she slept. Bied would miss her when she was tossed out.

'What are you carrying?' Bied said.

'Bess's gown.' Tess offered the gown for inspection. 'It's too long for you, but it was all we could do in such short notice. Your gown isn't available…for obvious reasons.'

Shakily, Bied pulled herself up and leaned against the wall. It was stone, and cold which helped clear her head.

'Why would Bess give me one of her gowns?' Bess hated her.

Tess grinned. 'I'm the only one who knows of her great embarrassment. Once I reminded her of that, she was more than happy to. Pray now, it's been some time since I overheard Jeanne in a panic and this tarrying might cause us grief in my great plan. He's been barking orders all morning, entirely not pleased at all.'

She didn't understand half of what Tess said, and when had Steward ever been pleased? He must be in a mad fit now. Broken goblets and sick all over the floor. Hers *and* Galen's.

'What are you doing?' Tess said.

'Rising. The kitchens need cleaning.' It was the least she could do for her friend before she was forced out.

'Already been done. You're fortunate you were drunken enough to not experience the full misery.'

Bied experienced enough of it to feel guilty, but Tess seemed unharried by the wrecked kitchen which meant some time must have passed since she'd cleaned it. 'What day is this?'

'The same day. You do have it horribly.' Tess tossed the gown on her bed and went to the tray. 'Maybe you should first have some repast.'

Bied eyed the bread which would undeniably get stuck to the roof of her mouth. 'Anything softer?'

Grabbing the bowl, Tess handed it to her. 'No ale or wine for you. I thought this infusion might help, though.'

The warmth felt good in her hands and the herbs smelled like mint. Bied took a sip. She truly didn't deserve such a friend. Shouting in the kitchens, Tess coming to her defence, then cleaning up and taking care of her?

If Steward was in a rage, he'd take it out on the servants. He always did. 'You shouldn't have defended me.'

'The whole castle in an uproar and this is what you say to me?' Tess scoffed. 'I didn't defend you. I was merely trying to…hold you back some.'

Tess might be strong, but if Bied wanted something, nothing could rein her in. 'I'd like to see you try.'

'I think the entire kitchens would like to see that. Can you imagine?' Tess laughed, and Bied winced.

'Was that too loud? My pardon.' Tess winked.

Taking another sip, Bied grabbed the roll which was too fine for servants. Tess took a risk serving this to her. Her friend took too many risks and that included her being here in the middle of the day, feeding and caring for her.

Bied had to move now or both would lose their occupations. 'I cannot give my thanks enough. I truly do owe you a favour that I will repay.' Though she had no idea how she would get non-existent coin to Tess past a guard who was likely to break an arm or two as he tossed her out the gates.

Tess snorted. 'What did he slip into your ale? Did you taste anything odd?'

Bied wasn't following this conversation. 'Galen was sick as well.'

'That's true.' Tess frowned. 'This isn't good, then. We might have to look at the supplies.'

Which meant they were busy and she needed to go. To wear a gown that surely had fleas purposefully put in there since Bess was forced to give it to her. 'I'm sorry for everything. I never meant for any of that to happen.'

Tess shrugged. 'I can't be sorry— I loathe those goblets. You can't fit many on a tray and they're far too heavy. I was glad they toppled, although I do hate that they will be replaced. Seems—'

'Wasteful.'

'Odd,' Tess said at the same time.

Bied had scrambled for every scrap of food, every rotting board on their tiny house, every stitch of clothing. The cost shattered across the kitchen floors would have fed her family for a year, probably more than that. What did she know of goblets? Her cups had been wooden and shared with Margery.

Margery! Bied's roiling stomach plummeted. Nothing to be done for her actions or to correct the wrongs done. Her intention to help her sister had failed.

Bied drank the rest of her infusion. She needed to hurry now and face whatever punishment Steward deemed suitable for her before they tossed her out the gates. 'Why do you say odd?'

'Steward left,' Tess said. 'When was the last time you saw him leave?'

It was odd. Steward roamed every bit of the fortress, and land, and he'd never walked away from a disaster. Even the tiniest mistake, he'd hover over the perpetrator to harangue them until they felt smaller than a speck of dust. But then what did she know?

'I haven't been here long.' Bied tore into the rest of the bread. Not as long as she needed to make everything right.

'It feels as though you've always belonged here.'

That had been the point of her displaying her more… humorous side early to the servants. To ingratiate herself to everyone, so they'd allow her more freedom and she could save her sister. Certainly, no one would bar the jesting, harmless Biedeluue from traipsing up one staircase or another? Opening this door or that?

Usually, she hid her pranks, until she'd slip up and then needed to look for another position elsewhere. But to save her sister, she tried to remain subservient around the Steward, and around the servants she showed her true self. Now all of it was lost and the guilt of not telling her friend the entire truth of why she was here felt especially heavy now.

'I liked belonging here.' Bied gave a last hard swallow of bread.

Tess eyed her warily. 'Do you think you can keep your food down? Because we need to get you dressed.'

We. It wasn't as if she could help anyway, or even if they wanted her help now that she'd ruined everything. Still, she needed to rise because she didn't want Tess to get in trouble for tarrying.

'I wanted to tell you how grateful I am for the time we've had together.' Bied pushed off the bed and raised her arms out.

Tess threw the gown over her head. 'This is an odd

conversation for the task we must do. Suck in a breath, I thought Bess's gown would fit around you.'

Nothing contained her chest, and this gown was indecent, but better to be extremely improper than naked in front of an angry Steward. Maybe if she pushed up her tits, he'd be lenient with her and Tess.

'If I had been given more time here, I'd show you.'

Tess loosened a few of the laces. 'Show me tomorrow if we're both still employed after we've delayed like we have. I told Jeanne to hold him off, but she's probably fainted by now.'

Delayed? If she had moved any faster, she'd be flat on the floor. She felt ill now knowing she'd failed her sister and would lose a friend. Humiliated at merely knowing she'd be soon standing before a crowd with her breasts exposed.

'No tomorrows for me,' she said.

'Are you always this maudlin when you're sick?' Tess tied a lace and then yanked her to face the other way. 'I'll have to re-evaluate our friendship. I thought you'd be brandishing daggers like you did that goblet. That is an image I'll regale in old age.'

Each tug of a lace jiggled her breasts, jostled her stomach. Maudlin wasn't what she felt. Desperation and despondency, however, came at her in great waves, but that was because of her sister. She never wanted to fail any of her siblings. 'I simply meant there's no chance for me to be here on the morrow. Do you honestly believe Steward would order me dressed to praise me? Tess, he will march me out of here.'

Brows shooting up, Tess said, 'That's the last drink you'll have. There is no Steward. I told you, he's left the estate. Truly departed, straight through the gates. You can't remember anything?'

Apparently not, but then it wasn't as if Tess had started

from the beginning, but maybe she'd missed that, as well. 'Then who is reprimanding and marching me out? Who ordered this gown and has been asking for my presence?'

Tess yanked her the other way. 'Louve, who is the Usher, and now possibly Steward, needs you. And he's not exactly asking for you. I got you the gown. After I stopped Jeanne—'

'Louve?' Bied was certain Tess's spinning was meant as torture.

'Louve. That man you yelled at like a spitting cat?'

Images. Unfounded, surely, because she remembered someone who was too handsome to be true, but perhaps he was real. 'He exists?'

'Very much so,' Tess said, 'and, according to our new Usher and temporary Steward, your presence, not exactly you, but hopefully you, is needed in the kitchen. However, given your skin is some shade of grey, I'm afraid for the floors. They barely survived this morning.'

Her stomach was moderately better from the food. Her head, however, wasn't piecing together everything Tess was saying, but there was something she desperately needed to understand. 'That man who entered the kitchen is now in charge and he doesn't want to reprimand me?'

'Oh, he certainly wants to reprimand you, but we'll convince him you're the woman for the task.'

Tess needed to start again. 'What task!'

'You're so prickly like this. You'd think you'd be grateful there's a chance to keep your position here after what you did in the kitchens. More than your position if we can fool him.'

After what occurred in the kitchens, no steward, even a new one, would keep her. 'Are you saying he wants me?'

Tess tied the last lace, and tugged the fabric in place. 'Have you not listened to a word I said? Jeanne, the chambermaid, came to the kitchens, and told me Lord Warstone wished to dine in the Hall this evening. No one can rouse Cook, so I begged her to stall and ran to get Bess's gown—'

Bied grabbed Tess's hand. Her heart! Her heart could barely take it. There was a possibility, a slim infallible chance she could still help her sister. She couldn't believe it, couldn't quite comprehend her fortune, but if Tess believed she hadn't lost her position here, that she could stay… Hope was quickly overcoming any of her nausea.

Tess didn't know of her sister, though by now Bied believed she could almost trust her with that truth. But even if Tess only meant her to keep her occupation, that was more than enough. 'I can work and you've been letting me sleep, delaying coming up here, allowing me to eat, to *dress*?'

'That's what I've also been telling you.' Freeing her hand, Tess looked pointedly at her chest. 'Although the dress part is still in question. Are you remembering matters now?'

She was, but Bied didn't care about her thoughts or her lack of covering. Not for anything or anyone. Lifting her skirts, she darted out the door.

Chapter Five

Louve had made many mistakes in his life. But this one had to be the most foolish. Why? He was trapped. He had willingly gone under the portcullis with no means of escape. He had laughingly walked past the watch guards and porter.

The ease of which raised an alarm in him which could be delayed until he could plan, but the behaviour of the Steward was something he couldn't sweep to the side for later. No one hired someone without asking for recommendations or testing him. It wasn't possible someone agreed to take a stranger into the home without walking the grounds and designating tasks.

Ian of Warstone couldn't have survived this long with a careless household. The Steward was worse than neglectful, he was unbalanced. Who left an unknown, unverified usher in charge of this type of hold for mere drinking wares?

But as the morning progressed, as Louve ordered and assisted the servants in the duties that needed to be accomplished immediately, it was all too obvious that is exactly what the Steward had done.

As Usher, he held responsibility, which was a setback. The intention here was to be an insignificant servant so he could go about unnoticed and search rooms, chests, cabinets. If all else failed, he'd capture a man who had the will and resources to murder his own family.

The woman, Biedeluue —for that was the name the man Henry who assisted him up the stairs and into the room had called her—had changed all that.

Hours later and it still galled him he'd ordered assistance when he wanted to carry her himself. But his pride wasn't the only emotion that pricked at him. For inexplicable reasons, he despised another man touching her in any way. Thus, when they reached the servants' quarters, he'd ordered Henry away. To have her all to—

No. No more. This morning was enough of an interruption, his continual thoughts too much when the mission needed his all. But…

She would have to be watched, for she was in good standing with the servants. Enough that the costly game was encouraged by her peers. She, a servant, had some influence. But he wasn't certain what to do with her, if he even could. Only time would tell. Until then, he'd give her a certain leniency. So, disaster in the kitchens? Clean it for her. Drunken, let her sleep.

When she was well again, he'd have her show him about. For a moment, he thought to flirt with her, but threw that idea away with the immediacy of how much he wanted it. No, he didn't want anything as harmless as flirtation. He wanted to seduce her and, if his reaction was this instantaneous, there was no way to contain it, at least not for long. No certainty to control it, at least not the way he needed to.

Just thinking about the lushness of her body wasn't enough to assuage his thoughts when the next image was him shoving her against the nearest wall, scooping a hand underneath her knee and—

'What is it?' Growling, Louve pivoted, only to be confronted by a trembling girl. Yet another servant he did not know come to harass him about more trivial matters.

'I'm J-J-Jeanne, sir,' she stammered. 'I've been sent.'

No Steward, no order, and he cared for none of it. He wasn't here for seduction or kitchen duty.

'Sent by whom?' he said. 'And for what?'

'Lord Warstone, sir,' she whispered. 'He wants food in the Hall this eve.'

He waved his hand. The kitchens were full of servants who had their duties. Despite the morning's chaos, they could still conduct their responsibilities. No one was stopping them, least of all him. 'Do what's necessary, then.'

She cleared her throat. 'We haven't had dining in the Hall.'

He'd assumed food had been served before he'd arrived and, in the haste to understand Warstone's fortress workings, he'd forgotten about the midday meal. If there was a midday meal. He had no time for any of this, but this girl, as timid as could be, wouldn't let the subject go.

'What is the usual hour to dine, then?'

'There is no…usual…hour, sir.' She trembled through her sentence.

He didn't care when the Lord of Warstone liked his meals; he needed the fortress to work as it always had and he was within moments of taking it out on the frightened messenger because he'd had enough of these interruptions. 'Simply do what has always been done and leave me be.'

He took three, four steps away from her at the most. But the flutter of her hands and the bowing of her head was in his periphery, and something that couldn't be ignored.

'What else?' He spun on her. She jumped. Again. Once could be dismissed. Twice spoke to a deeper issue. One of fear or constant retribution. She expected anger or punishment. This woman needed protection. But he was no avenging mercenary. Now he was a servant, glorified though the position was.

He gentled his tone. 'What else do you need?'

'There's been no dining in the Hall.'

'Today, yes, I know, but—'

'Ever!' she squeaked, huffing out a breath. 'The household, the guards, yes, but Lord Warstone? Not for a year, sir.'

The tension building since he had approached the guards this morning vanished as Balthus's words tolled: *They know. They always know.*

'Jeanne, are you informing me you've been sent to announce Lord Warstone desires to leave his private chambers and dine in the hall with his men...tonight?'

'His mistress as well.'

He ignored a gasp behind him. There were so many people milling about doing nothing it was a miracle anything got done.

What this trembling servant was telling him far outweighed kitchen duties. For it was lethally evident the Warstones did like their games. No steward present and a stranger was allowed to take his duties? The lord of the manor deciding to dine in the Hall for the first time in a year? Indeed, Ian of Warstone knew he was here.

Which meant Balthus was at risk and he couldn't warn him. At least the youngest Warstone wasn't dead. If Balthus had been caught, there would be no need for games, Louve would also be killed. There was no reason for Ian to keep a mere mercenary and servant alive.

Still, if he rushed towards the stairs and forced a confrontation with Ian, he'd end up tortured or dead and nothing would be gained. If he played a Warstone at his games, he could still lose, but information regarding the parchment, their entire reason for being here, could be obtained as well.

Given his skills, he was effective at discovering information, as well as serving food. Now he felt what he always did when approaching an enemy: anticipation.

'Jeanne, get me the Cook,' he said.

'Cook?' Jeanne darted a glance behind him.

Ah, yes, Cook was that lump in the corner. That would need to be addressed, but in the meantime, he was needed tonight.

'The Cook,' he said. Voices were behind him, but he ignored them. They could wait. Ian and his games were the priority. If the great Lord Warstone wanted to dine in the Hall, Louve would meet him there. 'Regardless of the past, he's needed tonight.'

She glanced behind him again and his annoyance flared. There were people behind him vying for his attention and distracting hers. In the years he'd been a mercenary he'd forgotten how vexing the bombardment of distractions could be.

Looking wildly around and then at her feet, Jeanne mumbled, 'Cook has only prepared food for the private chambers. He hasn't organised the Hall for weeks. Not since—'

He waited, but Jeanne didn't raise her head or her voice. Why Cook hadn't been doing his duties was unimportant for tonight. If Ian wanted to play games, he would be more than happy to play along. And those people behind him were much too close now. He'd take his frustrations out on them soon enough.

'But you stated the guards and household have been fed,' he enunciated slowly. 'There's food. If Cook hasn't done his duties for weeks, who has been in charge of the kitchens?'

'Biedeluue.' A voice behind him forced through his conversation.

A name, among all other names, he knew.

'The woman…with the goblets,' Jeanne announced helpfully, unerringly. Finally finding her voice, though it wasn't needed.

Of course it was her. Louve turned.

The woman he'd carried to her room and laid in her bed, the woman he alone had partially undressed and tended in her sickness, stood before him, a tilt to her chin he recognised in only a day. She looked…better.

Another woman stood at her side. Tall and with wild curly blond hair. This one had yelled and added to the chaos. She also stood with an almost aggressive stance, as if she was preparing for battle. No one, not even the most skilled servant, would ever approach their superiors like these two.

Which lent itself to so many possibilities and all of them in his favour. Provided he could determine exactly who Biedeluue was here, because she was more than a conscientious kitchen servant helping the cook

The way she'd rallied the staff behind her games this morning and under the watchful eye of the guards and Lord Warstone himself! If the antics she did hadn't clashed with his objective here, he'd…admire her. It took courage and a certain wildness to conduct such a spectacle.

For a moment he thought of Reynold's well-orchestrated households and the absolute irreverence in this one. Barely hiding the curve to his lips, Louve knew just how he could be victorious here.

Welcome to the games, Ian.

Bied's heart thumped in her chest and she was certain the entire household could see it, especially since there was little fabric holding it back, but she didn't care. Everything Tess alluded to was true. Her sister would be in the Hall this evening. She could get word to her. Could see her, talk to her, at least convey somehow that her older sister was here to rescue her. Everything she'd been hoping for, for weeks, was almost within her reach.

Yet how was she to do the rest of it? Tess had announced she was in charge of the kitchens. She had no such responsibilities. Over the last sennight, she'd swept, cleaned knives and goblets, did odd tasks to support others. She didn't meal plan, or source food, or direct the baker what to bake. The Steward did.

Without him, she had no idea how to start, but she'd do it, she'd do anything for her sister. Even if she had to lie and cheat her way through this.

The only problem was she could omit the truth, but any falsehood and her pale skin blushed.

'You,' he said. 'You've been in charge of the kitchen?'

'I've been helping, yes,' she said. Still all true, but she could feel the heat beginning, and she took a deep breath. Or as deep as she could within the constrictions of her gown.

'Helping,' he drawled. His eyes stayed with her, but she swore she felt that gaze elsewhere. As though he had taken in her appearance, the too-tight gown, her hastily secured hair, the fact that mere hours ago she'd been in a drunken sleep.

This man made her all too aware she'd slept the morning away. Louve, such an unusual name, but fitting. A wolf with his gaze that told nothing of himself, yet somehow conveyed what he thought of her. A liar. Or at least someone who hid something. Which she did.

'Sir, I'm head baker and, if there is to be a feast tonight, I need to get to the ovens,' Tess blurted out.

Bied jumped.

Louve's eyes never left hers. 'What must be done?'

Bied knew he was testing her, but what did the bakers do except make bread? What more did he want? 'Obviously, the trenchers.'

'Which were done yesterday, but the pasties and tarts must be prepared,' Tess added.

Louve nodded. Bied didn't dare take her eyes off of him, though she did move towards Tess to block her. She needed her friend here, to lie for her when she couldn't.

'I'm assuming this is not your gown,' he said.

Of course he'd mention the gown. She didn't need to look down to see her chest was a proper shelf, but it shouldn't matter to him, though it obviously did. Which irritated her. Still, she tried to keep to the role she'd been playing here as an obedient helpful servant. She was able to keep that persona with the Steward, so why not the Usher? 'It's borrowed.'

'You have no others?'

'Her only gown is with the laundress, sir,' Tess replied. 'It should be dried by tomorrow.'

Louve appeared to keep his gaze on hers, but she swore he looked down. Which, after this morning, was too much, and she snapped.

'This is perfectly suited for the kitchens. It won't—'

He eyed Tess. 'Leave…for now.'

Eyes huge, Tess spun. Her friend seemed half-amused, half-panicky. Bied was certain her glare conveyed how she was all panicky and not a bit amused.

The rest of the kitchen staff whirled around them. Not with the usual activity as when the Steward was here. Not anything close to what was needed if she was to prepare food fit for a man who personally knew the King of France and England, and probably all the other rulers in the world.

'Trenchers, hmm…' He stretched his back, before it collapsed again. 'How exactly have you been helping?'

The start of a blush was beginning, but she wouldn't back down. This had to be done. How hard could it be to fool a man who knew nothing? 'Wherever my help is needed.' When his eyes narrowed, she continued, 'Which has been much over the last few weeks. With Cook and all.'

'Who exactly are you, then?' he asked. There wasn't a note of curiosity in his voice. There was only a demand. An order.

Hours of sleep since this morning. Food in her stomach, freshly washed, dressed. More prepared than she'd ever been to face any adversity, Bied faced this man called Louve.

But her answer didn't come tripping off her tongue. Because although the usual and expected words were being said, his far-too-intense eyes seemed to be asking for more than her name.

For one foolish moment she wanted to answer him with the truth. That she had a sister trapped upstairs and he actually had the ability to help her. This enigmatic, unknown, irksome man had the power to release her sister and all the desperation in her welled up at the thought. The overwhelming feeling of desperation to tell this stranger terrified her, so she did the one deed she always did when she felt vulnerable.

'Who exactly are you?' she countered.

'Pardon?'

'You ask a question of me, though it's a strange one. Some time has gone since this morning and Tess just told you.'

'The same logic could apply to you. Some time has gone on since this morning—why ask me who I am?'

Why, indeed? Had she thought this man simple? That thought had come unquestionably from the ale. 'I've been asleep.'

'You haven't been asleep. You blacked out on your— are you still ale-addled? Is that why you couldn't answer my questions?' He leaned in and sniffed. 'You don't smell drunk.'

No, not drunk, but momentarily stunned. He smelled like steel, like the forests outside her childhood home. It wasn't her imagination that conjured how glorious this man was. She wasn't prepared to face him at all. But she wasn't here for him, she was here for her sister.

'I'm not drunk,' she said. 'My friends have taken care of me. I'm clean, dressed, fed and prepared to work.' Although he didn't need to know that she'd been undressed and dressed by Tess, or brought food. But he did need to know her name and she needed to not antagonise this man whose expression changed from glowering to something else as she told him what her friends had done for her.

Did he resent that they took care of her? 'You won't punish them for taking care of me? If it wasn't for them, I wouldn't be here now.'

'Your friends helped you,' he said, a certain tenseness vibrating through him as his eyes darkened before he looked away.

Oh, no, he intended to dismiss her just as she'd told Tess. All because she'd been acting like herself. She'd blame it on the worry for her sister, but if she'd acted like this in front of Steward, no amount of begging would have got her an occupation here.

'Sir,' she said, changing her tone, and the way she stood. When had she placed her hands on her hips? 'I'm no more or less than a servant helping in the kitchens. They call me Bied… Louve.'

A light to his eyes, a twitch to his lips. That did something to him. Changed that blue, dark gaze of his to something more…natural, effortless. As if humour was innate to him and he hid it. But that glimmer was there and gone within a blink. Now she wasn't so certain he didn't intend to toss her outside and—he couldn't toss her. No one man could. And she truly needed to remember who she was here for. Her sister.

'I've been helping in the kitchen. Fare has made it to the tables for staff and guards. Lord Warstone when he is in residence eats in his private chambers.'

'And where are those chambers?' Louve asked. 'It might be helpful to know the distance to determine the temperature of the food.'

She frowned. 'His chambers are up the narrow staircase on the far side of the Hall.'

He nodded as though what she said was of the utmost importance. 'And how many guards are up there in case they wanted food?'

'I feed the guards in the Hall,' she said, again. It was an odd question and one she had no time for. 'Now, if Lord Warstone desires to eat in the Hall, I need to begin.'

'Am I being dismissed?' An arch of one dark brow over blue eyes that seemed lit with some light.

His words were harsh, but the tone—it was almost as though he was amused by her words.

She was dismissing him, but how to state it and why was she acting like this? All the years of travel from village to village. If she wanted work, she knew to appear meek and grateful for a position. It wouldn't always last—eventually, she'd insult, make one too many suggestions or play one too many pranks, and she'd be off to search for another job.

For two weeks, when it came to the staff here, she'd been herself. When it came to her superiors like the Steward, she kept the mantle of a docile servant. It wasn't always easy, but the stakes had never been so high. She'd turn herself into a completely other person if it meant she'd free Margery.

But this man kept meddling and prodding until she reacted, but not as a servant. And if she couldn't remember to be a servant with him, what other parts of herself would she forget? She was here for her sister, yet she continually saw him as a man. He needed to do his duties and leave her alone.

'You wish for me to do my tasks, do you not?' she retorted.

One word between tightened lips. 'Indeed.'

Bied just kept back the breath of relief as he stepped to turn. Which was good because he pivoted again to face her.

'One more matter,' he said. 'I want the dishes to be served sequentially.'

'Pardon?' she said, watching Louve adjust his back. She had seen him do that before. Perhaps it irritated him and that was why he hunched.

'Tonight, for Lord Warstone, there will not be the first, second and third courses with the variety of dishes at the table at once, I want the dishes to be one after the other.'

She might know nothing of food preparation or menu planning, but she knew service of food and sweeping floors. Depending on if it was a meat or fish day, the three courses would have multiple dishes set on the table for the diners to serve themselves.

This Usher wanted the dishes to be brought out one by one. She'd never heard of such manners, not in all of France.

'You don't understand,' he said.

'I do,' she said. Still, she couldn't help but ask, 'But wouldn't that extend the length of the meal? With the guards, it might be midnight by the time the meal was complete.'

'Exactly. Can you do it?' he said.

'Of course.' She'd do anything, even serve a disaster of a meal the incorrect way. But why did she feel like this was a jest?

Chapter Six

The feast was underway, with the guards coming in from their duties and Ian and his mistress already descended. The water was prepared for the handwashing, the table set with utmost care. Goblets such as they were, already on the tables. Ale and wine placed on the side table for service.

The details for tonight needed to be to Louve's exact specifications. All customs not forgotten, but wholly disregarded. They were in France. The Warstones were half-French, but Louve… Louve was all English. If Ian knew he was here, well, they'd serve in as much the English style as they could. An offensive move on his part in the games started.

All that was needed was food, which thankfully smelled as though it was being prepared. But that was the only fortuitous detail in the kitchen. The rest? The scents weren't mouth-watering, more eye-watering. The cleanliness he had secured he once again destroyed. Pots stacked, peelings on the floor. Something vile spilled down the sides of one buffet. Perhaps it was wine with sops, perhaps it was something he'd rather not know.

Bied's hair was wildly sticking out from her cap. Her stature didn't allow for space between herself and the pot and her borrowed gown was plastered to her body. Did she have no shawl, some square piece of linen? The stretch of the fabric would be any man's undoing. It was certainly his.

She was a woman who was all his fantasies and nightmares in one. Fantasies because of her enigmatic hair and eyes, because of curves she couldn't and didn't hide. Because of the way she lifted her chin and demanded answers.

Nightmares because she lifted her chin and demanded answers. Because she was reckless, and someone determined and reckless took risks and didn't care about consequences. Someone like that wasn't…containable. And the familiar stab of lust that thought brought about was dangerous to the mission. To him.

She thought her friends had undressed her. What would she say if she knew it was he who'd ordered Henry to leave the servants' room? That it was he alone who'd carried her to one of the beds and had wrenched her soiled gown from her body and bared her to her chemise?

That he had taken a warm cloth to her hands, to her face, noting in the most intimate ways the smattering of freckles across the bridge of her nose, the tiny scar along her jawline, the plush, almost decadent lips that would leave any man wanting until he kissed them.

Every act he did was in her care and concern. No movement untoward or indefensible. Though, in truth, being alone in her quarters was wicked, a distraction he could ill afford and had no answer for if some woman servant stormed in the room and shrieked.

Yet, he'd stayed, and prepared to announce he'd unbound her hair from the bun so her head might rest more easily on the thin mattress, which was all very true, but did not explain the heat of desire as he felt the thick plaits.

Nor did it justify the wish to sink his fingers into the thick locks to know the texture, to know...

That smell.

Pulled from thoughts that had no place here, even if her hair curling around her cap was intriguing, Louve inspected the various dishes on the nearest table.

Turning at the sound of his clattering platters, Bied started and a splatter of soup sizzled into the fire. 'I don't know why you keep jumping into rooms. When did you get here?'

'Does it matter when?' he said. Her complexion was even lovelier flushed from the heat. But more than he liked that, and hated that he liked it, her first response to him was a retort. 'Aren't you more concerned with why?'

'If you're here to inspect my food, it's mostly done, so there's no changing it.' She eased a pot away from a flame.

Three vegetable dishes, but instead of chard with almond sauce or potatoes with mustard sauce, there was cabbage on one plate, onions on other. And something... He leaned down... Something that could not be served.

There was meat being roasted and turned by two boys, but there was no glazing of wine or spices. Further, it was fast becoming over-charred, for one boy half slept and the other had twigs for arms.

At another table where there might be meat courses, there were pasties thanks to the baker, and what appeared to be an omelette with sticks of rosemary. And the dessert table. Tarts with fruit, but nothing else. No pears with comfits, peeled nuts or wafers. Nothing.

There was plentiful food. Enough to feed the mass of people in this fortress, but the quality wasn't there. And the smells from the soup...

He peered over the pot rim. 'What is the first course?'

She huffed. 'Shelled beans. There's no substituting these either. They're done now.'

Beans, but not soaked in cinnamon or sprinkled in thyme.

'Any seasoning?' he dared ask.

She stretched to serve another pot and, before he could alter the course, his gaze riveted on the stretch in her gown. Masking his reaction, he adjusted his hunched back. 'Is there salt?'

'In the pantry.' She peered into another pot and the steam turned her complexion rosier.

Of course, seasoning was in the pantry—he wouldn't expect there to be no salt in a home such as this—but that wasn't the point. The point of it also wasn't noticing her too-tight gown and lovely skin. The point was, 'You didn't use the seasoning?'

'Do you have the key?' she said.

The Steward likely did and that useless man left without giving him one, but that wasn't what caught his attention. It was Bied's reply; quick, sharp with just a bite. A tone she'd used when she was drunken and waving a goblet at him.

He...liked it. More than liked it. He shouldn't. This wasn't the time, the place, but he wanted more of her stubbornness and more of her hair turning curly with steam, so he asked, 'If there's no access to the pantry, what of the tarts and sugar?'

She gave him a sidelong glance, perhaps assessing if he was simple or taunting her. Whatever was in his expression, she turned up her determined chin and returned to her pots.

'Sugar!' she said. 'As if I've ever seen that. That's in a chest inside a chest inside the pantry. Honey might or might not have been used.'

Unsweetened tarts. Perfect. Everything was perfect from the locked pantry to her lack of reverence. To the dear fact Ian of Warstone, as wealthy as any king, was to dine on a lengthy and quite unflavoured meal.

Louve laughed.

Chapter Seven

Bied's back had stopped protesting hours before, but her feet continually reminded her she'd been on them for hours beyond hours. Halfway through the serving and her mind was wandering from the task. She was used to labour, but that very morning she'd drunk ale and was sick and her stomach still felt uneasy.

She felt uneasy. Tess was correct, she'd drunk such amounts before and had never been sick. She wondered if there was something wrong with the ale, but if there was, wouldn't the guards or Lord Warstone have mentioned it?

Then there was her sister. So much nearer than before and still so far away. The serving of courses slowed the meal, giving her time to cook, to plate such quantities, but it allowed her no time to slip up the stairs and see Margery.

Dessert was next. She needed an excuse to present herself or at the very least to swap duties with a server. All the time she cooked the old cabbage and onions, her sister's message burned in her mind worse than the turnips that had to be thrown away. And she was mere steps away! Bied cursed this absurd meal, the foolish Steward and the maddening Usher who forced her to toil at yet another task she hated. But mostly, she cursed those cursed goblets.

Louve was inspecting the oven preparation for the morrow when Jeanne approached him as a mouse would a cat. One of her cheeks was red as if she'd been slapped.

He saw red himself before he heard any of her rushed words—that Lord Warstone requested the appearance of his new Usher.

Louve wanted to bound up the stairs, draw his sword and exact some revenge on Jeanne's behalf. If such injury came to a young woman, then it was likely other servants were also treated poorly.

When he strode through the doorway, he waited in the shadows to take measure of the Hall. And what he observed... The guards. They were cavalier at the gates, arrogant in their superiority, but their behaviour in the Hall went far beyond inconsideration.

Guards pushed, shoved, great platters of food were upended, unruly conversation thrived. Two warriors at a table played some game of strength while bets were being taken. In between the benches, servers were mauled and tugged on to laps. Some laughter from both parties, some shrieking with alarm.

In the far corner, a man's back faced the room. His trews were undone and around his knees as he rutted a woman against another half-dressed man. Other men stood around them, cheering or waiting their turn.

No sword, no men at his side. Louve wanted to defeat them all, but instead he swung his gaze to the high table.

The Warstone resemblance was uncanny and unmistakable. Ian of Warstone lounged in his chair, one hand absently caressing the cheek of the woman sitting next him, the other wrapped around one of the last remaining goblets.

He was listening to a tale told to him from a giant brute of a warrior standing on the opposite side of their table. Ian appeared somewhat amused, his mistress...

Sitting unerringly still, her hands in her lap, she neither

ate nor drank. She didn't appear to be listening, though the warrior's antics were comically exaggerated. Instead, she actively avoided gazing at the warrior at all.

She was like that rabbit who knew it'd been spotted by the fox; she was, as well, singularly stunning. Hair the colour of gold, large eyes framed with lush lashes. Lashes wholly unneeded, for even from this distance the colour of her eyes was a mesmerising violet, like lavender made into clear gems.

But her beauty could not hide the corner of her slightly swollen lip. The demeanour of a woman who had been damaged and knew she'd be hurt again.

There was a familiarity about her that irritated him because he could not remember meeting one such as she and not doing something about it. However, something about her features drew his curiosity, but that was it. Beauty that she was, she held no candle to—

'What do we have here?' Ian's voice boomed out to the crowd.

The brute immediately stopped and turned; his stance was wide to protect his master. Scarred face, ruthless hand drawing his sword.

'Come now, Evrart, no need for protection in my own house.' Ian announced to everyone until his eyes locked on Louve's and then there was a stillness in the room, in the middle of his chest. Thus, Ian's next words were clear even above the roaring in Louve's ears. 'Is there need for protection in my home, Usher?'

Yes, Louve answered silently as he strode out from the doorway towards the dais. He hadn't been asked to approach and he refused to wait for it as a servant would. He did, however, keep the role he chose. That of a hunched usher and one who was not trained with a sword.

Ian might, through his spies, know of him, but Louve could almost guarantee he hadn't seen his appearance.

Appearing weak, without being so, was an advantage he'd keep as long as possible.

Ian of Warstone kept the same empty expression so there was no telling if he was amused or angered. He did, however, lower his hand from his mistress's cheek and place it on the table.

The woman breathed deeply as the large warrior strode to Ian's other side. Louve had never seen a man that size before, not even his childhood friend who stood taller than most. If he had to face this man, Louve would be greatly taxed.

As for Ian, he wore all the arrogant and privileged markings of a Warstone: raven-black hair and the blank stare of a predator. But Ian's eyes weren't like his brothers'. Where theirs were differing shades of warm grey, Ian's were much paler. Almost white and utterly malevolent.

'You're the one my Steward hired before he journeyed south,' Ian said.

Ah, so this was how it was to be played before an audience, with them both pretending in their roles. Fair enough.

'I had come looking for other work, my lord,' Louve said, 'but it appeared my services were needed in a much broader capacity. I hope you have found everything satisfactory.'

'I can assure you I am most satisfied with your presence,' Ian said. 'Delighted, in fact. It has been far too long since I had an usher and can see the position holds much merit. After all, how amusing it was to be served dishes the way they do in England. To savour flavours one by one by one. I can think of few things that I relish as much as food. This, perhaps...' Ian scraped his finger across his mistress's shoulder '...or perhaps that thrust of a short dagger in an enemy's heart come close.'

The woman wrapped a trembling hand around her goblet and took a drink. She set it down just as slowly, her mouth moving even after she swallowed as though she was tasting something she didn't like.

There was much about this situation that Louve didn't like, but if Ian thought he was as trapped or vulnerable as this woman, he was mistaken. He'd bide his time until—

A guttural groan from the back drew Ian's pointed gaze and he flicked a finger to the corner. Without a word, there was the scraping of a bench, the thud of fists, the mad pattering of a woman's bare feet against fresh rushes.

Louve refused to take his gaze away from the enemy.

'Excuse my men for their lack of manners.' Ian smiled at him. 'It has been too long since they fought and released their...liveliness. You can understand what that can do to a man to be so pent up.'

He was there when Ian's men last released their liveliness. His friend, Eude, a fellow mercenary, had been killed before he reached Reynold's door in Paris.

'In theory, yes,' Louve replied formally, exacting. In these games, it was best to mimic the other player for it revealed less of himself. 'But I do not have the penchant that warriors have, hence my duties to serve have fallen in other, but no less meaningful, ways.'

Ian's eyes roamed over Louve, who kept his hunched demeanour. Not too much—he could never sustain the ruse—but enough to bely some weakness.

'Hmm, yes,' Ian said. 'But I do not believe those duties pertain to the actual food that graced my table this eve.'

'Was there something the matter with the fare?'

'Oh, no, nothing wrong with it.' Ian waved his hand. 'The meat tasted of meat, the fava beans were shelled properly, but that comes to the issue. I am often gone, but when in residence, I like my privacy and to stay in my rooms.'

Ian expected him to comment, but Louve inclined his

head instead. If there was a point to this banal talk of eating, it was best to get on with it.

Ian's lips curved and he continued, 'Over the years, my cook has prepared me particular dishes a particular way. Masking the true flavours of food with green twigs from the garden and salt from the pantry. Now I can see that was of no benefit. Thus, I can only surmise that it wasn't Cook who prepared the meal?'

Louve didn't trust or like the direction of the conversation. To tell a lie wouldn't benefit his game, to tell the truth could reveal a weakness: Bied.

'No, Cook felt poorly and thus your staff had taken over his duties,' Louve said.

'My staff? You mean the ones who served the food, the baker, who appeared to make the same pies? No, no. This fine fare must be your doing, and thus, you must have directed the person to feed me in particular this evening. After all, what usher wouldn't want to impress a Warstone? Come, tell me who it was, or better yet, go fetch them so I can thank them personally.'

Never. Not in a thousand years. Ian didn't wish to thank the person who prepared the food. Ian wished to know who had fed him, to mark them in case the fare was poisoned. To track them, spy on them in case the person was of some import to Louve or Reynold.

However, if he appeared to defend Biedeluue even in the most insignificant of ways, it would mark her death.

'It is, and has been, one of your staff,' Louve replied. 'I'm surprised you have not dined on her food before. For I am new, but she is not and willingly volunteered for this evening. If you'll allow my leave, I'll bring her forth.'

Ian waved his hand. 'No, no. You've worked too hard. I will have one of my men fetch her. Name?'

'Biedeluue,' Louve replied readily.

The mistress jerked and the smallest morsel of omelette, balanced on her knife, flew across the table.

They all watched it fall to the floor except the culprit who immediately dropped her gaze. 'I'm so sorry, my lord.'

Ian's smile and eyes were almost indulgent. 'No worries, my Margery. Now let's see this new cook.' Ian tilted his chin at a guard who immediately strode to the back of the room.

He burned to warn Bied. She most likely would be surprised and terrified upon the guard's approach, could possibly stall or deny. He was surrounded by men who could easily kill him and Louve prayed that Bied for once wasn't the determined, stubborn, courageous, reckless person he knew her to be.

Chapter Eight

Raucous noises above her, the floorboards rattling the kitchen timbers. If she stayed still, she could feel the vibrations through her own feet. Bied rubbed her sleeve over her forehead and lifted the last pot from the oven. Not all needed to be cleaned because the fire burned anything off, but a few were worse than usual. What had she spilled?

'Let me help with the cleaning,' Tess said.

Bied jerked her head to get her hair out of her eyes. 'Where have you been?'

'I'm up far earlier than you,' Tess said. 'Most of my duties were already done.'

'Hence when you asked to be excused because there was so much to do?'

Grinning with a wink, Tess grabbed a broom. 'It turned out well, no one has died from your cooking.'

'Not yet. There's still your dessert.' It wasn't possible to stay annoyed at Tess, but she did lace a bit of it in her words. 'I couldn't believe putting me in charge was how you intended to keep me employed here.'

'You've been industrious in the kitchens. How difficult could it be to do a little more?'

'A little more! For a sennight, I've been sweeping

floors, washing pans, and serving food. Regardless of Cook's…situation, I've never fed this many.'

Cook, whose son had died a few weeks before. He was grieving and lost and hurting. Everyone tiptoed around him, including Steward.

'What will happen with Cook? He's never not been here at all. He at least arrives to prepare Lord Warstone's food, talks to Steward about the menu and then leaves. I can't keep this up if it's only me.'

'He'll come…' Tess's face fell. 'I don't know.'

It helped that Lord Warstone, when in residence, wanted simple meals served to him in his private chambers. Bied hadn't even seen him. And those few dishes Cook had continued to prepare and serve, which had left meal planning to the Steward. Feeding the rest of the household was a matter of quantity versus quality, but even that took planning on a grand scale.

She could pull meals together for a little while, but when the Steward returned with the goblets, expectations would be different. This occupation kept her far too busy to reach her sister. It wasn't in her nature for this much delay and wondering.

'What are we to do with the new Usher?' Tess said. 'He's…'

Far too handsome? Intriguing? Everything in her said she should and shouldn't trust him. She didn't even know how that was possible. He was more than competent as an usher, probably knowledgeable enough to be Steward if he had the proper lineage. Yet…she didn't know what it was, but he wasn't what he appeared.

It wasn't much, but why would an usher change how to present the food? Why did he ask the questions about Lord Warstone and his guards? If she had to choose between truth or falsity, she'd swear he was lying.

As for the rest, dark hair, blue eyes. Even with that odd

hunch, his build was far too noticeable. Strength without bulk, though he dropped her earlier today...that just made his presence and actions more suspicious to her. 'He's—'

'Cook!' a voice boomed from the stairs.

Both of them pivoted to the mercenary on the stairs.

'I think he means you,' Tess whispered.

Bied brushed her hands against her gown. She didn't know why she was called. The food wasn't perfect. Perhaps she'd be ridiculed or punished. Perhaps she'd be told to pack her belongings and leave at first light tomorrow.

If so, she'd sort all that out later. For now, she'd soon see her sister. Her sister! Unfortunately, the guard's thick back blocked her view when they entered the Hall. Yet, though she couldn't see, something was different in this room. A menacing anticipation pricked at her skin.

It was similar to the warning feeling she had got when Margery raptured on about Ian of Warstone, the same feeling that made her warn her sister not to become involved no matter his wealth or charm.

But now that feeling was amplified, causing the hairs on her arms to rise. But she shoved the feeling away when the mercenary stepped to her side as they walked between two long tables and she finally saw her sister.

With Lord Warstone's eyes on her, Bied could only give a cursory glance, but it was enough to see the dark circles under Margery's familiar eyes, and her lips looked... swollen.

Ian, however, from his pale eyes to his effortless manners, was as Margery described. He seemed to be discussing matters with Louve, who stood on the opposite side of the table.

Louve with dark hair, but not raven black like Lord Warstone. The Hall's lit torches revealed that there were warmer tones in it. And from this side, without Louve's arresting gaze distracting her, the little twist he did to stretch his posture before collapsing it again took on a different light. Perhaps he adjusted it because he was forcing the poor posture. It looked wrong on him.

It wasn't only the angle of his wide shoulders giving that impression, but the rest of his build. His height, the tapering at his waist, the strength defined in legs encased in breeches that no tunic or boots could hide.

'Is this she?' Ian said.

Louve peered over his shoulder, his eyes steady on hers. Not cold, or warm. Not empty. Surprised. Because she was here? Not possible; he'd known the mercenary came to fetch her.

But what? So little time together and too many facets to this man. Was he an arrogant usher or a someone else? He sometimes acted like the guards who trained for hours every day and, at other times, he'd sound more subservient than those who cleaned the garderobes.

Moreover, he kept prying and interfering which made her want to respond, to forget the servant role she played and…tie all his boots to the rafters. She needed to understand, to—no, she needed nothing from this enigmatic man. A man who appeared dark, but wasn't when the light was shone on him. Purposefully weak, when his body was strong. Irritated there was no seasoning for the food until he laughed…that laugh! She wanted to share it with him even having no idea why he did it or why she cared.

Only her sister should matter. Margery, whose hand fluttered about her as if wanting to eat, though she didn't, so she drank and… Was her sister swirling the ale around her mouth and grimacing before she swallowed? Her lip was swollen, and looked cut!

The bastard had harmed her. To have something to injure him with! The guard who still stood next to her had a sword—why couldn't she?

But she couldn't, no matter how much she longed to. Rumours of Lord Warstone, which she only truly understood right this very moment, were enough to know none of them would survive if she attacked. This man was possessed by his own demons.

There was no negotiating with him while she was empty-handed. She couldn't attack when he was so well-guarded. If she attempted or said anything, she'd put her sister in danger. But there was one offence she could make. Because as long as Margery was alive and within reach, she'd answer any challenge. 'I am she,' she answered.

Ian's brows shot up and Louve shifted to keep Bied, the guard next to her and the brute behind Ian in his sights. Here he was, a hunched waste of an usher with no sword in his hand and in a situation as fraught as when he faced adversaries on a battlefield.

It wasn't customary for the Cook to reply directly to the lord of the manor. By doing so, she'd not only insulted Ian, but his position as well.

'I don't remember seeing you before,' Ian said, easing back in his chair.

'Is there anything of the meal that displeased my lord?' she asked. Her eyes not on Ian, but on the mistress, who seemed to be sampling her brew as her wide eyes stayed locked on Bied's.

Louve widened his stance, prepared to fight. Bied provided Ian with neither a direct answer nor a gaze. If he could, he'd caution Bied on her obvious disobedience. No Warstone would allow it.

'It isn't possible that I haven't seen you before,' Ian continued as if he hadn't been slighted.

Bied slowly shifted her eyes from the mistress to Ian. 'I help in the kitchens and am far from the private chambers, my lord. I hope my food revealed that I have some skill when it comes to your household?'

'The food was adequate. In—'

'The drink, perhaps,' Bied interrupted. Louve watched her eyes go from Ian to the mistress and back. She needed to focus on the true threat, to have some sort of subservience. Quickly, and with much haste, for Ian had noticed her interruption.

'The drink,' Ian pronounced slowly, carefully, 'was passable. Barely, but only because I allowed it.'

Louve waited for her to understand Ian's warning. Instead, Bied raised a determined chin and moved so the guard next to her was in a better position to knife her in the back when Ian gave the command.

Louve ached to say something, to stop the volley of words and deeds that were causing only harm. Instead, she continued, 'Any improvements there, my lord, for the ale, which is only passable, or suggestions from your—'

'You're new,' Lord Warstone said, his words sharp. Definitive and almost ugly. He leaned forward like a hawk whose beak had made the first stab into its prey. 'You're new, which is something I do not, ever, tolerate. Who—'

The mistress cried out, a clatter of a knife, and all attention pivoted to her. Eyes welling with fetching tears, she sucked the finger in her mouth.

'A cut, my dear?' Ian asked with a disconcerting concern.

Keeping her finger in her mouth, she nodded. Louve breathed a sigh of relief that the attention on Bied had been luckily averted. Now if he could only extricate her from the Hall while Ian's attention was solely for his mistress.

'Here, let me help ease your mind of that.' Ian grabbed the fallen knife, grasped the maid's other wrist and made a shallow cut across his mistress's palm.

She cried out. Bied hissed.

'See, one cut is worse than the other. Isn't that better?'

Ian crooned, while tenderly wrapping a linen around the hand he'd damaged.

In the madness, Louve had only moments and turned to Bied. 'You're dismissed. See that dessert is prompt.'

He must appear uninterested, heartless, as he faced Bied, whose eyes brimmed with an emotion he never expected her to feel, let alone to hide from their rapt audience: wrath.

Instead of outrage, instead of leaping across the table or any other ridiculous actions he could envision, Bied pivoted towards the kitchens.

'Wait,' Ian called out.

Louve hoped upon useless hope that Bied would pretend she hadn't heard Ian. To keep walking to the kitchens and out the other door. Towards the gates, where if she was fortunate they'd open them and she could be free of all this.

But Bied turned. Her eyes flicked first to the mistress, to her hand Ian held against his chest, and then deliberately slowly to Ian's paler ones.

Ian's eyes weren't like his brothers'. They weren't brutal, like Guy's, young like Balthus's, nor were they searing with intelligence like Reynold's. They did, however, hold the same mad Warstone light that was all too familiar. But this time the promised madness was actualised.

Those eyes feasted on Biedeluue while Louve stood there. He could do nothing to protect her, to warn her, nothing without jeopardising everything. Bringing down the entire Warstone family was the deed necessary to end wars. Casualties were merely part of it. Reynold's mercenary, and his friend, Eude, had died because of this war. This brave woman, he feared, would be another.

'I expect to be fed on the morrow,' Ian said, cradling the bleeding palm to his jawline as if to soothe it before he set it on his mistress's lap and stood. At his waist were keys he unhooked and tossed towards her. They fell far short of her feet. To reach them she'd have to step closer to Ian, to the guard who stood near the high table.

'I expect the food to taste to my specifications and to be served in the way of my family. Do you understand?'

Louve didn't breathe. Bied was trouble, wrecked by a joyous recklessness all of which he envied even as he needed to crush it. But if she displayed any of it with Ian, he would injure her.

Taking two quick steps, she snatched the keys off the floor and straightened. 'I'll do as my lord wishes and am deeply honoured to provide him and his men with my humble fare.'

Ian's eyes narrowed. 'Find that it's not so conceitedly humble tomorrow or it won't be to my liking.'

Two steps, that's all Louve needed to disarm the guard who gaped at Bied's bosom when she bent for the keys. Two steps to grasp the sword and thrust it through his stomach. To toss the smaller dagger towards the eye of the guard next to Ian. Those would be the only two manoeuvres he had before his own life, and Bied's, would be forfeit if she challenged Ian now.

But Bied only clenched the keys, nodded once and with quick short strides was out of the Hall.

'Usher,' Ian said, 'I don't think you're needed any more this evening. Feed my men dessert and have water and fresh linens brought to my chambers so that I might care for my love's fresh wound.'

A game. One he could forfeit now and be no better off or continue to play. 'As you wish, my lord.'

Chapter Nine

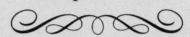

'Stop!' Louve commanded.

Bied yelped, the wooden ladle flew, the entire contents of ale arced above her head and she ducked.

He bit out a rapid curse as the ladle hit the wall behind him.

She spun around, just as he straightened from a crouched defence. 'Did you get any on you?' she said.

He brushed his hands down his front. 'No, and—'

'Let me grab this and fill it again.' She rushed around him and snatched the ladle. 'You deserve to be soaked. What are you doing sneaking up on me like that? Do you make any sound at all?'

'What am *I* doing?' he said watching her fill the ladle at the barrel and take a sip, then another.

He knew she was up to something. Warstone's malevolence permeated every stone of the fortress. Bied was reckless, but no fool, and had to know who the enemy was, but she'd kept looking at the mistress, kept asking about the ale. Now she was drinking it!

Pointing the empty ladle towards him, she said, 'There you go, repeating everything I said. You know, if I hadn't been working with you, I would think you were simple.'

She was spouting words, but he had absolutely no comprehension whatsoever. After the feast, he went to his room to rest, knowing he would need to be prepared for whatever Ian had planned for tomorrow. When he could sleep no longer, he went to walk, to think. Perhaps he could tell Balthus of the danger, though there was really no opportunity. That's when he saw her slinking around shadows and against walls.

'I'm simple,' he said.

'Right there, repeating again.' She filled the ladle again and drank. 'It's a terrible habit you have. You have to stop or no one will take you seriously. I certainly didn't, but I know better now. I'm relieved that I can tell you about it given the comradery we've developed.'

'We are not friends. I don't want to be friends. In fact— you're shifting the subject.' He didn't want her as a friend. He wanted more. Dangerous thoughts. Distracting needs. He took a step back, rubbed the back of his neck. 'Stop. Just stop. Biedelune, I followed you. And you're here drinking ale in the middle of the night.'

'The middle of the night was a few hours ago.'

'Bied.'

'It's true, it's almost morning.'

She prevaricated. What was she hiding and how to keep a fine line between what he'd come here to do and the irritating role as Usher? 'You're giving me no choice but to report you. You can't possibly be that thirsty. You've met Ian—you have to know I cannot falter in my duties.'

She swung the empty ladle between them, her hands and fingers deft on the instrument. 'Does anyone else know?'

'Anyone else know what?' His eyes wandered to her hands, to the ladle and her now wary expression.

'That I'm here—did anyone follow you? Did you tell someone before you followed me here?'

There, right there. She acted as though she didn't understand the nature of the household she laboured in, but then asked a question that indicated she did. Her coming to the cellars at this time of night meant she didn't want to be seen, meant she knew she wasn't supposed to be here and that she wanted to keep it hidden.

Which only indicated they were in more danger than he understood because Bied had an agenda—but what and why? 'Is it true that you're new? Is Ian right in saying he allowed no workers here?'

'How can that be true, he hired you.'

But Ian had had his own agenda when he set the trap for Louve to enter. By Ian's reaction, Louve knew Ian hadn't expected her. Not that anyone could. She was wild, clever, intelligent, but he'd spent years employed with intrigue and knew when a person deflected.

'Why are you here?' he repeated.

'To work.'

'Where are your family?'

'Asleep, most likely.' She swung the ladle, filled it. Drank again.

Games! 'Give me some of that.'

She shrugged and handed it to him. He sniffed and took a sip. Drained the rest when it tasted as he expected. Bied's expression and eyes weren't. She was too curious about his reaction, too wary.

'This ale seems fine,' he said.

She scrunched her face and scrutinised the other barrels. 'I think this one is, too.'

'Then what are you doing with the ale?' he said.

'I'm…tasting it,' she said.

He could see that she was tasting it, but in the middle of the night and alone. Only two possibilities existed and neither sat well with him.

What did he know about her? That she was a terrible liar, that she didn't know her way around the kitchens.

That even though she was new she had the support of the servants, who held a power of their own in a house such as this. He could still use her to help his mission, but asking her directly wouldn't foster trust and seducing her, if she was at all amenable, would only weaken his own defences.

This woman. If he had met her in any other time, even a few weeks ago, he would entice her from her secrets, then out of that taunting gown. As if he needed the crest of her breasts to desire her. He wanted her every time she *moved*.

'Lord Warstone accused you of being new. Let's assume he's right,' he began.

She held out her hand. 'If true, I did the task you wanted me to do, so what was the harm? It was fair to think you would rid the house of me after what happened to the goblets and the baker Tess tried to secure my position.'

'You lie horribly,' he said, handing her the tool.

She swung the ladle once again. 'I know.'

'That's how I know you're telling the truth, at least in part. If all you're doing is tasting ale, that can be determined quickly. You'd be gone by now.'

'Maybe I'm being diligent,' she said. 'When I came to the gates requesting work, the guards turned me away. Tess, however, sponsored my presence and I need to prove myself. Most of the staff were born and raised here—in fact, I don't know who hasn't been—but Cook hasn't been well and the kitchens were in trouble.'

'What's wrong with him? And before you try to shift subjects, you're drinking in the cellars in the middle of the night. I need some answers.'

'Cook's young son died less than a month ago. Choked on a bit of food Cook popped into his mouth. He's been blaming himself…grieving. Drinking and trying to forget. Since then Steward has been organising meals and Cook has mostly prepared Lord Warstone's meals, but… we've all been helping.'

She cared for others—that was also a crack in her defences and could be used against her. But it was also a crack in his. He couldn't be an usher with this woman. She wasn't a servant to him and he could never order her about. Even if he could, she wouldn't let him.

'I knew,' he said.

'Knew what?'

'That you were trouble.'

Tilting her head, she grasped the ladle with both hands. The shape, the way her fingers danced along the wood, stopped almost all other thought.

'And you're not?' she said.

He wrenched his gaze to hers again. 'You're very direct.'

She huffed. 'I'll repeat, you're not?'

He needed to return her irreverent tone. To bend her wit to that moment of awareness when, with just a glance, they acknowledged what it was they both wanted.

He wanted this woman. Not now. Too dangerous. He needed to be outside this mad intrigue and betrayal. To leave behind lies and games. To have a home of his own, a wife...some peace. Instead, he was in the very centre of mayhem with a woman who would only cause him more.

'You think I am direct?' he said. 'Not this time...no.'

'What is that supposed to mean?' she said. 'You're an usher, aren't you meant to order tenants and villeins about?'

She teased. Flaunted. Couldn't be contained. That alone he'd take advantage of if he didn't want it for himself so very much. For the rest? She *cared*. How could she be in this household, even with so little time, and still care? She'd lied her way into this position, for security, a roof over her head. There was nothing safe here.

'Don't tell Ian—'

'Ian?' she interrupted.

'Lord Warstone,' he corrected. 'Any of this. Before you ask the reasons, remember I was there in the Hall when he talked to you.'

'He didn't seem to like that I'm new,' she answered. 'But he didn't berate you.'

He had to lie, at least somewhat. 'The Steward left. His need for someone to manage is greater. Though I don't have a family to support, I'm not born to nobility and need the position.'

Bied grasped the handle with both hands once again and ran her fingers along the smooth sides. 'Do you intend to report me?'

His eyes went to her long fingers straying along the curved handle and locked on them. Try as he might, his body refused to have him look anywhere else. Not even to fully understand what she was saying. 'You want to be reported.'

'Certainly.' She wrapped the handle in her fist and stroked up.

'Do you need that ladle?' he choked out.

'No, why?'

He cleared his throat. 'Because I don't trust the direction my thoughts are going.'

Giving him an odd look, she presented it to him. 'I'll need it back, if you let me stay.'

He stared at the ladle in his hands, tracing along the handle where her fingers had been. It was warm still from her touch, but not nearly as warm as him, not nearly as hot as he needed them both to be. At that thought, the temporary easing in his breeches he'd felt when she handed him the ladle vanished.

'You told me you didn't need it,' he said. Under no uncertain terms could he give the ladle to her again.

She looked curiously at him. 'I wanted to explain myself first,' she said. 'And I could see there was doubt on your part, so it seemed easier to give you that.'

Barely holding back the growl, the need to tell her why he wanted it, wanted her, became almost too much. 'Bied, there is more than doubt when it comes to you. There's more of *everything*, truth be told.'

'That doesn't make sense. Again.'

No, it didn't. 'I am Usher and am in charge of the pantry and all that crosses the Great Hall. Ian of Warstone is not someone who would tolerate anyone tasting or...altering his ale.' He stopped. 'Did you smile?'

'Lord Warstone doesn't like me and you saw how I reacted to him, yet you didn't say poison.'

Louve stilled. 'What?'

'You don't believe I'm poisoning him.'

Two forceful steps towards her. 'Keep silent. Just silent.'

For reasons Bied didn't know, she did. Most likely because the look on Louve's face... Sometimes he was angry, frustrated or wary. Sometimes she was certain he played at being meek and awkwardly humble.

But this low growled command—no. That sound, that look—made goose pimples scatter across her arms. She felt like a rabbit who finally and far too late spotted the fox.

'What is it?' she whispered.

A quick shake of his head. Another wait while the odd sounds of the night filtered through: a scampering of rodents, the hiss of cats, the crunch of soft rushes, the creaking of the floorboards. Nothing else.

But the staying still allowed other sensations to permeate her senses. Like the dank cold of the stones. The urgency of the cheese wheels. The sharp vinegar tang of old spilled wine. And this man in front of her who had his own scent, one—

'Tell me it's not true,' he whispered harshly. 'No games. No confusing word play.'

'I can tell you I'm innocent, but wouldn't that be something a liar would say?'

He dipped his chin. She loved and hated when he looked so directly at her like that. Even in this dim light from the flickering torch she'd brought, there was no mistaking the piercing blue.

'Bied, I can't protect you if—'

She started. 'Protect me?'

A muttered curse.

When she waited, and he said nothing more, she gave in. 'Fine. No, I'm not poi—

'Don't say the word.'

Strange man. Not simple at all, but sometimes, like now, she wished he were. Because what he was, most certainly, was complicated. He wanted no word plays, yet she wasn't supposed to say a word. He wanted the reason she was here; however, she couldn't say why she was here.

'I was tasting the ale because I think it's already...' she waved her hand '...you know what.'

'What?'

She put her hands on her hips. 'The word you told me not to say.'

He took a step back, another. Immediately, she missed his warmth that she hadn't realised was there. 'You think the ale is already altered. Tell me.'

'Why?'

'I'm Usher.' At the doubtful look she gave him, he continued, 'And to keep my position, it might be useful to tell Lord Warstone.'

She didn't entirely believe him. 'Like me, I think you've got secrets and you're too new to care about your position with Lord Warstone.'

At his suddenly alert expression, Bied averted her eyes.

'What do we have in common?' Louve said. 'Secrets, or that we're new?'

Why did she say that? She hadn't drunk that much and, in truth, this ale didn't seem any different than anything else she drank.

More than that. Why did she want to tell him? It couldn't be something so simple as he had a secret, too. There was something odd about his behaviour and she had too many seasons not to know when a man was lying. But even with the secrets and the behaviour, he hadn't immediately jumped to the conclusion she was poisoning the ale.

A typical usher would have questioned her. The Steward, despite her help, would have had the guards punish and then discard her outside the gates. Did he truly trust her, or did he have something to hide himself?

After tonight, she wanted to trust someone. Weeks being here and she knew the task was too great to do alone. She'd been tempted so many times to tell Tess and hadn't. First because she didn't know her, then she worried she'd embroil her friend in something she could get punished for as well.

But this man was different. He was an outsider, like her, and he was in a higher position. Moreover, there was something else about him…almost a quiet strength, a surety, underneath it all that called to her. Of course, she couldn't entirely be certain her willingness to trust him hadn't to do with the way his dimples flashed when he smiled, or was angry, or frowned. Like he did now.

'Tell me,' he said.

She arched a brow at him. 'Because you're an usher, or something else? If you want me to say anything, you tell me first.'

So many emotions crossed through those eyes of his, fleeting and gone. But when he remained silent, she couldn't wait. 'Will you tell me?'

'You're not unpredictable,' he said.

She wasn't. Couldn't be. Usually, she'd attempt to be deferential to those who fed and clothed her, certainly not tapping her feet with impatience. He glanced at her foot before he shook his head.

'I have always worked for others. In the past, I have managed another's estate.'

'And?' she prompted. 'I can already guess from what you have done that you've done it before.'

'You're observant. Couldn't your observations of my character be enough?'

She shook her head.

He gave a rough exhale. 'You are correct in thinking Lord Warstone is approaching me differently.'

She waited. When he didn't continue, she said, 'You're simply telling something else I observed.'

A quirk to his lips. 'But the reason is…he is playing games with me.'

That terrified her. If Lord Warstone played games with this man, he'd play games with Margery. 'Do you know him?'

'I have never met him before.'

'Then why would he—'

'That's enough.'

'Because you want to keep your secrets?' She noticed the sudden tension. She remembered the word he'd used before. 'That isn't the reason, is it? You said you want to protect me and keep me safe. Me, who is a complete stranger. Even so, aren't I already in trouble for being here when I'm not supposed to be? Or simply by being here in the cellars in the middle of the…almost morning? Nothing is safe here.'

He kept his gaze on her, nothing of his thoughts in his expression or any movement. 'Your turn,' he said. 'You tell me you believe the ale to be altered. Tell me why you think that.'

'There are a couple of reasons. The first was the day of your arrival.'

'That was only yesterday. And in that little time you decided to be here?' he said. 'Do you not remember that only yesterday you were ill?'

'I wouldn't have played the game if I thought I'd lose,' she said. 'The amount was not unusual and Galen was also sick. But then at the feast with the lord and his…lady. She drank and smacked her lips afterwards. She then peered down into the goblet and swirled the contents about as if she were looking for something. That gave me the idea that the ale is…you know what…or at least something is terribly wrong with it.'

His brows rose. 'You determined from a distance observing a woman licking her lips that the ale was wrong? Did she speak to you?'

This was getting into the territory she did not want to talk about. 'No, but she's beautiful. Beautiful people are discerning, aren't they?'

When he didn't answer, she asked, 'Did you find her beautiful?'

She wanted to kick herself for asking when ultimately, she always knew the answer. But this was different because this man didn't know they were related. No…that wasn't the reason.

She wanted to know because Louve kept looking at her and making her feel something she shouldn't. So she wanted to hear it from him and remind herself she shouldn't be thinking of dimples, blue eyes and dark hair that fell across his eyes just so.

'I know you can't actually confess to finding another man's wife or mistress comely,' she said. 'But surely you noticed the shade of her hair and eyes. Isn't a woman that beautiful discerning? Look who she's with—Ian of War-stone is certainly handsome and powerful.'

He examined her so long, she was certain two years had passed before he spoke.

'Are you telling me you came to the cellar in the mid-dle of the night to determine if the ale was altered?' he said slowly. 'You wished to examine that by yourself with no assistance as you drank the ale, even though you were ill before?'

Expecting him to talk of her sister, but feeling as though his question was a deception, she answered with the truth. 'Yes.'

He went to hand her the ladle, but when she reached for it, he held it back. 'What other misconceptions are you toiling under?'

They weren't misconceptions, they were truths, and she had a mad thought to tell him so. Even though she had no idea who he was and a feeling that underneath everything he was good wasn't enough to risk her sister.

With her sister well-guarded and Lord Warstone suspi-cious of her presence, she had few choices. Her slipping up the staircase and releasing a locked latch as she originally thought would be impossible in this fortress.

'Lord Warstone wasn't pleased with the food I pre-pared, because of your suggestions,' she said.

'Not happy with your presence,' he added. 'The food and service were fine.'

She snatched the ladle back. 'I thought if I tested this, and it was altered, then I could stay.'

She had no intention of staying—she wanted to bargain for her sister. Ian of Warstone didn't truly need Margery. Surely, he'd be so grateful for her saving his life that he'd do anything. Especially if she found who did it, which shouldn't be difficult. There were only a few people who had access to the ale barrels. And if it wasn't from the barrels, then in the ale house, or maybe in those ridiculous goblets she drank from.

His eyes narrowed. 'You would risk your life so you could stay in an occupation you've held for two weeks?'

'A difficult one, and I'm not from a noble family with wealth.' She threw his own words back at him.

A beat of unerring silence before he said, 'You're quite faithful to him.'

'To whom?' She filled the ladle again and lifted it to her nose. This cold damp room was perfect to store wine, ale and the wheels of cheese that permeated the air with a rich pungency, but it masked the ale's aroma.

'Ian of Warstone,' he said. 'I'm assuming that's why you're testing the ale. Why else?'

'I can spout as many questions as you. Why aren't you stopping me from drinking this? Why aren't you reporting me immediately? Obviously, you can as Usher. Shouldn't you be protecting the supplies or throwing me outside the fortress gates for being somewhere I shouldn't?'

'What if you're right?'

She ladled more and drank again. 'That's why you're here, to see if I'm right?'

Did the flavour seem odd? No, but she'd been drinking this same ale for weeks. It could be a possibility that the poison was weak and she'd have to drink so much she'd be sick.

She'd know soon enough. 'You were there in the Hall—he doesn't want me here. I'm trying to prove my worth so I could have a roof when winter comes.'

'He let you go after the meal,' he said. 'Being a servant would mean you telling him you think it's altered, not drinking it yourself.'

He snatched the ladle away.

'I think it's the quantity that matters,' she said.

'Quantity?' he said. 'If you are right, it'll affect someone immediately. That's the point of it.'

'What if it's in tiny quantities from a person who doesn't want to get caught? You said this is not what we've been drinking. It's been watered down.'

'Sometimes, I'm not certain who you are,' he said.

'We're merely servants who need these positions so we're not out on the streets,' she said.

'You are right,' he said. 'You can hold your ale and you were drinking before I came in.'

His look was all too knowing. As though he was unravelling some string and soon he'd have it all straight and it would be she who was revealed. She could hold her ale, but...the more time with him, the more of his voice she took in and that way he looked at her, the more she risked her sister.

'I feel no effects,' she said. 'We should try another barrel.'

'Where are the cooper tools?'

Nodding her head towards the door, she jammed the bung in, but it'd need a mallet.

'What happens when that one is also unaltered?' Louve struck the bung and moved on to the next cask.

She wouldn't wait for his cooperation. They'd shared information, enough for her to know he wasn't telling her everything. But she didn't need to know everything about him to save her sister. If he helped her enough, she'd take it. The sooner she could rescue her sister the better.

'There are over twenty barrels in this cellar. What if it's not in those? What if it laced the goblets that only the lord and his mistress use?'

At the helpless sound that somehow escaped her throat, in her heart, she knew she'd made a mistake.

The few torches she'd lit were enough to see the room

and more than enough to see surprise, then a wary comprehension, flit across his features.

'Who are you trying to protect, Biedeluue?' he said.

'I'm not trying to—'

'I haven't known you long, but I know you well enough when it comes to this. This is far beyond trying to keep a roof over your head. You're testing this ale. You're putting your own life in danger for someone you care about.'

'How could I care about anyone? I haven't been here long.'

'You care about the Cook. Inebriated, yet you were waving your arms shouting about protection of the children. You told Tess to be quiet so she wouldn't be punished.'

She moved to get past him, but he blocked her.

'You didn't give yourself away, not until I mentioned the goblets. It isn't Lord Warstone you care for, it's the woman.'

'It's Lord Warstone. I'm loyal to him, like you said.'

'You didn't ask me about him. You asked about her. There are only three people in this fortress who weren't raised inside these walls or just outside. Who is she to you?'

He searched and searched, and she could turn away, but Bied knew it was too late. Still. She tossed the ladle on top of the barrel. 'I'm tired and there's nothing wrong with the ale. Since it is almost morning, I must begin in the kitchens.'

She pivoted to get around him and, for one brief moment, she thought he'd let her go, but just as she went past, his hand clasped hers.

His hand was warm, firm. She could have yanked it out of his grasp, but the easy possessiveness of his grip, the tips of his calloused fingers brushing against her inner wrist and something other than annoyance rippled through her.

Something strong enough to hold her still. Hold *him* still. Blue eyes riveted where they touched. A forced inhale through a clenched jaw. His hair cutting across the high bones of his cheek, pointing to the almost softness of his lower lip and casting shadows where his dimples would be.

He was close enough for her to scent wool, leather, and something like sunlight in forests. Something of...him. His lips stayed clenched; she felt her own part. At that moment he raised his eyes to hers, blinking as if it was she who stopped him from leaving the room.

'Who are you?' he said.

A sister. Always a caregiver, but at this moment she felt like his. 'I told you.'

His gaze cleared. 'Who is she?'

Tension stabbed through him, through her, and it jerked her from his spell. She wrenched her hand, but his fingers clamped hard.

'No,' he said, a firm shake to his head. 'Deny it.'

'She's my sister,' she said.

Chapter Ten

Louve felt the floor drop, envisioned the time involved, the coin spent, the secret discussions and strategies wreck against the cellar walls. Felt his own heart pain in his chest from a wound she gave him. Then felt everything change with a few words.

'Damn you.' Yanking her wrist towards his chest, he catapulted her against him. Soft curves unwillingly given; he crushed his lips against hers. It wasn't to taste, to seduce or discover, but to punish. To claim. To take possession on the secrets she held and shouldn't have. They were his now.

Yet as he felt her softness, caught her breath, the punishment he meant to give her became his. As his body tightened, as his blood pulled and pounded, the claiming became hers. Her free hand laid against his chest, denying him the entirety of her body. The need for more becoming too much. The heat from her fingers not nearly enough before she gave a hard bite of her nails and shoved him away.

He let her go this time and she scrambled back. Her eyes darted behind him, noticing he stood in front of the only exit. She wasn't going anywhere.

Seeming to know his thoughts, she held her wrist in

her hand and rubbed. Her confession, the fact he'd injured her, sent him down a seething path he'd never been before. That of frustration and self-loathing. Pivoting around her, he went to an ale barrel, ripped on the seal until it popped and froth poured out.

'What are you doing?' she said.

'Tasting this myself while you tell me everything.'

He liked that she stood there. Partly in surprise, partly because she was still fighting him. He liked that more than was good for either of them.

'While you don't tell me anything,' she said.

He shrugged. 'Not fair, I know. But what you told me is far worse.'

'How could my telling of family—' She released her wrist. 'Because Lord Warstone is playing a game with you.'

Her mind… When she was like this, he didn't need perfect light to know how she felt, it didn't matter if her eyes were…lavender. That was the colour threading throughout the blue. Her eyes had lavender like her sister's. And her hair had the golden colours, but so many others. He liked that infinitely more. He liked her.

'Why are you here for your sister?' He drank.

'It's no concern of yours because we could be gone this very day. Aren't you going to ask why I'm here to take her away?'

'I saw her in the Hall, it doesn't take much to know why you want to rescue her.'

She flexed her fingers at her side. Was it from her thoughts or because he hurt her? Those wrists, the grace of her fingers. The fact he could have crushed either… He wanted to cradle it, press his lips to soothe… Images of Ian slashing her sister's palm turned his thoughts ugly.

'I owe you,' he said.

She waved her hand. 'I don't know you— I don't need

to be involved in your games. I have enough problems of my own.'

'Don't we all?'

She eyed the door behind him.

'Try it,' he goaded.

She crossed her arms, which threatened the last thread of the gown holding her in, and he was tempted to tug.

'As if you could possibly stop me,' she said, 'you're hunched—'

He straightened to his full height and cricked his neck.

'That's what *I* thought,' she said.

He gave her that victory, but that would be the last. 'Now tell me.'

'No, there is nothing that is yours. My sister is my responsibility. She's younger than me, gentle, and needs me. I can't imagine how she's surviving! I will get her out of here. Obviously, whatever games you play with Lord Warstone will only complicate it.' Her eyes widened. 'You didn't pois—'

'Don't!' he whispered harshly. They'd both hugged the walls and shadows to get here, but the fortress was well-guarded and nothing could be left to chance. 'Do you honestly believe we're two people alone in the cellars at this time of night? That there couldn't be someone on the other side listening?'

In dawning horror, she surveyed the room and closed door. 'Why did you follow me here?'

'Because no good could come from you being here. What are you planning?'

'Because I know that the ale is altered, I intend to use it to negotiate with Lord Warstone to release my sister.'

'You're clever, you have to know he'd want more than information.' Louve cursed. 'You intend to find the culprit and bring a prize for exchange.'

'It would work—'

'If you weren't dealing with a madman. You can't know he didn't alter the ale himself to trap someone else in his games.'

'Why would he harm himself for some game?'

She truly didn't know the Warstones. 'Was he smacking his own lips at the altered taste?' At her expression he added, 'Does he know you are related?'

'You keep asking me questions. You keep telling me these matters, as though I can believe any of them,' she said. 'You kissed me…and who are you? You're no… usher.'

He had kissed her and he felt the burn of it now. When she fell into his arms, he had not wanted to let her go. Now that he had had the barest taste of her, he only wanted more. 'I am only Louve and you and your sister are in far over your heads. You can't trust me, yet you must. I'm not the enemy. Ian's the man you have to defeat.'

This man, this stranger, had kissed her. Her lips still felt the bruising press, her body the giving away against his hard length. She had curled her nails into him, wanting to explore where he only took before she broke them apart.

It was true, Ian of Warstone wasn't who she was expecting. She knew from what Margery had told her that he wasn't good. When Ian summoned her, when she saw his Hall for the first time…

For the fortnight she'd been here, the men had eaten in the Hall, but the behaviour wasn't like she'd seen this night. It was always loud, messy, the dogs having free rein. But the giant warrior animatedly telling a story before the dais, those men in the corner, the fight in the other—it seemed they were amusing Lucifer himself.

'I have to trust you…because why?' she said.

'Tell me why you're here.'

'Margery sent me a message. That's how I knew she

was in trouble.' At his surprised look, she continued. 'Writing became essential with my family when I had to look for work. We're close. Margery was taught how to do sums, reading and writing. She's far better at languages than any of us. She taught us with a stick and some dirt.'

Out of the slit she'd made in the hem of her chemise, she pulled out the tiny bit of precious parchment, watched his mouth purse before he handed it back to her.

'Her penmanship is beautiful,' he said.

Of all the things he could have said to convince her, that was it. 'I don't taste anything different with this ale, can we open the next one?'

He set the ladle down. 'Your sister is unique looking.'

It had been years since they were together under the same roof, but the sting of a male asking about Margery was still familiar.

There was a time when she was hurt because she didn't carry the beauty of her sister. But as she got older, she began to appreciate what she did have and pity Margery because hers came at a price.

'You're angry.' He straightened, filled the ladle and took a taste. Sipped some more. 'Is it because you've rescued your sister before?'

Grabbing the ladle, she took a sip, though she wasn't concentrating on the taste. 'Everyone notices her. I could never be angry about that. It's not her fault.'

'You're not angry at her, but her admirers.'

'We've all had to protect her.' It seemed she had to protect her from Louve as well.

'Ian might have noticed her because she's comely, but that's not why he keeps her.' Louve's eyes strayed to the ladle gripped in her hands, his expression curiously pained.

Irritated at that look, she dipped the ladle in the barrel

and swallowed several gulps. She thought Louve would be different. Foolish idea. A man who looked like him was used to women who looked like her sister.

'Do you believe she's beautiful?' she said. The thought made her ill. Or…was it the thought?

His gaze darted to hers, his brows drawing in. 'You said so, but—'

'But?' she repeated. Was he lost in reverie thinking about her sister's eyes, her hair? She'd been a child when she'd last had this doubt about her appearance and quickly rid herself of it. This man was making her question herself. Something wasn't right.

'Margery's beauty represents—' Louve inhaled sharply, straightened his shoulders.

'Are you feeling well?' Bied said.

'Though her beauty can't compare to yours.' Louve's eyes darted to the barrel.

'What?'

Louve rubbed his forehead. 'We didn't drink that much.'

'It's the same as last time.' Bied tried to focus on Louve, on his words, but she must have heard it wrong. 'This ale's altered.'

Louve gave a long exhale, leaned against the wall. 'We have to mark that barrel.'

If she lifted her arms, her body would revolt.

Bied had paled. Louve's own skin felt flush and cold. They hadn't had much of the last barrel, but apparently it didn't take much.

They must get out of here. Soon. If either of them was sick, there was no pretending they weren't there. The evidence would be too obvious.

He pushed off the wall, staggered, released the dagger at his waist. On the underside he made a long scrape so it would look natural.

The room spun when he straightened and he noticed the tap. 'This barrel's already been marked.'

'What's that sound?' she said.

Sheathing the dagger, his movements were clumsy. Too much ale and that sound!

'You...haven't heard it before?' he said. 'That's the herald. The gates are opening.'

'The gates!' she said, swallowing hard. 'The gates haven't opened since I've been here and it's not yet morning. Who would travel at this time of year and in the middle of the night?'

It was almost morning, bitterly cold, and the person travelling would be someone who wanted to hide until they knew it was safe. Safe because they were among their kind. Their kin.

The horn played only a few notes, a singular familial tune for one family in particular. Unbelievable. Inconceivable and, absolutely, certainly, the worst that could happen.

The Warstone family had come for a visit. Despite everyone knowing this was merely a game, it must be played out.

He, as Usher, was duty bound to serve the family home and lord. Which meant he should already be at the gates, should already be shouting orders to servants. He should have already known they were coming so rooms were prepared. Simple duties and yet if not done as was customary, then a certainty that he was a fraud. Ian might know, but did anyone else?

To leave the cellars when everything between them wasn't finalised wasn't wise. She knew nothing, not truly, and that could cause further problems. He had to warn her somehow.

A wave of nausea hit him and Bied staggered. They needed to leave. Right now. To face a family who declared massacres and burned their own children all while his stomach threatened to empty its contents and his thoughts turned increasingly vague.

If the poison was meant to fell enemies, it had caught its prey: him.

Chapter Eleven

His stomach roiling, his thoughts full, Louve watched the procession out of the corner of his eye. Ian might know who he was, but in the game, the players played. And Louve intended to play the Usher until either he won, or a sword cut through his heart.

That eerie horn sound had stopped, but he swore it reverberated against the stone walls of the fortress, against the plumes of cold air lit by torches. Reynold had never allowed a display of his family crest. He had certainly never wanted the horn signal that heralded his family's arrival. But one time, he'd whistled it for Louve.

Maybe it had been the storm slashing against the small hut they'd found shelter in, maybe it was the lateness of the evening or the amount of drink. But sitting before that fire, and between sips of the last flagon of ale, Reynold had whistled it over and over as if he couldn't stop.

Louve had never seen his friend that way before. When the fire dimmed and their cups were emptied, Louve plucked the empty cup out of the warrior's hand and set it down. He'd left Reynold in the giant chair, knowing he'd provoke him on the morrow. But that night, the song haunted Louve's sleep and neither of them talked much the next day.

No, Louve hadn't forgotten that horn's unique signal and it had saved him and Bied as they left the cellar and rushed along the wall's edges. The only people he knew to avoid were the Warstones themselves. The guards and servants were too embroiled in their own lives to worry about others.

They had to separate when they reached their quarters. Though he tried to warn her along the way, he hadn't been certain she listened. No time to worry about it now, he had to prepare.

His room was large, luxurious by any servant's standards, and the privacy it provided was welcomed right now. Eyes burning, he forced his stomach to empty in a bucket. He went to the basin, poured cold water and splashed it on his face. Fresh clothes would hide most of the night's events, chewed mint would relieve the foul taste in his mouth, but the distractions in his head were a weakness he could ill afford.

He was tired. There were long days where travel was rough, the weather cruel, then there were days like this. He'd never had a day like this. And it wasn't entirely caused by the Warstones or the intrigue, or someone trying to kill him.

But Biedeluue. What to do with her, how to protect her without compromising his position? If he ignored her and her situation, she'd be safe, or as safe as Ian allowed. He hadn't liked that Bied was in this fortress, but had seemed to prefer to keep his mistress. For now, it was questionable whether Warstone knew they were sisters. They weren't similar unless you scrutinised both. He knew which of them he preferred.

He needed to think of Balthus, of Reynold and the Jewell of Kings. He should ignore the woman who'd come to rescue her sister. Yet he had to help her. In this vast world, what did it mean if one person didn't help another? Ian wouldn't let go of Margery without some exchange and she was too heavily guarded to make an escape.

A negotiation was needed. While he still had breath in his body, he wouldn't allow Bied to face Warstone. It was up to him.

Clothes straightened, he hurried down the hallway to one of the outside passageways. Ian would have heard the horn; he'd want to greet whatever family member deemed it necessary to arrive this early in the morning.

There were enough torches and sunlight peeking on the horizon to flood the courtyard. Enough illumination to cast shadows and count the members, to see the others who flaunted the Warstone golden crest.

Ian wore it. That was one. A thin tall woman, her grey hair plaited in an intricate coil on top of her head was another. Next to Ian's mother was, undoubtedly, Ian's father, a stout warrior who rode alongside her.

But the figure right behind them, riding a horse Louve had seen yesterday with the same carelessness that had become all too familiar over the last weeks that he'd ridden beside him—Balthus rode behind his parents as if he'd always belonged. If Ian didn't kill him, Louve certainly intended to.

Bied hung her head over the nearest garderobe. They hadn't been cleaned for a day, so the smell that wafted up helped heave her stomach's contents down the narrow hole. Her body shuddered, but once she knew she could stand, she did. Bracing one hand against a wall, she waited until she didn't need the facility again.

Warstone's family. Bied had only had a glimpse, but the wealth was staggering. Maybe thirty or fifty people, mostly guards all dressed in the same garb. Plain, but for a band of red silk on the bottom of tunics.

She'd always been fascinated by that red band. Thought

it a useless bit of frippery that served no purpose. If one sat behind a table no one could see it. But she'd thought it was restricted to this strange household.

Louve's role here was as Usher, but what was his other purpose? He said he was playing a game with Ian…but there was no hint of a friendship and he'd said it was dangerous for her and her sister to be here. If he hadn't distracted her with his kiss, with his accusations, with his very presence, she would have realised nothing was revealed.

What did she know of him? Nothing. His accent belied his English heritage and he had the look about him, but he didn't reveal where he came from. Had he a wife, parents or siblings?

As for his motives, he hadn't discussed those either. No, it'd been her revealing everything. He knew she cared for people and loved her sister. That she learnt reading and writing by sticks and dirt. She'd become vulnerable to him. A stranger. She knew better than to believe men.

Her stomach pained her, but was tolerable. Her head pounded and her legs felt shaky, but she was infinitely stronger than she was a few moments before. Pushing off the wall, reminding herself to report a cleaning before—

'What are you doing here?' Tess proclaimed.

Tess! Bied slammed the garderobe door behind her. 'Do you need to go in there?'

'No,' Tess said, 'I was looking for you. You were in bed last night, but when I woke up to do the bread you were—'

'Shh.' Bied looked down the hall. It was empty, but she could hear the household greeting the visitors.

When they left the cellars, Louve had urgently whispered warnings. How she wasn't to break the role they played, that he was nothing but an usher and Margery a mistress. To try not to speak, to nod and curtsy only. On and on he'd whispered instructions, hastily given protec-

tive words. She was wary of the visitors, worried over
Margery, had barely heard a word he said, but why hadn't
she demanded answers?

'Everyone is in the kitchens which is where you needed
to be, although you should know...' Tess stopped, tilted
her head. 'Were you sick again?'

Bied nodded.

'I know there is something amiss.' Tess crossed her
arms. 'I took a chance and let you in. The Steward was not
pleased, but with Cook... Don't even begin to say nothing is happening. Are you—'

Bied grabbed Tess's arm. 'I'll tell you, but not here.'

When Tess relented, Bied quickly walked to the servants' quarters which were empty at this time of the day.

How to begin? Margery's message was foreboding, but
the information Louve voiced was menacing.

Her earlier thoughts still rankled. Since those fateful
days when she was much, much younger, when had she
ever relied on a man to help her? She knew better. Her
father abandoned her family; the village men offered assistance at a price. That man riding through the village,
spotting Margery and...taking her away with him, then
Lord Warstone trapping her. Men were not to be trusted.

'You were right, there is something wrong with the
ale,' Bied said.

Tess's jaw dropped. 'You tested it by drinking it yourself!'

Bied threw up her arms. 'Why does everyone keep
questioning me on this?'

'Everyone?' Tess said. 'Pray, you are new and we don't
know each other well, but I feel as though we have some
understanding.'

Bied did, too, and perhaps it was time to confess. She
needed her sister right now, to talk about...rescuing her
sister! It was past time to confess to Tess.

Tess cleared her throat. 'I hope I can tell you what I believe—you're trying to prove your worth. That's what you're doing, isn't it? You don't have a husband or children and not two coins to rub together either.'

'You think I drunk pois—bad ale to prove myself.'

'You couldn't have done it for the result or the taste. Or...' Tess paled. 'You're not... You're not...'

She thought she wanted to be dead. 'I didn't intend to get sick. It happened a bit more quickly this time.' What could she say? She'd been holding off telling Tess anything and, now with Louve hinting at danger, it wasn't easy.

'I know what this is,' Tess said.

Bied started. She did? Perhaps that's why she felt such an affinity with Tess. 'I wanted to tell you, but I wasn't certain how to begin.'

'I had an aunt with the same wariness as you,' Tess said. 'I know nothing can be done now. Since you're here, obviously you have some control, but sometimes... I think she needed to tell someone. I want you to know I will listen.'

Bied had nothing under control and she needed far more than mere listening, but it was a beginning. 'Your aunt had family in trouble, too?'

Tess's brows eased. 'Her husband wasn't kind. The village she lived in allowed it. Of course, under the sanctity of marriage her husband was within his rights to do what he did, but...she lost an eye. It was yet another fight, yet more wounds, but he had a wooden spoon in his hand and when he went to strike...'

Tess shook. 'When she healed, she left. We all woke up one morning, she wasn't there any more and we never saw her again.'

Bied could only stare. What Tess described was horrific, yet she'd also said her aunt reminded her of...her.

'When you arrived requesting work,' Tess said, 'well, no one comes here, either because of the Warstone repu-

tation or the knowledge we never open doors for anyone
new. I was raised here and as I watched you look around,
I remembered my aunt. You seemed fearful, so I let you
in. Was it a husband, a father? Who hurt you and do we
need to do something about it?'

If Biedeluue could have conjured up a friend, Tess
would be it. Mostly because of how much Tess seemed to
understand her and wanted to help. But Biedeluue wasn't
here for friendships, as badly as she wanted one. She was
here for her sister.

'There's a reason I am fearful,' Bied said. 'There's a
reason, too, that I'm testing the ale.'

At Tess's look, Bied continued, 'I have a sister and
she's here.'

'Tell me,' Tess said.

Bied did. When she was done, she only had to ask,
'Will you help me get Margery out of here today?'

'I'd be insulted if you didn't ask.'

Chapter Twelve

Ian took his parents to their rooms, so it wasn't difficult for Louve to meet Balthus in an abandoned room near the root storage.

What was difficult was believing that the youngest Warstone had purposefully trapped himself in the Warstone fortress and seemed amused because Louve was disturbed. His stomach was moderately better, but now his head pounded.

'What are you doing here?' he said.

'The whole party were travelling not far from where I hid,' Balthus said.

He could have lost Balthus and not even known it. 'They spotted you?'

'No,' Balthus scoffed. 'I actually let my parents pass right under me, so I was at their back when I greeted them. You should have seen their expressions!'

'What of the other men?'

'Still hidden. Still safe. There was time for instructions before I joined my family's hunt.'

Hired mercenaries, men paid by coin for dangerous duties, were protected while the one man they were all meant to protect greeted the sword point.

'It's not too late—your family are occupied, you can leave.'

'Why would I do that?' Balthus said.

'That's obvious. What isn't obvious is your being here.' At Balthus's expression Louve added, 'Please do not tell me it was for your amusement.'

'I was bored waiting.'

Louve had been gone a day.

'What role are you playing here?' Balthus said.

'I'm Usher, but the Steward left to secure goblets and my role has expanded.'

'Goblets?' Balthus said. 'What importance is that?'

'It's a long story and I, too, am suspicious of his departure, but haven't had time to make enquiries.'

'Do you have the parchment, then?' Balthus asked.

'Are you jesting? Were you always this impatient and impulsive?'

'You left early enough. Regardless of the threat my brother represents, he does sleep and he can't be everywhere at once.' Balthus crossed his arms. 'Reynold trusted you on this. Given his proclivity, I expected more from you.'

He'd got a few hours of sleep. Not nearly enough for everything that had happened. Arriving to chaos, to games, to a reckless woman and poisoned ale. In between, he'd conducted Usher duties.

'As I've said, I've been occupied,' Louve said.

'This is why I am here,' Balthus said. 'This parchment is crucial, and any delay could be our undoing.'

Louve took one look at Balthus's haughty expression, of him barely containing a laugh, and swung his fist.

Balthus ducked, lost his footing and fell to the floor. Not as satisfying as a direct cut across his jaw, but the humiliation provided some comfort. Unfortunately, the sudden movement reminded him he'd been spitting bile in a bucket less than an hour before.

Balthus stayed on the floor. 'You don't look well.'

'That's because I'm poisoned.'

Balthus merely leaned back against the wall, resting his elbows on his knees, his position as casual as if they dined in an open field under a summer sky.

'No reaction at all?' Louve said.

Balthus huffed. 'I've been poisoned too many times to count. Warstones would recognise the different subtleties and some of the effects. Do you have any with you?'

'It's in a barrel in the cellar.'

'So that's why you don't have the parchment, because you've been drinking…with Ian?'

No, with a woman he'd tried to warn, but hadn't. She was a distraction from the mission, a distraction because… her sister. Had he told her to not do anything? He couldn't remember, but, knowing Bied, she was probably charging ahead, and with the entire Warstone clan in residence, it was a nightmare.

'I have to get out of here.'

'I unquestionably liked you better when you weren't so serious.' Balthus stood. 'What is occurring here and don't tell me it's the useless parchment?'

Not the useless parchment, but Bied trying to save her sister. He didn't even need to think about the point where his priorities had changed. It was the moment she'd spread her arms and shouted about protecting the children.

His life had taken a different turn and he'd been too distracted when she told him of her sister. Then they'd got sick. He was certain now he hadn't told her he'd help her.

'I have to do something else—you'll need to acquire the parchment.'

'I don't want the parchment and have no intention of searching for it.'

'Then what are you doing here...?' At Balthus's grave expression, Louve had only one word: 'No.'

'He tried to kill me.'

Balthus was here, in Ian's home, so he could murder his brother. This was exactly what Reynold didn't want to happen. 'Reynold was clear—you are to be protected. I can't protect you if you threaten Ian.'

'My very existence threatens him.'

Louve pinched the bridge of his nose. 'That has always been the truth, why hasten it now? Why not wait in the woods as we agreed?'

'Because it's convenient.' Balthus said. 'The whole family is here as witness, and we can end at least one dispute.'

Dispute. Louve was unfazed by Balthus's word use. He'd been involved with the Warstones for so long that talking of fratricide was simply another conversation. 'Is it possible Ian is trying to poison himself and blame someone else?'

'What are you talking about?' Balthus said.

He had to be overthinking this. Ian couldn't be putting poison in his own barrels in the hope of poisoning someone else. Someone had to be slipping the poison in the barrels, but the protection here was unparalleled so how could it happen?

Truly, the poison was the least of his problems. 'There's a cook here and she shouldn't be. Ian has trapped her sister and she's attempting a rescue.'

'Someone's here on a mission at the same time we are?' Balthus said very slowly as if he was trying to understand it. 'You're jesting.'

Louve wished he was.

'You're poisoned and you're telling me about a cook you care to help,' Balthus said. 'You do remember I'm a Warstone and you're handing me a weakness of yours?'

Louve mockingly arched his brow. 'You do remember that you're trying to prove you're one of the good ones?'

'If this is a test, it's an easy one. Ian's only ever cared for his wife and two sons.'

'The wife and children who are kept far away from him.'

'As the rest of us are.'

'Your parents are together,' Louve pointed out.

'When you see them today, you'll know why. They hate each other, but their need for power and a united front to protect it keeps them close.' Balthus shrugged. 'Harder to plot intrigues against the other if they are constantly in the same room.'

Balthus was wrong. Louve would never understand the Warstones. A quiet wife who accepted him, a small plot of land of his own, peace. He'd keep chanting that until it became true.

Even if Ian cared for his wife enough to keep her away, there was something possessive about his behaviour towards Margery. 'The cook, the sister, still wants to rescue her from here. Until that is done, neither of them is safe.'

'The mistress should be safe...unless...' Balthus went quiet.

'What is it?'

'Ian talks in his sleep. He might be keeping the mistress because she knows something.'

Then Margery was in true danger. 'We need to get her out of there now.'

Balthus shuddered. 'This *we* reference rankles as does doing good deeds, but it doesn't matter. If Ian wanted her dead, he would have already done it. Although it is curious why he has her so well protected in his chambers.'

Louve didn't find it curious at all why a man would want Margery. Even he could admire her beauty. Admire it, but not...crave it like he was beginning to crave a certain woman who could stack goblets and challenge a room at the same time.

'The mistress might be protected, but I am unsure her sister is. Ian wasn't pleased she was under his roof. He's sent out messages—I am certain at least one of them was to gain information on her, and that cannot happen.'

Balthus gave a curt nod. 'Let me assuage your concerns—if this cook dies suddenly, what does Ian gain from it?'

He'd have Margery, but he already had Margery.

Balthus sighed. 'Our brother, Guy, might have murdered and been murdered without thought, but the rest of us are more discerning. Ian will only kill if it gains him anything. Unless…did either of these women poison the ale?'

He didn't know. Bied hadn't, but what of her sister? She certainly had reason to. 'Neither of them did it—the cook was testing the ale because Margery was drinking it.'

'Was my brother drinking it?'

'I only observed him once and, at that time, he wasn't.'

'Poison in a Warstone home can only mean death for someone, but who?' Balthus said, then laughed. 'Probably you. Perhaps Ian knew our location and anticipated your arrival.'

'I can't think this way.' Louve rubbed his forehead.

'That's because you're weak with whatever you drank.' Balthus added, 'He could have set you up. Poisoned the ale, so he could have you killed and no one would question it.'

He wished there was a window, or they could leave the door open. Anything to get fresh air in a room that was suddenly too stifling. 'What would he gain from my death?'

'You're Reynold's friend.'

'He'd deny it.'

'As would I—I refuse to be friends with someone who can be loyal within a day.'

Bied. He shouldn't leave her alone like this. Was she feeling as ill as he? Louve looked to the door. He hadn't said enough, kissed her enough. She could be doing any reckless activity now.

'Reynold won't react to my death,' Louve said.

'He'd be wise not to, but from what I saw he's attached—it might hurt, which would amuse Ian.'

'Can we think along the lines of Ian not poisoning the ale to kill me for his amusement?' Louve said.

'His servants wouldn't dare do it,' Balthus said. 'Most of these people I've known since I was an infant. They worked for my parents and then under him, and suddenly they decide this?'

The most likely to blame were the three people who were new: Bied, Margery or himself. He'd assumed Biedeluue hadn't done it, but had she denied it?

'I need to leave. We've been too long as it is.'

'Exactly,' Balthus said pointedly. 'You've been here a day, which was apparently enough to develop feelings for a servant. I'm beginning to think Reynold kept you for entertainment when his dull books wouldn't do.'

Everything was a jest for Balthus. Everything used to be a jest for him. What had happened? Bied.

'Your brother won't appreciate you're here,' Louve said. 'You need to be far outside these fortress gates.'

'You're not worried about my brother or me, you're worried about that cook. I can't wait to meet her. I wish I had taken bets on this! I could use the coin now. The new mercenaries are fierce. Perhaps Ian would play—'

'You're not playing games with them,' Louve interrupted. 'They'll murder you. Ian already tried and he's likely to do it again.'

'He did seem pleased when I rode up to him.'

A nightmare.

'Do not worry about Ian,' Balthus continued. 'I'm my mother's favourite and he won't do anything in front of her. My father, moreover, will enjoy pitting brother against brother and would be annoyed if that entertainment ended too soon. While I'm keeping them occupied you can find the parchment.'

'Balthus, I was to protect you.'

'You were to obtain the parchment and you need my help. You can't face my parents and Ian on your own.'

He couldn't face himself now. Land of his own, a quiet accepting wife, peace. None of it he could conjure now. Nothing that would cease his rolling thoughts. Every one of them could die a horrific death and there was nothing he could do to stop it because the entire world had gone mad.

He might as well join them. Wrenching open the door, he forced words through his clenched teeth. 'When this is over, I want never to hear from any of you again.'

Tess was true to her word. Bied should never have doubted she was a good person and now friend. If she had trusted Tess earlier, she could have rescued her sister before Louve ever arrived with his confusing smile and reports of danger. They'd be home now instead of further trapped because the fortress was overflowing with curious people.

But the scheme they came up with was simple. While the family were occupied and servants were preparing rooms, Bied would simply be another servant in the private tower. Jeanne even agreed to help, though she didn't know why Bied asked her to remain in the kitchens while she carried refreshments up to the private chambers. But she didn't question it too much, so that was fortunate.

The only issue was since the fortress was full, many people would need refreshments. Feeding the fortress was easier when Steward made the menu and Cook helped with Lord Warstone's personal dishes. No Steward meant the burden fell on Cook, no Cook meant Biedeluue needed to be at her station. However, she would be upstairs, so Tess needed to cover the kitchens. Which might work if Cook, who'd arrived, stayed.

Oh, but Cook didn't look well. His robust body moved sluggishly, his gaze not quite meeting anyone else's; however, he stood at his station and directed the staff. Bied and Tess exchanged glances, but no one was mentioning his arrival and it seemed he preferred it that way.

'The trumpets most likely alerted him,' Tess said.

They alerted everyone. She'd never seen the kitchens so full.

'When was the last time there was company?'

'Years, and never both the parents and two brothers.'

She thought of her own family and how they wanted to stay close, but couldn't. And this family had everything, large homes to live in and all the wealth and prosperity anyone could want, but they all stayed apart. It was heart-wrenching and frustrating.

As was Louve. Who was he, exactly, and why was everything he did a contradiction? He helped her with the ale, told her she had to trust him, yet hadn't offered help with her sister, hadn't revealed his purpose in the Warstone fortress.

Playing games with Lord Warstone could mean anything and, if she were wise, should mean nothing to her. Her concern was her sister. And with the Warstones here, for better or worse, she needed her sister back home.

'I'll walk out with you until you reach the stairs to the private tower,' Tess said. 'If anyone questions our presence, I can stop and divert them, while you walk right up. It's the third door down on the left.'

Bied lifted the tray with its delicacies. The luxury was

completely frivolous, but tempting enough to offer to any Warstone who wanted it.

'That's two favours I owe you now,' Bied said. 'One for getting me Bess's gown so I could keep this position and now helping me with my sister.'

'Two!' Tess scoffed. 'Three. I argued with the porter and Steward to allow you into the kitchens in the first place.'

Bied rolled her eyes. 'I'm not so certain you did me a favour that day.'

Chapter Thirteen

'**W**hat are you doing here?' Tess cried out.

Bied woke to see a dark figure standing inside their room and she opened her mouth to scream. Two heavy thuds of feet and a calloused hand against her mouth prevented it. His body blocked out the slim light, but the forest scent of him...

'Come with me,' Louve whispered and stepped back.

She glanced at Tess, who sat, but stayed still. The others in the room remained lying in their beds. Asleep or listening? She didn't know. If they were to pretend he was Usher and she was a servant, she had no choice. Pushing the quilt aside, she heard the rushed breath of Louve before he left the room.

He was standing in the hall, pacing, when she emerged from the room. The rest of the servants were already rising, the day beginning.

'What did you need?' she said, plaiting her hair.

His mannerisms not easing even after she was at his side made her look over her shoulder. Sounds everywhere, only a few torches lit as sunlight began to filter through the empty hallway.

No one else about. He had come early, but only just. When she turned, she caught his eyes roving all over her and she looked down. There was nothing to adjust. She'd dressed in the dark, but all the ties were done and, since the gown was her own, she was adequately covered.

'What did you do yesterday?' he said, his voice almost raspy. 'I was too far away, but I saw you carrying that tray. Tess was by your side and you were walking towards the private tower.'

More voices behind the door she'd closed and he indicated with his chin for her to follow. Why would he want to talk of yesterday, the failure of which still hurt her heart? No, he must mean something else.

'Did nothing but my duties, sir,' she mocked. 'The family wanted some food and—'

'Don't,' he said, opening a door and peering in. When there was no one inside he opened it for her to get past him. Maybe he didn't open it enough, maybe he was in a hurry, but she went in sideways, her gown, her body brushing against his. She felt the heat, the strength of him before he pushed the door closed and the rush of cool air hit her skin.

The miniscule room itself had several shelves, mostly empty, except for a few linens not used. It wasn't meant for two people to stand in the middle. Thus, she leaned against the shelves at her back, her hands gripping a shelf for support. Still, her feet practically touched the man she'd thought of all yesterday.

He'd kissed her. In anger. When had a man ever done such a thing? Never. And…she'd responded, but she hadn't been angry, she'd been upset. It had been a distraction in the moment, but had he meant it to distract her still? Right now, she was almost intrigued by that scar under his left eye.

'We only have a few moments and shouldn't be risking these,' he said. 'Why did you go up the stairs to the private chambers yesterday?'

So not ale, then—he wanted to talk of feelings? She owed this man nothing. 'Why do you think? My sister was there.'

'That woman—'

'Tess,' she offered.

'Does she know?'

'Yes,' she answered, although it was none of his concern. Even so, it seemed to agitate him for he took a step to the side, the room denying him any more movement. At least she had the shelf she could grip.

'What are you muttering?' she said.

He stopped. 'I'm not muttering. I'm reminding myself of what I want when this is all over.' He looked to the door. 'We don't have time for this.'

'Tell me.'

'There's no point. You told the baker about Ian and—'

That's what he thought? 'I wouldn't concern her with your *games*, whatever those are and whoever you are. She knows I have concerns about the ale. I want to get my sister back home and Tess agreed to help.'

His exhaled roughly as if she struck a blow. 'Did you see her?'

'Tell me what you were muttering.' She crossed her arms, which was a mistake because it put more of her in front. He kept his eyes on hers, but she swore he took in her new posture, how much closer she was to him.

'You're the eldest, aren't you?' he said.

'What is that supposed to mean?' she said.

'Demanding,' he said. 'If you must know, I was reminding myself what I want when the games are done. Land of my own, an accepting, quiet wife, peace.'

If he had said he wanted to fly, she would not be more surprised. 'You purposefully lied to be inside this fortress, pretended to be someone else, which you still haven't told me, and all the while Lord Warstone is playing a game with you. A man like him doesn't play games with those lesser than him. You report you're not from noble blood, but I wager you have skill with a sword, are learned and are devious.'

He did shift then, from one foot to another. If there was space, she knew he'd step away. For her, she released her arms.

'We do not know each other,' he said.

She pointed, almost poking him in his chest. 'You said games, not game. Which means whatever this is, it isn't the only time you've played against each other. Been doing it a long time, have you?'

He glanced at her finger, so she put her hands behind her again.

'Tell me if you met with your sister,' he said. 'Did anyone see you?'

'I didn't see her.' But she'd known that she was on the other side of a door where two watch guards stood. The other rooms along the hall were thrown open so she couldn't hear her sister even if she called out, but she liked to believe she heard steps. That perhaps Margery heard her.

'Did you talk with anyone?' Louve said. 'Something slight that you might have missed.'

This wasn't about her. His questions were all about… whatever it was he was doing here. 'Why should I help you?'

His chest expanded, his eyes determined as if he faced an opponent on an empty field. No one had ever gazed at her that way. Whatever it was he was about to say… he meant it.

'I'll help free your sister from the Warstones.'

His expression was one of a monumental challenge. But all she felt was disappointment. Tess had already agreed to help without demands attached. The way Louve was looking at her now, she felt that he would attach so many exceptions. Her sister would be locked behind a door for ever, guarded by men who meant to do her harm. If Bied could scale towers, if she had coin to bargain, if she had anything else, she wouldn't be standing here with this man, who…she could stare at the rest of her life and could never trust.

That took her beyond disappointment into irritation. 'And I'm to simply believe you.'

His eyes flashed. 'I said I'd do it.'

'That's all you've said.'

He clenched his jaw. 'I'll help you escape as well. Both of you.'

That went without saying. 'Before I tell you anything, give me something of you.'

'Something of me,' he said slowly as if the words were simple, but the meaning wasn't. 'Such as…?'

'What are these games?'

At his expected silence, she asked, 'Who truly are you?'

When he merely kept that calm, assured demeanour of his, she said, 'Fine, how do you know how to run a household like you do? And don't tell me you've done this before. Something…meaningful.'

'We don't need to know each other to get what we want. I'm from—'

'You're English,' she retorted. 'I won't waste a question on what I already know or what is safe. If I'm to trust you, I have to know you.'

He was right, she didn't need to ask him personal questions, and a part of her was surprised she did, but…she'd revealed too much of herself to him while in the cellars. Too personal. He knew she was poor and learnt to write in dirt. That Margery was the favoured child and educated, and no person of her station should ever have been taught to read and write.

But there was more than just her pride—she wasn't altogether certain if her asking came from trusting him or wanting to know him. And that was the most worrisome because since when had she wanted to know a man, any man?

'This is ridiculous,' he said. 'You don't know this family, or you'd accept my assistance immediately. We can't get caught.'

'Then why did you pull me in here?'

'You're stubborn, you know that. I also don't have to help you—you know that as well.'

Despite understanding what he meant, she didn't have facts or trust. 'I know. I still want to understand. She's my sister and I can't risk her to just anyone.'

He dropped his head, looked down at his feet. Because she leaned back against the shelves, her feet had slid even closer and she fought the sudden need to pull them back.

'I have a friend who owns a large estate in England,' he said, not looking up. 'He left for several years and I managed it for him.'

'Did you like it there?'

He exhaled roughly. 'It was challenging, beautiful. A battle against the weather many times, but…all the tenants were in it together.'

It sounded ideal to her. It also sounded like a time and place he cherished and wouldn't have willingly left. Why would anyone leave a good life? 'When he returned, he evicted you.'

He gazed up through his lashes, a look she practically felt, when they were this close together. She wanted to thread her fingers though the lock of hair that fell across his cheek. Wanted to…kiss that scar under his left eye.

'What would you do, Bied, if my friend evicted me? Would you have come to my defence?'

* * *

The look on Bied's face was worth that needless question. Part surprise, part umbrage. Part of Louve truly believed she would come to his rescue from eviction. Most of him liked that idea.

To have a woman defend him. No, to have *this* woman defend him. He'd like to see that very much.

Why had he dragged her in here; why did he offer help? Nothing of this was as intended, but even with Bied and her sister in the game, waking her up early, dragging her into this room wasn't intelligent.

He had to protect Balthus, find the parchment, not notice that this woman's gown was so perfectly tied he wished to simply…unravel it.

The small linen room was no distraction, its minuscule size only enhanced so that he could almost smell the slumberous warmth of her skin. A scent which caused an ache that could only be assuaged by him pressing his face into her neck, kissing and tasting the skin there until he'd wrung more of those tiny sounds she made when he forced their first kiss.

Even her drowsy eyes, and the deft way she plaited her hair as she yawned, called to him. He couldn't stop staring, there wasn't anything else in this room, in his entire life, that was near as enticing.

'He didn't force me to leave the estate, I left voluntarily.'

'You didn't dislike it—you would have stayed.' Her eyes narrowed. 'Something of it hurt you.'

Enticing…and all too astute.

'Nicholas and I were friends since childhood and I still hold his and his wife's friendship dear.' When she looked doubtful, he added, 'I'm telling the truth.'

'But not about everything.'

'Now is not the time for everything.' But there was

a compunction in him to tell her the rest. He'd already told her his heart's desire for a family and a home of his own, but he wanted to tell her more. Would she defend him still? Confront the woman he'd cared for, who never loved him in return? Storm after Reynold and Balthus for dragging him into their games and this cursed mission they were on?

He'd like to see that, too, but imagining or wanting it wasn't good for either of them. Instead he said, 'What else can you tell me?'

'Tess and I went upstairs, the hallways were full, I had supplies, but… Lord and Lady Warstone believed they were for them and confiscated it all. I couldn't return after that. There were guards everywhere.'

There it was. The crack in her voice, the slight sheen in those eyes that was there, then gone.

'How many guards in the rooms?' he said.

'Five, six?'

He'd already counted the ones who came in, but others went upstairs, and he didn't know how many. 'Did they all wear the red band at the bottom of the tunic?'

'No. Why is that important?' she said.

It meant not all of the guards had been proven because their loyalty hadn't been tested. Either the Warstones had grown negligent and they travelled with anyone who'd work for coin, or the final test to be part of the official guard was yet to come.

Thus, it wasn't an answer he'd give her. Unproven guards could mean they could be persuaded to his side or…would like to prove their loyalty to the Warstones. He didn't like the odds.

'We need to get your sister out of those rooms,' he said.

She made some sound of frustration. 'I don't know how to get her out of that room! There were guards… everywhere.'

'This is not a situation where caring matters.'

'You said you'd help.'

'I will,' he said. 'We need to leave.'

'I can't simply believe you. I can't. I have my friend and she'll help me.'

She meant those words. What would any Warstone do at this point? Walk out. It wasn't important that she trust him. But…she couldn't involve more people. That would mean more chaos, more distractions, more danger for all of them.

Determined. Stubborn. With certainty if he simply walked out, she'd do this without him, and that, for whatever inexplicable reason, didn't sit well with him and not only because of the danger she'd cause.

'Whatever you do, don't invite Tess to help you. What else do you need from me?'

She swallowed, tilting her chin. When she parted her lips, he imagined tracing his thumb along the plump lower one until she darted her tongue to taste him, or he cupped that chin of hers, lifted it to his own where they took one breath, two before they—

'Tell me of someone you cared for,' she said.

A quick stab through his errant thoughts. A slash to his conscience. An ache in his soul. 'No.'

'Never cared for anyone,' she said. 'Why would you bother?'

Was that where this conversation was going? 'I've *loved* many.'

'Of course you have. Look at you.'

'Well, I am appealing, but what do you mean by it?'

'Did you just jest?' She scrunched up her face. 'I'm not going to tell you what I thought now since it appears you're vain and have probably had numerous women.'

He was half-thrilled at her remark, half-exasperated. Was it possible she was envious he'd had other women?

Was it possible the connection he felt with this woman wasn't one-sided? For her to feel the pull...

Balthus would laugh at him if he knew the entire mission rested on convincing Bied to believe in him. But somehow it was important she trust him and, because he wanted that frown to leave her face, he thought to tell her his most embarrassing moment. 'Yes, I've had women. Even two at once. Is that what you wanted to know?'

She blinked and he was delighted to see a slight pink blush creep up her neck and over her ears.

He laughed low. 'Trust me now?'

She frowned, shook her head. 'That's not what I meant and you know it. You're... I thought you were serious?'

'Not that night. I was drunk, slumbering. They had each other. Apparently, many times. Maybe some day I'll have you meet the mercenaries who know the facts.'

She slapped a hand over her mouth, laughter spilling over, the light in her eyes returning, but then she gasped.

'Is that what you are? Not some usher, but a mercenary. What are you doing here? Who hired you?'

Too much, she was too intelligent and he knew better than to hide the facts. 'Not always.'

'But you can...get my sister out.'

'I can try. Let's go.'

She held up her hand. 'Wait! You having skills doesn't mean I trust you.'

'Are you...negotiating with a mercenary, Biedeluue? What will you negotiate with?'

Oh, he liked that wide-eyed wariness mixed with challenge in those unusual eyes of hers. He loved the way her round cheeks flushed and her hand went to her hip and then off again as if she, too, had several roles to play. What would they be like if they were themselves?

'Can you just be...forthright?' she said.

Her words. She wanted him to converse, but her words

heated his blood, tightened his body. They were so close; he liked this tiny room very much. And if his mind had to guess how'd they be, his body already knew.

'I didn't start as a mercenary.'

Her eyes took him in and he let her. He wasn't ready to tell her everything, but he wouldn't lie to her. Not when she already had so much at stake with her sister here and needed to rely on him.

Very slowly, keeping his gaze on hers, he engulfed her hand in his own. Traced the lines across her fingers, the folds along her wrist. He was fascinated by her hands. He was fascinated by her.

'I truly did start by managing an estate.'

'What…?' She licked her lips. 'What made you change?'

He wasn't prepared for that question, but she didn't take her hand out of his as he scraped the tips of his fingers against hers. He was reluctant to let her go so, against his better judgement, he told her. 'Her name was Mary and she was a tenant on my friend Nicholas's estate. She had twelve acres of her own and a home. She was a widow. We were together for years, but I wasn't the one for her.'

'Were you too young?' she said softly. 'Not a good kisser?'

He wanted to laugh, more at her tone than anything. But bringing up Mary, even in this context, even as superficial as telling a woman he didn't know merely so she'd trust him, was too much. It wasn't Mary herself that was the issue. In truth, it had been many years since he'd thought of her in any way. It was, however, what she represented that pained him. A home, a wife, peace. Something he yearned for, but which seemed out of his reach for ever. He wasn't going to find that while on his friend's estate, he'd only find it by creating his own. Which was the reason he'd left.

As the silence stretched between them, Bied folded her

fingers around his until he wasn't certain if it was he who held her hand or she who held his. 'Did she still love her first husband?' she whispered.

He refused to look up though he knew she wanted to gauge his reaction to her question. 'My ego liked to think that. In the end, I knew others laid with her, ate at her table and slept in her bed. Sometimes the linens were still warm.'

Her brows drew in. 'Because she had to pay taxes?'

'What?'

A bang as a door slammed. They both looked at their closed door, listening to the beginnings of the day, voices, activity. This room was small, the shelves were mostly bare, but someone might need the few linens left. Might wrench the door open and see them in here.

He released her hand and finally dared to look her in the eyes. 'If we're caught here, there will be no saving your sister.'

She was so close he couldn't hide anything from her, but he tried. And he knew he'd succeeded when her eyes lost that searching look and instead turned hesitant.

'We can pretend we're in here for...' She swallowed, looked at his lips, then back into his eyes. 'So we could...'

He hoped she didn't finish that thought. He hoped someone caught them so he could pretend, except it wouldn't be anything but true.

Reckless. Irrelevant to the danger. There wasn't a breath of space between them and Bied kept gripping the shelf behind her, which only displayed every curve given to her. That gown might cover her skin, but not his imagination.

What he wouldn't do to grab the shelf above her head, to lean forward until the board bit into the curve of her back and he would need to press a hand there to soften their press of bodies which wouldn't be soft at all. All so that he could kiss her as he should have yesterday. Not in anger, not in any emotion except for…this need.

Small space, distracting thoughts. Even looking at the floor wasn't safe when he saw their feet almost touching. Touching her hand was a mistake, revealing anything of him was a mistake. Not taking the danger seriously was a mistake.

He knew she didn't understand what was at stake and, if all went well, she never would. It was up to him to remember the danger. To be resolute.

Her lips were slightly parted now, wet from her tongue that she darted out. Her eyes heavy lidded as if he'd already kissed her. He wanted—

'Where did you get that scar under your left eye?' she said, rushed, light, all too feminine.

'In the fields, teaching some boys,' he said. The flush in her cheeks was calling to him. 'Where did you get that one under your chin?'

'A hot turnip,' she said.

He parted his own lips to ask, but she looked at his lips again and he was lost.

'Biedeluue,' he said, cupping the back of her head, her hands and arms immediately reaching behind his neck. Her fingers cool against his neck, his body shuddered as he wrapped his other arm around her back and pressed her against him.

He wanted, needed to kiss her. *She* needed to stay safe. Breathing out to settle his body, he said the words that needed to be said. 'We need to leave this room. Now. Separately.'

When she nodded, when he could release her, he added, 'I have one favour to ask—stay in the kitchens. Stay there even when everyone leaves. I can't offer much protection, but I'll stay close by as long as I can.'

One hand gripped the latch, the other a linen, when she told him, 'There's something you should know about me—I hate the kitchens.'

Chapter Fourteen

'Usher,' a voice commanded.

Louve fought the urge to pivot immediately. If he did, it would only look as though he had something to hide. And right now, he didn't. His thoughts, however... Biedeluue and the way he felt about her must stay hidden. If Ian of Warstone knew he was beset by the kiss they'd almost shared that morning, Ian would make Bied's death the evening's entertainment. Or worse, the parents would make it theirs.

All day, his heart had beat unsteadily, his senses staying on alert, as the Lord and Lady Warstone surrounded Balthus and never left his side. If he watched too long, he swore he could see them circling their son like vultures. But Ian, who was reported to be the favourite at least with the father, was always out of reach.

Oh, he was sitting in the same room and conversing with them, but by the angle of his body, the position of the chairs or simply by the way they stood showed that his parents didn't dote on him as they did Balthus.

Which made up, down and nothing safe. Louve questioned everything. Balthus in Troyes apologising to Reynold, reporting that Ian had attempted to murder him. Vowing that he'd do anything to bring down the Warstones. Now it appeared as though he'd been welcomed back into the fold.

Who was the villain? Did he have any allies left or should he depart at first dark and leave the parchment behind? With the full fortress, there was no opportunity to search for it. There was no one to watch his back and if he let his thoughts drift this way, he'd certainly go mad. He had to trust his friendship with Reynold, needed to give some faith to Balthus. Or else...

The poor servant standing in front of him was quaking and Ian was still waiting to be acknowledged. Louve spit out a few more instructions as he pointed behind him, as if the boy needed to know where to go. But he took the hint well enough and left immediately.

When Louve turned, Ian was at his back.

'Balthus is occupied.' Ian's pale eyes were without emotion. 'My parents rest and we need to talk.'

Where was Balthus? Louve didn't hesitate to follow Ian to more private chambers. From the back he so reminded him of Reynold. Slim build, black hair, clothes that cost what a tenant made in a year or two.

It was far past time that he and Ian came face to face without an audience. Now it was a matter of if the game continued. He'd learnt to play this game by waiting. He needed for all their sakes to keep the upper hand.

Except, after sharing that one kiss with Bied and being left wanting more, the game didn't hold any allure for him right now. Distractions. There were too many players and Bied and her family needed to be taken off the board, immediately. Negotiating with the eldest Warstone brother was the only way to do that.

Down a long corridor they walked to a room Louve had never entered. It was dark, unlit except for the slice of light coming in from the archer's window where Ian strode to look outside. Louve kept his back to the door and closed it without turning around. Warstones struck at a moment's notice. He wouldn't give Ian the chance.

'You walk like your brother, though your movements are less refined than his,' Louve said.

Ian turned on a chuckle. 'I didn't know what to make of you.'

'You think one sentence provides you with the answers?'

'It eliminates some lies, which helps reveal a truth. Or at least the truth for now, which is all we ever get.'

'Do you read the great philosophers as well?' Louve said.

Shaking his head, Ian said, 'No, nothing like my brother. How is Reynold?'

'Alive.'

Ian raised a brow. 'Loyal, but I already knew that.'

'You asked me here— what do you want?'

'Impatient. Which I didn't know.'

Louve crossed his arms and leaned against the door. If they played word games, it would be an excruciatingly hazardous conversation. One where either of them was bound to make a mistake and expose a vulnerability.

Ian sighed. 'I want to be your friend.'

Louve just bit back his laugh. It would not have been one with any humour and completely out of place, but the words…from a Warstone!

'I see you're surprised. Perhaps friend was too strong of a bond?'

This man as an ally? Never. 'You say the word *friend* and all I'm waiting for is a dagger to be thrown.'

Ian stared, his brows drawing in. 'Would acquaintance do? Or ally?'

Louve shook his head. 'All are equally unacceptable and completely without merit. What am I doing here, Ian of Warstone?'

'Aren't I to ask the question of why Reynold sent you here? I have guessed it has to do with my death.' He spread his arms wide. 'Here I am.'

The temptation was there. 'Why did you allow your Steward to leave and your parents to arrive?'

Ian smirked. 'My Steward is off obtaining my favourite goblets, of course. But his sudden absence was clever of me. Whatever you're doing here, you'd need more of a challenge. Distractions such as the Steward's departure are useful, but deadly ones are better. And my parents are deadly, don't forget.'

Something wasn't right about the Steward's departure. He'd been eager to leave the fortress before he had talked to Ian to gain permission to do so. Perhaps it was always Ian's intent for the Steward to leave when Louve arrived, but it was too convenient. The Steward's mystery, however, could wait.

'Your parents seem attentive to Balthus at the moment,' Louve said.

'That bandage has been too long on his hand—I hope it is not ruined. But at least he has the other one, hmm?' Ian held up both hands for Louve to inspect.

The deep scar made from flames on the left hand was there like on all the brothers. Except Ian had one on his right hand as well. Both hands held to fire to prove Warstone loyalty.

Standing near the lone torch, Ian waved one hand after another over it. His expression was pleasant, as if this was some pastoral day with blue skies and birdsong. The room filled with the stench, but Louve refused to comment.

For years, he'd surmised the Warstones were mad. The risks they took, the games they played. He feared he'd go mad merely playing along with them. But with utter certainty, Ian of Warstone was conflicted.

'My mother burned my hand so frequently, I can't feel

anything,' Ian said. 'I was the first, you see, and she did it differently with me. Not for as long as my brothers, certainly not like Balthus, but more frequently. I've kept my movement as a result, but now anything could happen to these hands and it wouldn't matter.'

That woman was in this house, with Biedeluue, with Tess, with a red-headed boy and the cook who grieved. The need to protect burned through Louve, shocking him with the intensity and the rightness of it. But he feared anything he said would reveal that, so he kept quiet.

'Do you know what it's like to feel nothing?' Ian said. 'I suppose you don't. You weren't raised by monsters.'

What he had seen of Ian's father... He seemed jovial, almost happy to be in his sons' company. His mother had the imperious voice and needs of the privileged. Monsters? He hadn't seen it, but apparently, he hadn't been looking closely enough.

'We all have parents who are different,' Louve said. 'What is the point of this conversation?'

Ian took his hand off the flame and sat on the lone bench. 'Aren't you tired of it all?'

'Tired of what?'

'All the games.' Ian rested his hands, palms upwards, on his knees. 'Every day. Every breath taken has been a game. I have had to ask since I was three—will this be the last time I see the sky? I'm the one who married and had children first. I'm the one who wants something better. If I die...what is to become of them?'

'Why tell me this, and not your brothers? Balthus is right here.'

Ian studied him in that Warstone way. 'You're cunning. That's a surprise. I thought it was your loyalty Reynold saw in you, but there's more, isn't there?'

Louve stayed quiet, all too used to Warstones voicing their reflections. To others it would seem like mere intimidation or very one-sided conversations. But after years in Reynold's company, he realised that it was indeed how they talked. As if they enjoyed revealing a little of their madness. It was the direction of their private thoughts, the ones they never voiced, that terrified him.

'I can't simply interact with my brothers. Guy was the worst,' Ian continued. 'I could not approach the mercenaries surrounding his gates, let alone the man himself. Balthus is too trusting and so can't be trusted. Not until he knew I was sincere. And it might take some time for Balthus to forgive me after I sent the archer after him.'

'What of Reynold?'

'I tried to contact Reynold.' Ian raised his brow. 'You don't believe me? I know he received my messages and I know what he did afterwards. Just this year, in Paris, I let him know I was near in case he wanted to talk.'

'You sent no message to Paris. I was there, why would you lie?'

Ian's brows lowered. 'No lie. It was my arrow that felled that messenger by his gates. My brother would have known that that was my arrow for I made the notches myself.'

Louve felt sick. Even after all this time, and all the acts he had committed to survive, in the hope for something better, this one act almost brought him to his knees.

Eude, a fellow mercenary and friend, was always restless and needed the long journeys Reynold required of him. He was a good warrior, an excellent rider and absolutely begged not to do stable duty.

'You killed a man because you wanted to leave a message?' Louve sneered. 'Isn't that the most idiotic logic I've ever witnessed? Your brother never saw that arrow because I disposed of his body. He didn't learn of your presence until long afterwards.'

'Pity,' Ian said. 'That was as close as I ever dared to reach Reynold personally.'

No light of remorse or shame. Ian's eyes were as dead as they'd ever been and Louve wanted to slam his fist into his jaw until Ian's teeth disintegrated.

'Anger?' Ian said. 'You are fascinating. Especially since you've repeatedly insulted me.'

'Friends insult each other,' Louve said.

'So do enemies,' Ian said.

'Enemies don't tell each other of their family life,' Louve said. 'Would it help for you to know I came from a happy one? My mother sang, my father liked when the pork skin was extra crispy. When they died, I grieved. But my grandmother's calloused hands ruffled my hair and she could make this soup that tasted of home.'

Huffing, Ian stretched his arms and legs as if the chair was suddenly too tight. 'That wasn't nice.'

'We all have broken homes, Ian. Not all of us become the human that you have.'

'I'm eldest, I was the first they experimented with. They made mistakes with me that they didn't make with the others.' Ian shrugged.

'Guy's reputation was infamous. Are you saying he was a gentler soul?'

Ian laughed low. 'Guy scared me. His mode of cruelty wasn't taught. Some dogs in the pack are more rabid than others. That is also true of all families, no? Of course, I am no better. My reasoning slips year after year, so I trap myself in a fortress away from my wife, away from my children. It's why they stay away from me. I have become unpredictable even with them. Games have their own penalties.'

If true, what did that make the Warstone family? What did that make him as he played their game?

If someone came upon either of them now, there was no difference between them. Granted Ian's clothing was finer, but both of them were conversing in the middle of the day while servants rushed to the evening service and meal. All quite civilised as if they were acquaintances and not enemies.

A quiet life, and a home to withstand generations. That was Louve's goal. That was what he wished. Moments in Ian's insidious presence and he could feel himself moulding into something murky.

'Is it so terrible your wife is gone when it allows for younger, sweeter temptations to be by your side?'

Ian chuckled. 'You speak of my mistress. Do you find her a temptation? I have to admit she is interesting to watch. But not as interesting as that woman at your side.'

Louve inwardly cursed. Ian couldn't link Bied and Margery together. After Ian's response in the Hall, messengers had been sent out, likely to discover Bied's history. He intended to free the sisters before a messenger returned.

'You speak of an insignificant kitchen servant? You must not have done much research on me to know my tastes,' Louve said. Or Ian would know that Bied was every fantasy he had and many ones he didn't know.

'As if I want to know your tastes. My mind is full of useless information. Games are exhausting enough.' Ian exhaled roughly. 'The one between Reynold and I was at a stalemate until you arrived. If Reynold didn't listen to my messages, maybe he will listen to you when you return to him.'

What to believe when everything appeared to be opposite? Ian now wanted his survival and Balthus visited with his mother and father. 'Is my continued well-being agreed upon by your family as well?'

'I can't speak for them,' Ian said.

'I have to admit, I'm seeing a different side of them from the stories. Your mother has a charming laugh and your father a fine sense of humour. Do you miss them?'

Ian huffed. 'Why are you alive and freely roaming my home?'

'Because you want to be my friend.' Louve smirked.

'A word I can't use around you without your waiting for a dagger to be thrown, remember?'

Louve lost his humour. In truth, he hadn't fully appreciated Ian's instability, but why had he said such a thing?

'There are other words we could start with,' Louve said.

Ian's eyes narrowed before he dropped his gaze. 'I know what you're doing here and what you want. I invited my family to thwart you from ever getting an opportunity to search my rooms.'

The parchment. Ian knew he was here for the parchment. If so, how? Had Reynold sent a message ahead, or was Balthus right? That Warstones had ears everywhere and always knew?

He was frustrated at Bied for not trusting him, yet could he blame her? For years, the company he'd kept was riddled with mistrust and malevolence until he didn't even know who *he* was any more.

He didn't know who he was with her. He certainly wasn't carefree as he had been with any of his childhood friends, but he wasn't joyless, dark or scarred like the Warstones.

He was a playing piece that was being moulded by the game. He knew it, too, when he questioned everything. Could he believe the parchment was here simply because Reynold said Ian had it, or because Ian reported he didn't want him searching rooms?

It would be like them to not have the parchment here so his searching could amuse them. In the end, however, it didn't matter if the parchment was here or not. It would be impossible to obtain with Ian's family here. The parchment would have to be abandoned. Now, it came down to Balthus's safety. What would it take? Trust between him and Ian?

'Why would I want anything to do with your rooms?' Louve said.

Ian huffed. 'Games are all fun until you realise you're stuck on board with the same players who won't ever let you stop.'

'When we win, the game will end.'

'You...like the games. Now, that is unexpected.' Ian exhaled roughly and waved in front of him. 'It might be too late for you, but I'll give you this warning—get out before you're as much a prisoner as I am.'

Chapter Fifteen

'Are you certain you want to stay?' Tess said not for the first time since the Warstones had arrived yesterday morning.

'I'll merely prepare a few more dishes before tomorrow. To help Cook in case he arrives again.' Bied wiped her brow with the back of her arm. The kitchens were much cooler than they were all day, but still warmer than the rest of the fortress. Now that everyone was gone, however, she piled her hair on top of her head and loosened some of the ties holding her gown.

Cook's presence immediately helped even though he only directed. His first order was to light all the ovens. The heat at its peak was unbearable, but to see him standing, aware, even if his shoulders sloped, was heartening. He was there for several hours before he walked out again as silently as he'd entered.

Tess gaped at the mess still to be cleared. 'I'm exhausted and can't believe you stayed here the entire day.'

Other than to wash her hands and face, and to cool the back of her neck with a wet linen, Bied had stayed in the kitchens. She hadn't been lying when she told Louve she hated the kitchens, she did, but she'd do anything to help her sister. Louve had told her to stay here and she would.

'I'll leave soon enough, don't wait up.'

Tess was already shuffling towards the stairs. 'I couldn't wait up, even if I wanted to. Not only am I tired, this place isn't...pleasant when everyone is gone.'

The door closed behind her friend. Isolation echoed off the timbers and through the empty rooms. When was the last time she was this alone?

There was more to do for tomorrow, and though the kitchens weren't quite clean, she had no intention of doing much. In fact, she didn't want to do any of it. She was here because she waited.

With any hope, Louve would not make her stay much longer. He had been one blessed distraction to the monotony of cleaning pans and sweeping. True to his word, he had stayed close most of the day. Distracting, welcoming. Comforting with that strength of his, though he'd avoided looking her way.

She'd been here for so little time, and she'd known him even less than that. A handful of conversations with him. Both of them oddly laced with secrets she'd never told before. She'd blame the fact she told him so much on her worry for her sister, but she also knew part of it was him.

She knew better than to believe in anyone other than her family, especially men who took advantage of such trust, but...there was something about him that eased her mistrust.

It was in the way he was there and every time she wanted help, he offered it. She still flushed to think of the questions she'd asked him and of the answers he'd given her. Never in her life had she been so bold. Because she'd travelled, she'd kept most of her life private and didn't pry into others.

But within moments she was demanding an absolute stranger something of himself just so that she could trust him. Her belief in her father was broken, but not in her family, so her asking anything of him was unfounded. Yet, equally confusing, he did it. He told her far more than about a love for a sister or a shame that Margery was taught by wealthy benefactors, and all the connotations that meant. Because there wasn't a benefactor in all the land who would teach a beautiful girl her letters without expecting something in return. To this day, Margery never confessed what she'd done to learn to read and write.

Louve knew it was unusual, his eyes had widened when she told him. He understood. But he'd been compassionate, too, and kept his counsel.

These matters she had told him and in return... He could have told her nothing of import, he could have told her nothing at all. It wasn't he who was in trouble, it was she. Would she truly have denied his help? She couldn't. Thus, her demands weren't because it risked her sister, but her pride. Which was laughable, for even that she would have sacrificed for his help. He had to know this, yet over and over she played his words to her.

He'd left a home he loved, a friendship he cherished because he hadn't felt as if he belonged. He hadn't said all as such, but it was in his eyes, in the facts. It was that woman. Bied wasn't prepared for the jealousy that scraped through her when he told her the name. Had he loved this Mary?

The more she asked herself these questions, the more she realised her fascination with Louve might be more than the way his dark hair fell across the back of his neck, or the way he dipped his chin when he looked at her. A worrisome prospect when she watched Ian take Louve away and she hadn't seen him—

'It's warm in here.'

She spun as Louve descended the kitchen stairs.

His movements were graceful strength and she loved that he didn't hunch in her presence. But the way he moved his body reminded her of the other thoughts that had snared her all day. The way his hand felt as he held her gently, firmly, the self-deprecation when he told her the story of the two women. Who did such a thing?

He told her there were mercenaries, but where were they when…? Oh, she couldn't think. Her imagination kept imagining and wouldn't stop. Not even as Louve slowed his pace, his brows rising, his expression turning quizzical.

It *was* warm in here. 'Cook ordered all the ovens fired since we were behind in roasting and pies,' she said.

A few more steps and he was there before her. His eyes were still as blue, his hair just as dark, his shoulders— did she notice those shoulders before? He was so much taller than her, but in a way that only made her want to—

'Is there something on my clothing?' he said.

She snapped her eyes to him.

'Nothing is amiss,' she said. 'You seem fine.'

One brow rose. 'I was not aware my condition was in question.'

His tone was strict, but humour fanned from the corners of his eyes. Too many conflicting facets to this man. Laughter, fierce frowns. A kiss meant as punishment and then, in the linen room, that almost-kiss…

The way he said he'd protect her and her sister. The way he had been protective of her all day. She might not understand why he did the deeds he did, but she felt them. Despite her past, she wanted them.

His humour eased. 'What are you thinking?'

'Nothing of import.' She couldn't stop.

'Your cheeks are flushed.'

'It's the heat,' she blurted. 'Where did Lord Warstone take you today?'

Pivoting away, he walked around a table. His profile

was no less intense as she watched him take in a deep breath. 'I wasn't certain I'd see you here after your telling me you don't like the kitchens.'

'I wasn't certain I was going to be here, but I stayed all day until the end.'

Why did she feel this way around him? Louve might not have told her where he went, but he had returned. Just as he said he would. Such a simple thing truly. It wasn't as if he traversed great lands or fought dragons, but he was here. He was here and she felt a ridiculous amount of comfort from that.

He ran a finger over the table that was barely wiped down and lifted the grubby digit towards her. 'What have you been doing all this time?'

She wanted to laugh. But the undercurrent between them that had started in the cellar and flared in the linen room was tightening. In the dark kitchens, with faint sounds of doors latching closed and the crunch of rushes as people strode towards their sleeping chambers, anticipation, not laughter, ruled her.

'I know you talked with him. Tell me.'

'We didn't talk of your sister.' He took a step, the scrape of his boots against the spilled grain overtly loud in the cavernous rooms. 'Why didn't you leave the kitchens today?'

'What do you mean you didn't talk of her? Are you intending to negotiate with him?' Bied didn't dare say Margery's name. 'I thought—'

'You can't negotiate with him unless you have something to negotiate with.'

'The ale,' she said.

'Won't work,' he said. 'Because Ian of Warstone has numerous people trying to kill him every day of the year. If he showed favour for any who tried to save him from a murderer, what's to prevent the very killer from setting up a scenario that he can pretend to save Ian from and therefore profiting from it?'

'That's—who thinks like that?'

'Warstones do.'

'Who is spoiling the brew, then?'

'I don't know,' he said. 'We might never know. I will try not to serve any to your sister.'

It wasn't good enough. 'Then what—what do you intend to do?' She almost trusted this man. Why? Because he said he'd help, because he stood around the kitchens and came back tonight? She was a fool trusting any man. 'You don't have a plan, do you?'

'There's a chance we can free your sister, but we have to choose the right moment. Talking to Ian then wasn't it.'

'A chance! I'm not doing it on a chance.'

'I will help you, I will,' he said. 'But there are other matters here, everything must be balanced.'

She crossed her arms. 'There's no balance when it comes to my family! I gave you a day. That's more than I should have given you.'

He took a step back. 'Everywhere I'm surrounded by impatience. I did talk to Ian and gleaned some information. Your sister is in danger, but so are you.'

To turn or not to turn. She tilted her head and almost saw him in the corner of her eye. 'What do you mean?'

'He sent out messengers to find information on you. As of now, I can't guarantee he doesn't know who you are and, with the entire family present, it's not safe. There's a war here, Bied. You might not see it, but you and your sister are a part of it.'

Part of what? She waited for him to continue, but wasn't surprised when he didn't. It was just another enigmatic remark from a secretive man. He was a mercenary who couldn't be trusted. 'Then I'll take my sister and leave.'

'Wait,' he said. Then she felt him, right there, right behind her.

'I don't have patience either,' he said. 'I'm here to prevent further harm, but my thoughts, my very soul, were preoccupied by this woman who's fierce, protective and so damn lovely, my breath catches.'

His warmth, the sunlight scent of his, the rumble of his voice, she took it all in.

'I know so little of you,' he said. 'Is there a husband somewhere, Bied? Do you have a man waiting for you?'

Physically, she didn't need to ask what was happening between them. He'd occupied all her thoughts today. They weren't even facing each other and she felt the need, the want, of that almost-kiss.

'No husband,' she said and stuck her tongue in her cheek before she added. 'Nor two men in my bed.'

A huff of breath. 'Now, there's an image I don't know if I like or hate.'

She tried to turn around for that, but firm hands held her shoulders. 'You can hardly complain when you told me.'

'You want to know why I hate it?' He lowered his head, his breath just behind her ear. 'Because if you have had two men... I wasn't one of them.'

That stilled her. This man...didn't mind she wasn't a maiden? 'You would...'

'Share? No, I couldn't, I am too hungry for you to share.' His words fell against her cheek, her neck, her ear. 'I love that you aren't contained. If I'm honest, I'm half-hard with your recklessness and the need to taste your lips.'

What were they doing? Louve was different, but this wasn't the time, and yet, when else? 'I'm not claimed by any man.'

'Except by me,' he said.

She wrenched around and Louve let her, but only so he could skim his hands over more of her. Only so he could see her reaction to his words.

Her eyes, such an unusual colour. Not clear like her sister's, but complex and layered with emotions. He liked that very much, liked the darkening of them as they searched the sincerity of his words. He liked that she didn't step back so he could feel the brush of her breasts with each breath she took.

Sweeping his hands on her shoulders, his thumbs caressing across her collarbone, simply that movement was all he'd allow himself until she allowed more.

'I don't let any man claim me,' she said.

He sensed that. Generous, loyal. Fierce, and yet along the way her trust had been tested. And he'd given her nothing to trust him on, not yet. They should wait. But he wanted more with her. Whatever was between them, he was incapable of ignoring it.

'What if you let me...borrow you for a bit?' he said instead.

Her lips parted as she comprehended what he meant. A flick of her tongue against a plump lip and he could not tear his gaze away. A slight flush beginning along her neck again and he wanted to know where that flush started. Did it begin at the tender place her heart pulsed, just there in the lines of her neck, or lower?

He didn't think he could wait. 'There are matters here that demand me to be one kind of man, but with you, I want to be that reckless male who kisses you...lies with you.'

He wanted more than that from her...for a lifetime. So little time, but what he did know, what she had inadvertently shown him as well, everything pointed to this being the woman. She knew some of his past, hadn't flinched when he told her he was a mercenary, seemed to have some humour of her own. Her protection of the people she cared for, her generous body which he'd work to feed every known delicacy to—he wanted everything about her.

He always wondered when or how he'd fall in love, how it would feel and what he would do. He'd watched in amusement as his friends struggled against it, but he already knew he'd run after it. He craved that one person to spend the years with, but he could never find her.

Until now. And, as Bied stayed in the almost-embrace of his arms, as she took in his words and the burn of his body, it seemed she shared at least some of his want and need.

He'd have her as soon as the cursed mission was over. As soon as they had freed Margery and were far away. He'd find a place for them both and she could break goblets and raise children. His daughters would be wild and—

'A man who…lies with me? Kisses me,' she said. 'No.'

One word, he immediately held up his hands and she stepped back.

She seemed as shocked as he felt.

'I can't simply trust you.'

Ah. She didn't know how he felt and he couldn't tell her, not yet. Not the way he wanted to. But he saw right through her defences. Soon, he'd let her see right through his.

This man was too potent. Too…everything. The first time Bied saw him, she couldn't believe a man like him existed, with eyes like his and that way he dipped his chin to look at her.

There was more, too. She wanted to *trust* him, even though she had learned her lesson in the harshest of ways with men and accepting their help. Yet, she wanted to believe him that he'd help rescue her sister and her. Ridiculous.

'You have your mission to do,' she said.

'Bied,' he growled.

She firmed her resolve against him. 'It's true. You're a mercenary hired by someone, but you won't tell me why or by whom. And all of it is entirely too much and puts my sister in danger. Even if it's to save kingdoms, it's not worth risking her for.'

He stilled. 'Why did you say that?'

'You keep talking that there's something more here. I might not be of noble blood, but we are in a Warstone holding. If it's more than this, then what more could there be?'

His jaw tightened. 'I won't be distracted this time around. We both have our reasons to be here. If this between us was something simple, it would be possible to say no. Does it seem like something you can walk away from?'

'We *should* walk away from it. I am a sister pretending to be a kitchen servant to save her. That should be my only role, my only want.'

At his expression, she hadn't any more words to fight him off, so she turned her back to him. She'd crumble if she faced him now.

But she knew he faced her. Could feel his eyes taking in the tension in her shoulders, the way the gown stretched across her broad hips.

'I'm a mercenary who is pretending to be an usher, but with you, Bied, I'm only a man.'

His voice was low, a roughened tenor that rushed the awareness she'd been trying to avoid through her. The wall she stared at wasn't interesting enough to ignore the man or his words. 'What has that to do with anything?'

'I thought we were throwing out opposites.'

She was throwing out excuses. *Reasons.* So many. Oh, she'd had men before when she wanted them. But there was too much with Louve. Too much fascination with the wave of his hair and too much want when he gave a smile that lit his eyes.

'Tell me,' he coaxed.

'Tell you what?' Her voice, she was proud to say, remained as steady as always. As long as she didn't turn, she could remain strong. He'd grow bored and leave.

'What's the opposite of man?' he whispered. Why did she have to face a wall with only a few pans and some herbs dangling from it? Did he know her heart beat that much more with his every word? That each breath drawn became that much more difficult as desire tightened her insides?

Woman was the answer she almost blurted. She wanted him and more so now the longer they stayed in these deplorable kitchens.

'Will you deny it?' He enticed her. And from the press of his body against her, he unmistakably wanted her. 'It's been there since the beginning.'

She swallowed. 'In the beginning I was drunken.'

'But I wasn't.'

That game! 'Stacking goblets isn't me.'

He chuckled and his breath rushed against her hair. 'Yes, it is.'

How could he know?

'What is it?' Louve said. 'You're…still.'

It was nothing, she turned around again. When Louve kept his hands resting along her arms, slowly brushing them up to her shoulders and down, she thought about stepping away. She'd told him no, but she needed that touch. 'I've had to work all my life.'

When he dipped his chin in that way of his, she continued, 'I couldn't do enough at home. I helped my mother and brothers in the fields and then in the kitchens. But there were some…obstacles.'

'There usually are when you're running a household.'

He probably couldn't imagine what act she had to do to earn the use of her neighbour's ox. She didn't want to even think those thoughts now. Not when Louve's hands had stilled and he was simply rubbing his thumbs along the crook in her elbows, which was both comforting and…making her breasts feel tighter, fuller. 'I couldn't do enough, I had to find work in the next village to earn coin. Every payment I made at the inn, I walked back to my home and handed it to my brother. It was a good time and we were able to pay taxes, I was making friends, I was welcome there. Then…'

'You put thistles in someone's braies,' Louve said.

The comment was so far from her thoughts she could only stare.

Louve's face turned absolutely innocent. 'You poured a bucket of piss over someone's head.'

She slapped a hand over his mouth. 'No!'

When she realised what she'd done, she awkwardly pulled it away. Only to reveal a double-dimple smile, and her mind reduced to that one ridiculous word: glorious.

'Did you…?' Her voice was barely audible. 'Did you do those things?'

He raised one knowing eyebrow. 'I might have played a part.'

He seemed so proud of what he did, she knew he didn't understand.

'Well, I played a part, too, and it lost me my occupation. I was forced to go to the next village, then the next, and…here I am far away from my home.'

She could see from his expression, he understood then.

He wasn't from wealth or nobility, he'd had to earn his coin as well.

He squeezed her arms. 'Don't change. Don't even think it.'

'I have to, to stay. I can't keep getting further away from my family—'

'But you play here.'

Her heart dropped. 'It usually takes me months before I become myself around people. Here, to get to my sister, I was different with the steward than I was with the servants and what you saw that first day.'

His blue eyes softened as she told him some of her past. Oh, there was heat there, too, and the promise of more. It was there, as well, in the way he kept touching her, as if he couldn't stop.

She didn't want him to stop.

'How did you know it was me?' When his brows turned in, she added, 'You said earlier that you knew the game was me, but you'd just arrived.'

'Because anyone who can stack goblets while drinking must have been practising for a very long—'

'Stop!'

His eyes danced around her features as if he was mesmerised by her sudden laughter. Her whole body leaned into his expression and his hands settled close to her hips.

All the while, his eyes never stopped their roaming. From the tips of her ears to her scar under her chin, she didn't feel as though any detail was too small for his interest. So his next words again took her by surprise.

'Because there's so much of you,' he said. Then growled under his breath. 'No, don't turn away again. Stay with me.'

Whatever he needed to say, she'd let him, then walk right out. 'I'm right here.'

'You went away.'

'I'm here, only my back is to you. Again.' She turned a bit more so she couldn't see him.

'Turn the rest of the way. You face every other adversity and challenge. Face me and you can see that what I'm to tell you isn't any hardship. Bied, don't you know what I mean? How much you give away. Your protection. Your generosity. Your heart. Even to me.'

She spun on that, the movement insignificant, but he was close, so she brushed her front against him. He stiffened then.

'You,' she said, 'don't have my heart.'

A quirk at his lips. 'But I have all of your ire and you're generous with that.'

Humour, and that dimple given away effortlessly, as if he had done it often in his past. 'You like laughter.'

'I do.' He searched her features. She wondered what he saw there.

'How can you jest, be a strict usher, a deadly mercenary and on a dangerous mission?'

He flashed a grin. 'I can do many things at the same time. I also like to meddle and pry.'

'What happens when you pry and interfere with me?' she said.

He dipped his chin. 'You look as if you want to throw something at me.'

She almost snorted.

Smile widening, he swooped closer and whispered, 'But there's something else, isn't there? There's something underneath or just behind, or beyond what you feel with me.'

She felt the way his voice rasped across her ear, felt what that heat did to her. 'No.'

He pulled back. 'You told me some of your family, surely that means something.'

'I only told you a bit, you don't even know all their names.'

He exhaled, straightened his shoulders. 'If you mean it, if this is truly a no, I'll leave, Bied.'

There was no light of humour in his eyes. He meant these words, and she didn't want him to leave. She wanted it to continue, but it had to be temporary. He had his duties and she had her sister. Surely this was temporary. If so…they could have this night.

'I do feel something else with you.' At the ease in his expression, she added, 'It's annoyance.'

'Oh?' He walked around her, until he was again at her back. She was grateful to not be staring at the wide ovens, but nothing held her interest as much as this man.

'Undeniably, annoyance,' she said. 'You ask me to turn and then you're at my back.'

'Does annoyance feel like this?' He brushed his lips against the shell of her ear. 'Or perhaps like this.' His breath warmed the base of her other ear.

The kitchen blurred and then returned in focus. What did he want? She knew she didn't want him to do that again. If he did she was certain to turn and he deserved a wait. 'Not annoyance. Exasperation.'

A sharp breath as if she pleased him. In a blink, his teeth nipped around the shell of her ear and then he was at the other, whispering more of those words. 'Exasperation goes like that…or is it more like this?' This time, nothing was fast as he used his lips to nibble along the edges until her core clenched.

'Displeasure!' she bit out. Her voice caught between one breath and the next. She wasn't in the kitchens any more. She was only with him.

He trailed off her ear, continued with the same press of his lips, the same light nip of his teeth, the flick of his tongue behind her ear and down her neck. She wasn't moving now. She couldn't as he angled closer, as anticipation gripped her.

He brushed his nose across the nape of her neck and rubbed his roughened jaw up along the other side back to her ear where he began that same maddening pattern with his lips, his tongue, his teeth which drove her absolutely mad.

As did the hum he did when he nuzzled into her hair. It felt as though he was touching her in more places than the innocent brush of his chin at the top of her head. They weren't even talking. They'd merely spouted words that made no sense.

Yet all of it was too much, just like everything else with him. The way he used such simple contact, the way she felt now as he brushed aside some curl and stepped between her legs. Every touch maddeningly light as he pinched the laces of her gown between two fingers and lifted them into her line of sight.

She waited for the tug. It didn't come. She no longer pretended she didn't want his touch. He had to hear the shortness of her breath. With this too-tight gown, he had to see the thumping of her heart.

She could turn. In the past with men it was usually with much haste as they buried themselves between her breasts and then between her legs.

But Louve did none of that. Oh, she knew he wanted her. His own breath fell hot and fast against her bared skin. She felt the hard thump of his heart between her shoulder blades. The insistent length of him hotter and much lower than that.

He swung the laces before her. A tug, that's all he needed to do. A tug, to unravel, to shove the gown to her sides and it would collapse at their feet. It might not even take that, the laughable fabric hardly wanted to stay on her as it was.

'And this, Bied, what is this?' he said.

She didn't know. Were they talking of opposites? Or were these more useless words which held no meaning to her any more?

Grasping his hands, she forced the tug on the laces. Shoved his hands to the side and pushed the gown down herself. It fell in the front, but held up in the back, where his body pressed, where his leg held strong between hers.

'Annoyance,' she announced.

One hot, amused release of breath down her front and she didn't need to know where his gaze went. Her chemise was pulled tight across her bared breasts. Her nipples beaded dark against the light linen.

A breath in, before he pulled away, just that bit, and she felt a pinch in her gown before the fabric gave out and finally tumbled between their bodies. Leaving her almost naked and him fully clothed.

Again, she thought to turn, but Louve's stubbled cheek rubbing against the top of her head stopped her. His fingers snapping at the bindings of her plait, completely freeing her hair, extinguished any thought of forcing what she wanted. What they both wanted.

'Not annoyance, my goblet smasher,' he said. His voice deeper, raspy. Another indication that she wasn't in this alone. 'Annoyance isn't the word now.'

He gripped the chemise in his fists. Waited, and slowly, she lifted her arms above her head. When he pulled on the fabric, she wrapped her arms around the back of his neck.

Dipping his head, he took the invitation. Their kiss no more than an open taste of tongue and lips and carnal need. When he pulled back, she didn't release her hands on his neck.

'What are you doing?' he said, his voice no more than a rasp.

She leaned back that bit more, thrusting her breasts that he barely touched, rubbing her back against his torso.

'Feeling you,' she said.

He tugged on the fabric again. 'That was my idea.'

The greediness of his hands, the hard bar of him against her back, all belying her effect on him. He was tall and broad-shouldered, but she wasn't a slender maid. Though the chemise didn't truly hide her, it hid some, and she hesitated releasing the last of her covering.

She'd never been this way before, never felt this doubt. Something inside her knew it was different with him than anyone else…and so she hesitated.

'Bied,' he growled. 'I couldn't last time. Let me see you now.'

Her fingers loosened at the need behind his words and she looked up. Dark hair mussed by her fingers, his lower lip damp from their kiss.

'What do you mean you couldn't last time?'

If possible, his eyes turned more heated. Lit with unmistakable amusement. 'You think your friends took care of you that day? You think I allowed even for one moment that pup Henry to untie your laces and lay this lush body down?'

It was he. Louve had carried her to the room and removed her gown. 'You? We'd just met!'

'Under the circumstances, with your arms and breasts waving at me, we were more than acquainted.' He flashed both dimples. With the darkness of his eyes, it was more than distracting. 'You should see your expression. Trying to remember?'

'I don't think I want to.'

'That gown was off you much faster than this one, Bied.' He let go of the fabric and the chemise's hem whispered against her shins to the floor again. 'For I had you underneath me.' His hands were rougher this time as they swept across the fabric to her skin underneath, as if the image he spoke of her beneath him was a bit too much.

It was a bit too much for her.

'I worshipped those eight freckles across your nose, the way your chin tipped in defiance, the blush of your bottom lip.' He leaned his head to rest on her shoulder, his breath, his lips telling her the story as much as his words.

'I brushed that warm linen across already clean skin simply to have an excuse to touch you.' His hands swept underneath her breasts. Held the weight of them as his thumbs rubbed across the sensitive skin, as his fingers swept over the tips and ever so gently, tugged. At her caught breath and the sound she could not hold back, he did it again. And again.

'Madwoman that you were, spouting absurdities.' His hands swept down her sides, over the curve of her belly and across the tops of her round thighs. He touched as much as was available to reach with her body pressing tightly back, with her leaning on him for support, for *more*.

'I've wanted you ever since.' He gave her more roughened caresses, more tiny tugs at her chemise. 'Let me take this off. Let me have you.'

She didn't want his fingers to stop the digging at her thighs, his palms kneading at her hips. This time, she grasped the chemise to yank it off, so she could feel those hands against her bared skin. But when the hem brushed the bottom of her breasts, most of her body bared for that touch, something stopped her. Something good. Something right.

She tilted her head to look up at him. Liked the knowing light in his eyes. Liked even more the promise of retribution because she held up her gown for his touch, but denied his eyes from seeing anything of her.

His hands hovered. There was no turbulent touch, but she felt the heat none the less. It was there in every light shudder his body couldn't hold back. In the way his lips parted to take in a breath that seemed harder to reach. In the way his lids lowered as his gaze raked across her mouth and dipped lower. He couldn't see much, not with her hands holding out the chemise from her body. But he was imagining it. She liked that most of all.

'I know what this is,' he said.

'Frustration?' she quipped.

He flashed one exceedingly wicked smile. 'Ah, no. This… You… It's called provocation.'

A hard grip at her hip and he spun her around, ripped the chemise from her body, fisted his hands at her back and kissed her. Until she could barely stand, until there were no kitchens again, only Louve. He stretched her gown with a sweep of his foot and ordered, 'Lie down.'

She did and he followed, with his hands, with his mouth. None of her escaped his touch. Nothing. When he peppered kisses between her breasts, she fisted her hands in his tunic, desperate to take it off, and he helped her.

When he folded it under her head, she scraped her nails along his sides. He growled, kissed the large orb of one breast and then the other, his mouth as greedy as his touch.

'You know the words I'm thinking now?' he said.

She hadn't imagined his growing impatience. It was there as he gripped her thigh to widen the place where he pressed one leg.

'Ache.' He pressed down. Just where she needed it, the tips of her breasts brushing against the smattering of hairs that was the only softness on a torso etched by years of hard work, of dedication.

Too much pleasure. She cupped the outside of her breasts and pressed them together; he jerked his head up, his heated gaze assessing what she silently told him. To take, to kiss and grip and be as hungry as he wanted. To end this little game he continued to play.

'Ah, no, you won't have me that easily.' He blew cool air around one nipple, then the other. Curled his tongue around one breast, then the other. Cupped her knee and pressed it outward to adjust himself fully between her legs. To give weight and heat where his breath and kiss cooled. She couldn't still her hips.

Urgent touch, greedy kisses missing no dip and swell across her belly, down one plump thigh and up the other. His breath as much a caress, as needed as any of the words he spoke, any of the insistent touches he made.

'Need,' he growled. Both hands against her knees, pressing them wider yet, revealing her to his hungry gaze.

'So much desire.' His hips thrust once hard against the air between them as if helpless to his thoughts as much as she was helpless to his touch.

Hands sliding down the back of her thighs as he laid between, his nostrils flaring as he dropped his head. A light breath, a soft kiss, a knowing tongue. Flicking it along her folds, switching from one side to the other, opening her up to more of his kisses.

She wanted more. She wanted him. She wanted this. 'Louve, please...give.'

'Yes,' he promised. His lips following his tongue. Teeth nipping thereafter, a hint of the brutal force he held back.

'What else, Bied? What else do you feel?' he murmured against her damp flesh.

'Louve,' she panted, sinking her fingers into his hair. Feeling the crispness against her palm, the cool air against bared skin, the hot weight of his body against hers. The familiar tightening in her core.

'Tell me,' he rasped against her wet folds.

'Pleasure.' She broke, while he growled in satisfaction and she answered him in all ways.

When the last shudder released her from its grip and

Louve didn't get up, she laughed and pushed against his head. 'No more. No more.'

A hum of protest, a last attentive touch that had her body releasing one more spasm before he kissed her inner thigh. Then he kissed the other until she was nothing but another puddle in the kitchen. Louve seemed to come to the same awareness.

'Who cleans these floors?' he groaned. 'Please don't tell me that wine sop is still here.'

She giggled and curled into him.

'It's your fault for ordering such a strange meal. If I didn't know better—'

'What…you must finish that sentence.'

His cock pressed against her damp curls, as he held her tight, rubbed his chin along the top of her head.

She felt the vibrating need within him echoing in her own body. But for now, what they'd shared was more than she had with anyone. Knowing it wouldn't last, she revelled in it. This couldn't mean anything past right now and she wanted to prolong the joy that it was, as he rasped more kisses along her jaw and nuzzled into her neck. As her hands caressed and stretched to feel everything she could reach.

'If I didn't know better, I'd think you played a jest with that ridiculous meal,' she said.

He laughed low. 'Didn't you find the English serving amusing?'

She smacked him, the slap of her hand echoing as his laughter and kisses increased. She wanted to laugh again only for the joy of how he felt, how he smelled. She wanted it to never end, as his hands continued their exploration. She arched her neck, twisted her body. His fingers swirling traces along her spine, his mouth tasting the crook of her elbow, the dense bone at her wrist, the fleshy bit of her palm. And then reversing the path to repeat it all again.

'How do you like the kitchens now?' he murmured between her breasts. 'Still hate them?'

If there was laughter in them and not just the urgency of where the next meal was, she would. If he kept touching her like he did… 'I think I might see some point to parts of them.'

'Perhaps you want some of your own?' He nipped along her breast's swell, against her ribcage where she was most sensitive.

She was certain he wanted another play at words and meanings because they weren't truly talking of kitchens, but she only had enough thought left for the truth. He'd taken most of her ability to think at all.

'No, no kitchens.' She shifted again so he could gain access to the other side of her breast, and he hummed in approval. Then stopped.

Lifting his head, he peered down at her. 'You're not… playing.'

The cool air hitting the damp spots upon her breasts pebbled her skin. It chilled her without his continued kisses. 'Why would I want kitchens?' she said. 'You do all this labour and you simply have to do it again the next day.'

He gave her a quick kiss to silence her. 'It's called eating. Most of us like it.'

The sweep of his hand indicated the conversation could continue as they were, but she knew enough to know some matters needed to be understood. What they had between them was temporary and anything of kitchens was something dark from her past.

'I'm in earnest, Louve. If you have a family, the amount doubles, triples. In my case I had four siblings. What do you think happens then? You never leave the kitchens.'

'Is that why you don't season the food? It's faster to prepare then?'

That earned him a quick shove against a shoulder. 'That

had to do with the keys and nothing to do with my hatred of kitchens.'

'Ah, yes, no kitchens, then. But you don't like the outside either.'

'It's too cold to wander the gardens.'

'Bied.' He dipped his chin. A shock of black fell across his eye and she held it back. Kept her hand there as he kissed her inner wrist.

'No, I don't like the outside either,' she said. 'There's work there, too. Fields of wheat, or barley. Turnips and cabbage, onions.'

He brushed his hand through her hair, his gaze wandering there as if fascinated by the tangled strands. 'You're not idle, Bied. If you don't like the inside and don't like the out, what, besides me, do you like?'

'You think I like you?' she retorted, which earned her a true smile and dimple which she quickly kissed. 'I like the people I meet from one town to the next as I find work.'

He untangled his fingers. 'You like Tess. You treasure your friendship with her. I've seen it.'

Her friendship with Tess was unexpected. She'd made friends along the way in her life, but she never, except for her family, felt the closeness she did with the baker. 'I do treasure her. She's very dear…and demanding.'

He chuckled low. 'And you love your family.'

'More than I like you,' she replied. 'My brothers and sisters are everything to me. Always have been.'

'Tell me more about them.'

'You do like meddling, don't you?'

'I don't know all their names.'

She was loath to bring her family into anything between her and Louve when all she wanted was him. They were different and for the first time in her life she wanted to tell someone about her family. But it made her all the more wary because she knew this couldn't be more.

'Servet came after me,' she began. 'He was an old man even before he was weaned. Married, no children. Isnard was less than a year after that and when he reached two years that was all the maturity God ever granted him. Mabile married a village man, they have a pack of nieces and I don't think I'll ever see a nephew. But I wouldn't change them for anything.'

'You left out Margery.'

'From the moment she opened her eyes, she was more a worry than any sibling should be. There were times when I'd thought someone had stolen her. Neighbours would take her simply to stare at her. Even if I didn't indulge her, everyone else always did.'

'And your parents?'

She'd talked enough of her family. Talking of her parents, of her mother's heartbreak and her father's abandonment. No. That had no place here.

He made some wondering sound. 'You care for your siblings, and family, yet you don't have one of your own.'

And there. There was the bit she did not want to bring between them. She'd lain with men with some caution, though it wasn't a certainty. She could be barren, but she always felt relief each month that she didn't conceive. After her mother's marriage, she couldn't imagine one of her own.

Louve, the way he searched her eyes, the way he tenderly touched her. The way he immediately offered help with her sister, deserved the truth.

She shook her head. 'No, I don't want a husband.'

His brows lowered. 'Nor a house, or a plot of land to till.'

'Never.'

'But—'

She pressed her palm upon his lips and silenced him. 'I've known myself longer than these few precious days with you. I've never wanted a husband.'

He dropped the hand touching her. The side of his body

was still pressed to her bared skin, but the beginnings of cool air fanned in as he disengaged himself from her.

'It's all I've ever wanted,' he said. 'Land of my own, a wife, peace.'

Peace, something that was ripping up between them as the conversation continued. She leaned up, grabbed her chemise and clenched it to her chest. 'That's what you've told me.'

'You don't believe me?' He pulled at the chemise, spread it over her bared breasts and belly. It didn't cover her completely because she refused to unclench her fist holding it, but she appreciated the warmth it gave. 'I've known myself far longer than you.'

It was true, but she didn't believe him. He'd left a safe home to become a mercenary, he talked of danger and there was something in his voice that though he warned her against it, indicated he liked it. But she'd only known him mere days, and in the end, this was always going to be temporary.

'You want land, a wife and peace and I don't. It's good you were only meant to borrow me.'

A shift as if something she said made him uncomfortable. 'If I'm to borrow you, I want it to be for an exceedingly long—'

She slapped her hand over his mouth, shook her head.

No dimples, no smiles. Just his eyes searching hers. He hadn't said anything, but she knew, she felt it when he touched her, kissed her. Somehow in these few days when she needed to seize her sister and run far away, she'd found a man who wanted to marry her.

She eased her hand away from his lips. But she didn't want to marry him. It seemed he came to the same conclusion for he dropped on his back beside her.

'What *is* on these floors?' he asked. But it was no longer humorous.

Chapter Sixteen

'Hunting. Are you mad?' Louve demanded.

Again, Louve had had little sleep, his thoughts plagued by Biedeluue and the impossible situation they were in. The fact he wanted the impossible with her. He thought… he thought the conflict with the Warstones would be all that separated them. He knew she'd had her trust broken, but he hoped if he proved himself, and after he explained all of these plots and schemes, these games, she'd see the possibility.

But she had turned away from him and all he could think was: Had he fallen for another woman who would never accept him, who only wanted him to keep her bed linens warm?

'I like hunting usually,' Balthus said. 'Not this time of year with the cold, but if I'm fortunate, I can release an arrow as the prey darts across an open field. It's been too long since I had that freedom.'

'That's because the last time you went hunting with Ian, one of those arrows released was aimed towards your back.'

He didn't need any of this. Breaking fast went well and there were no incidents as they continued to chapel. But in that short distance, he overheard Balthus suggest to his family a hunt on the morrow. A. Hunt.

It had stopped Louve in his tracks and he didn't follow them into the small building. He did, however, dare to make eye contact with Balthus, who took the hint and somehow found him in the frost-filled gardens so they could have this discussion.

Prayers would take time, but Balthus's presence would still be required. Louve couldn't believe he was using this precious moment to talk to Balthus about hunting versus finding the parchment.

Balthus hummed. 'It wasn't my brother who released those arrows. Ian's archery skills are abysmal. Further, if my sources are accurate, that particular archer can't be found any more. Ian will have to struggle taking me down. If I'm truly fortunate, I'll get to taunt him about it until the deed's accomplished.'

'Are they injuring you, is that it?' Louve said. 'Are you hurt somewhere and not telling me, and so you've decided to end everything? Or have they hurt your head when I wasn't looking?'

'There are ways they injure us that many cannot see,' Balthus said. 'You should know that by now.'

Louve did, very much. After seeing them retire for the evening and then resume their activities this morning, he had some idea of the damage. The father, jovial words, cutting expressions. And no beguiling grin completely overshadowed the rapier eyes.

But Balthus's mother… Serenity encapsulated her. Always her hands were clasped in front of her, or in her lap when she was sitting. Her words were soft, her manners graceful.

Yet she reminded Louve of a weever fish. Odd, he knew, when she was stunningly beautiful, but those dragon fish had venomous spines and buried themselves in the sand for their prey. She had that predatory patience about her, that calculating ability to wait and strike any vulnerable being that swam too close.

Balthus's tone when describing his parents was so matter of fact, so even, Louve mourned for whatever life he had had. 'What I can't understand is why any of you stay near.'

'They are our parents. If you think we have damned our souls for the deeds we have done in their games, what do you think God would say if, instead of honouring, we killed our mother and our father?' Balthus shrugged. 'Even if any of us decided to, and, in truth, I'm surprised Guy didn't try, they guard themselves even against us.'

'There are other ways to kill you. They'll find a way.' Louve walked farther into the garden. The orchard wasn't big and there weren't that many shrubs or plants to hide behind. Moving around was their best bet to not be seen or heard.

'Most likely, on the second attempt, Ian won't try to hide his murder of me,' Balthus said. 'However weak of me, I hope my mother hasn't plotted in my upcoming murder. As…twisted as she is, I do like pretending I'm her favourite and she might be irked at my death.'

'There will be no murder or your death.'

Balthus ducked under a branch. 'You're not God.'

'I don't have to be God, I merely have to be there,' Louve said. 'If you are insisting on this hunt tomorrow, I'll give you some time to get in front before I leave the stables to—'

'You have to stay in the fortress,' Balthus said. 'All of us will be out of the house. All of the danger and those with prying eyes. This is your opportunity to find information or the parchment.'

Louve hated the logic of Balthus's plan. Hated that it also let his treacherous thoughts go to Bied. Because, yes, he had an opportunity to locate the parchment, but he also had an opportunity to free Margery. All at the expense of Balthus's life and his friendship with Reynold. Nothing was without a sacrifice.

'I've already talked to your brother. He knows Reynold sent me here for the parchment. Right now, I don't know if he knows what it's for, but he's no fool.'

'What do you mean, you've talked to my brother?'

Louve clenched his eyes. How was he to keep track of all this? Despite his earlier thoughts, he had to believe that Balthus was good, Ian was not. Otherwise, everything was for naught. Everything, including those few treasured moments with Bied in the kitchen.

'The conversation was mostly about friendship. Ian extended an offer of peace.'

Balthus's mien turned dark. 'You're now telling me this.'

'Your parents were sleeping. Ian said you were gone… Where were you?'

'The day we arrived?' Balthus's frown eased. 'I was occupied. Weeks in the company of men will do that.'

'If you're not to take this seriously, neither will I.' They didn't have time for this. 'I won't trust his word.'

Balthus picked one of the few leaves on a tree. 'I wasn't intending to ask. There's no point. You're loyal to a fault and, even if you can't trust me or Ian, you trust Reynold. And fortunately for me, Reynold said to trust me.'

Louve did trust Reynold, but only after years together and careful observation. But that trust was sorely tested right now.

Reynold hadn't sent that message regarding the parchment until they left Reynold's home in Troyes. He and Balthus knew they were to confront Ian, or gather information. But could it be true that Reynold hadn't known of the parchment until half a day later? Or was it equally true he didn't want Balthus and Louve to know about it until they were away from their home?

Warstones and their games!

Balthus tossed the leaf, grabbed another. 'I can feel you thinking.'

'One of us has to.' Louve looked to the chapel doors which remained closed. Some servants were going about their duties, none were near here. But their luck would end.

'It doesn't matter the possibilities, the result is the same,' Balthus said. 'Of course, I thought that Reynold could have written that message regarding the parchment so you'd be forced to bring me here and Ian would kill me for him. There's also the scenario where Ian fed that false information to Reynold on purpose to lure us here, so he could kill us both. You see, the possibilities are diabolical and all of them probable, and none of them make any difference. The end result is the same.

'We had to come here. I have to lure my family out of the house and you must look. When it comes to Warstones the scheming possibilities are endless. We can only determine the veracity and truth by eliminating the lies. Unfortunately for me, these conversations and the hunt might end my life.'

That was the truth Louve fought. 'My task is to protect you, so I don't care what the possibilities are. A life, even yours, is worth more than a scrap of parchment.'

Balthus walked faster and Louve, shaking his head, was forced to follow. The youngest Warstone was trying to escape that Louve told him he was worth something. How often had Reynold discarded Louve's words of friendship? Too many times to count.

'You know this is beyond a scrap,' Balthus said. 'The legend existed long before either of us were born. Finding that parchment which could lead to a treasure must be done by us, not my family.'

'I can't allow this,' Louve said.

'Reynold won't kill you. Out of all of us, he knows sacrifices.' Balthus opened up the pouch at his waist and held out a folded parchment. 'I wrote a message you can give him.'

Louve held out his hand, realised it shook and snatched the sealed message. 'You're exactly like your brother.'

Averting his gaze, and looking up at the trees for longer than it took him to snap a few leaves from a branch, Balthus said, 'We're decided, then, on the hunt?'

Louve couldn't imagine Balthus's childhood. He'd had loving parents and grandparents. His friendships had been for life. Yet, somehow, he'd become involved with the Warstones, who actively avoided friendships or ties to anyone, who plotted against each other and wondered when a blade would be slipped between their ribcages. They lacked trust and, as arrogant as they were, they had an odd sense of worth.

He'd spent years with Reynold to build any trust between them. Apparently, it would be the same with Balthus.

Tossing one leaf, Balthus flashed a grin that didn't quite reach his eyes. 'If it'll ease your conscience, I should let you know I lost many bets to the mercenaries that you'll now have to pay. And if anything happens, just remember, you can't trust me. Any of this could be a lie to lure you to your death. Goodness knows, I've lured other men to theirs. So I am, indeed, no better than parchment. I am not even worth the seed that grew the tree.'

Louve inwardly cursed. Balthus had better return from the foolhardy hunt. In the meantime, if Fortune favoured, he would find the parchment and be one step closer to what he wanted: land of his own and peace. He knew now he wanted no other than Bied, but he had to put that aside until much later.

'When I said you were like your brother, I meant the good one.'

Brows drawn suddenly tight, Balthus tossed another leaf to flutter in the cold air. 'Which one is that again?'

Bied hadn't seen Louve since he'd left with the family for the chapel. Maybe he was in the role of Usher again, or in the role of mercenary or...what did mercenaries do when they weren't swinging swords?

Perhaps he was only ignoring her after last night. Not seeing him could be for any of those reasons. She'd rarely seen the Steward, who'd had duties throughout the fortress, and since Louve was near the kitchens yesterday it was conceivable he wouldn't be here today.

Cook showed up again, but his tentative gaze snagged on a pot or a spoon or something, and he'd let out the briefest, most agonised sound she'd ever heard a human give. Henry had rushed to his side and helped him outside. She hadn't seen either of them the rest of the day.

She thought she'd seen grief in all its forms, but she didn't know how Cook was making it through. If she had the freedom of the house, she'd give him some payment and let him go. Or if he wanted to stay, he could garden, or do something else. She could understand wanting to do something different from the past. It seemed he was trying to stay occupied, but every moment in the kitchens had to be agony for him.

Not seeing Louve also gave a certain pain to her heart. She still didn't know who he was, not truly. What Louve told of himself revealed someone who was complex. Underneath, he held a calm strength, while there also seemed to be an irreverence to everything he did. He said he played games with Lord Warstone, but now she wondered who instigated those games and how dangerous they could be.

And yet... There was truth when he'd touched her, kissed her with passion and humour. He'd looked at her as if he meant it. She'd never met a man like him. If her family was safe, if he wasn't asking for something permanent, she'd demand more with him.

He'd said he wanted something different than her; however, she questioned that. He was a mercenary and, before that, he took care of an estate not his own and cared for a widow who didn't want a husband either. The choices he had made were the absolute opposite of his desires for a plot of land and a peaceful life.

So where did that leave them?

She had to work to gain coin for her family. None of them were surviving very well. Granted she never meant to be this far from them, but one job after another she lost because she could never hold her tongue or her pranks. Their need for her didn't lend itself to building a family of her own, even if she wanted it.

Maybe she could persuade Louve he didn't want a wife. Maybe he'd want a travel companion. He was a mercenary and she never stayed in one location for long. They both had to earn their coin. Again, if her family was safe, she wouldn't mind some danger or some games. That was certainly far from her childhood of toiling in the kitchens, toiling in the fields, and it still not being enough to save her sister...to save herself. Maybe...if she could learn to trust a man, if...

No, she had refused Louve's offer to borrow her indefinitely and he'd taken it that way. She'd only appear a fool to change her mind. Even if she did, there was no certainty he'd take her back. She was on her own now, as it should have been from the beginning. All she needed to do was to work, to ignore her thoughts of Louve that there could be—

'You're late,' Bied said, as she spotted Tess slinking in and grabbing an apple.

Tess merely raised her brows and tossed her apple from one hand to the other. She was up to something. Bied wiped her hands across her apron and followed her into the small larder. Herbs hung over their head. She was short, but Tess stood with dried thyme hanging in her face, and Bied would have laughed if she didn't know Tess did it purposefully.

'What are you hiding from me?'

'Who says I am hiding?' Tess said from behind the thyme bundle before she leaned over and winked.

'Tell me,' Bied said.

Tess leaned down and whispered, 'Margery.'

It took a few heartbeats before she comprehended Tess's words because the delivery of them was far too jovial and everything to do with rescuing her sister was fraught with difficulties and Louve's secrets.

'Has something happened?'

Tess shook her head, peered over Bied's shoulder and lowered her voice more. 'Galen overheard the family talking of a hunt tomorrow.'

The family gone, including Ian of Warstone, meant her sister would be in the room alone. There might be a guard, the latch might be locked, but it was an opportunity she hadn't had before. The sudden relief of it all was overwhelming and she wanted to ask a thousand questions. Instead she squeezed Tess's arm. Eyes shining in understanding, Tess gave a quick nod and stepped away.

'Wait!' Bied said. 'How do *you* know what Galen overheard?'

Tess took cheeky bite of apple, flicked her hip up and walked away.

Bied laughed. When this was all done and she and Margery were far away from the Warstones, she truly was going to miss her unexpected friend.

Chapter Seventeen

It wasn't a sound that woke Louve from his sleep, it was a presence that skittered across his skin. Even that shouldn't have woken him since for years he'd slept in rooms filled with other mercenaries. He was used to other men's snores, the rustle of clothing and the minute movements of restless men.

So it was the sinister feel of the presence that alerted him to the danger. Of course, if the person standing in his room wanted him dead, he'd already be dead, so he didn't open his eyes or move when he said, 'Did it have to be this late?'

'I couldn't fit it into the day that we had,' Ian said.

Shoving the quilt down with his feet, Louve sat, and ran his hands through his hair. He'd hardly slept the night before and the night before that, and the night… When was the last time he'd slept?

'Why is it your entire household abhors my getting any rest?' he said.

Ian chuckled. 'Maybe we are afraid if you did, you'd think more clearly and leave while you can.'

Eyeing the Warstone who was barely perceivable in the dark, Louve stood and stretched.

'You sleep without any clothing?'

'Don't you?' Louve said.

'Seems like a luxury to me. When you have to escape with your life, having a tunic is useful.'

'Maybe if I had one as fine as yours, but I'm afraid I spend my coin on other matters, like the weaponry that is more functional when a life is at stake.'

'Those are the financial choices a mercenary has to make?'

Those were ones he made. Louve swept up his tunic and slid it on. 'Won't you tell me why you're here?'

'It's too dark in here for this,' Ian said.

'It's perfect for sleep.' Louve secured his braies and grabbed his breeches.

'But we need to talk.' Ian opened the door and returned with a torch to light the two in the room.

Maybe it was the lateness of the night, or the flickering torch, but Louve was again reminded that this enemy was also the brother to Reynold, his friend. They looked and talked so similarly—what went on in their heads, though, could be different. Louve needed to determine if Ian's flashes were madness or warnings.

Nothing about Ian's mannerisms now seemed tensed for attack and, in that brief moment that the door opened, Louve saw no one in the hall. Perhaps Ian truly was that secure in his skills, or this was another friendly, but odd visit.

'How was the conversation with my brother in the garden?' Ian said.

Louve wasn't surprised Ian knew, he was only surprised he'd been allowed any access to Balthus.

'He doesn't trust you and neither do I.' Louve adjusted his breeches.

'That'll take time, no?' Ian said.

Time wouldn't be enough. 'I have some wine here if you'd like.'

Ian moved farther into the room. 'I didn't think I allowed such luxury for my servants.'

'You don't.' But the ale was poisoned and it was safer to ensure he had his own wine in case someone had tampered with those casks.

Ian accepted the cup from him and drank, his eyes keeping with Louve's. 'What is it?'

'It's unnatural to have you here,' Louve said.

'What could be unnatural about conversing and sharing wine?' Ian lifted his cup.

It was unnatural because Ian kept seeking out his company. With Balthus and Reynold he'd been the one to pursue any relationship. It'd been the same way with Nicholas when he'd returned.

Louve rolled the wine in his cup. Too much of his life had been dictated by others. He longed for the time when it could be his own. He longed for the time when he could sleep through the night again.

'Surely you must have shared such time with my brothers,' Ian continued.

'A time or two.' Louve took a sip.

'I'm surprised either of them allowed you to approach my fortress.'

'Are you?' Louve said, indicating the chair behind Ian for him to sit, while he sat in the other.

'I'd think they'd be more protective of someone who decides to be a friend. I know I would.'

Had he chosen any of this madness? 'I think I'll decline your protection since it entails attempted murder.'

Ian settled back in his chair. 'Would you believe me if I told you I'm glad Balthus escaped?'

'You know the answer to that.'

Ian shook his head. 'True, it is right not to believe me since his death suits my needs. My parents' as well. Balthus and Reynold only divide our power and wealth.'

'You say this at the same time you talk of friendship and wanting your brothers back.'

'We might have no choice, though,' Ian said. 'Only one of us can survive.'

Louve slid him a glance and something flitted across Ian's face.

'I said that aloud, didn't I?' Ian said.

Warnings or madness? Louve observed the lack of confident smugness and notes of vulnerability in Ian's voice.

'I didn't mean to say that,' Ian repeated.

The Warstone appeared frightened. Louve knew he himself was terrified. 'You have no reason.'

'I do…right this precise moment. But as a precaution, where's your weapon?'

'It's near.' Louve didn't glance to his chair arm where he had strapped a dagger.

'I don't need to ask if you know how to defeat me. I know you can. First Nicholas, then Reynold trained with you. You've had practice.'

At the mention of Nicholas, Louve stilled.

Ian gave a scoffing sound. 'Don't be surprised by what I know about you, or who assisted in Guy's death. Although I was always surprised that a man as large as Nicholas of Mei Solis could move as swiftly as he could. Do you have his speed?'

'You woke me up in the middle of the night to talk of my fighting skills? I'm more likely to use them on you as a demonstration. Do you intend to do this hunt tomorrow?'

Ian stood suddenly. 'If my brother, Balthus, asked me to a hunt, why would I not go?'

'Because there will be consequences if he doesn't return.'

Louve braced for an attack, but Warstone only walked to the table and poured wine into his cup. So Louve raised his cup as offering to see what the eldest son would do.

Brows raised, Ian eyed Louve and with much flourish tipped the flagon until the remainder of wine filled Louve's cup.

'There are consequences to any death, but especially in one so dear. Balthus is dear to my mother.' Ian set the flagon on the table, but did not return to his chair. 'I am, as you said, losing my understanding. It's been occurring…for some time. I thought I had hidden it from my parents. They are not pleased by my mistakes, Balthus dodging an errant arrow being one. They've tried to kill me, you know.'

'As part of your childhood training,' Louve said for clarification. It wasn't possible that the Warstones recently attempted to murder their eldest.

Both hands cradling the crude cup, Ian strode to stand behind his chair. 'I have theories, but I'd like to hear why Reynold ordered you here and why you allowed Balthus to be within my reach?'

'Ordered. Allowed.' Never taking his eyes off Ian, Louve kept his right hand near the dagger. 'There are only moves on the board, Warstone—do you think any of us players can truly be influenced by another player?'

At Ian's unexpected silence, Louve considered his night companion. Ian's slips from one topic point to another weren't alarming, but ignoring a question and not making a reply was.

Louve didn't dare move, not when Ian suddenly sat in his chair and seemingly forgot Louve was sitting in the room with him. Not while he watched minute changes begin as Ian's open expression closed before pale eyes rose once again.

'It's not here.'

'What's not here?' Louve said as evenly as possible. Ian's voice was now cultured, controlled, and a sly cunning etched his features. It was subtle, but even the way he sat in the chair was different. The moment they had, the *right now* that Ian said he had, was gone. Lord Warstone had returned.

Adjusting himself in his seat, Louve prepared for whatever fight would come. 'What isn't here?'

The second brother, Guy, was reported to be a brutal killer with no remorse. It was apparent Ian suffered from his own demons all while he was aware of them. Was this the fate that awaited Reynold and Balthus? And what did that say about his own destiny?

'The parchment my brother seeks,' Ian said. 'Do you think I'd have it in my possession at the same residence I invite my parents to?'

This was the Ian who could strike at any time, the one who played games. The one who liked to reveal truths and then hide them again. Warstone had already hinted that he knew the reason Louve was here and that was to obtain that parchment leading to the treasure from the Jewell of Kings. There was no point to deny it.

'Why wouldn't you have the parchment in the same residence as your parents?' Louve said. 'They adore you. What parent wouldn't admire their firstborn who owns it while the other brothers covet it?'

Ian sneered, 'It's so they keep me alive.'

'It's merely one among your other notable attributes to keep you alive,' Louve said.

'Those are many.' Ian chuckled. 'Oh, but as long as my brothers live, my family could change their minds. It would be amusing if they, for example, try to kill me instead of them.'

Twice. That was twice that Ian alluded to his parents trying to kill him. Could it be true?

Ian waved his cup around. 'Hence why the parchment is far away. Don't think my dear mother and father wouldn't change on any of us if they gained the parchment regarding the Jewell of Kings. It's beautiful, you know. Not those torn slips of paper that Reynold has in his possession, but one complete page. Of course, absolutely useless unless one is also in possession of the Jewell and the dagger, but beautiful none the less.'

The crackling of the flames in the torches was the only other sound besides this eerie conversation, but Louve strained his ears to hear if anyone was outside the closed door, listening to this conversation.

Ian was a Warstone, and this information would come at a price, but he'd take it while he could. 'What do you mean useless?'

'I believe it explains the treasure.' Ian smirked. 'Ah, yes, I know of the treasure. My parents believe, and perhaps Reynold knows, that what I possess is a code which must be deciphered.

'Of course, my parents can never possess it—I'll keep it until I'm dead. Or they are dead. Or if everyone dies, I'll gather all the words, find all the meanings and have the power and treasure to myself.'

And thus power begets power and madness. A place where Louve could find peace seemed further away than the parchment. 'I would not wish for your childhood.'

'If we could change, I wouldn't wish for yours.' Ian arched one brow. 'Surprised? See it from my point of view—how dull yours has been. Secure in a home and estate where you're respected and cared for. Happy, but not interesting. Worse, it appears Reynold is building such an existence for his own children! How far he's fallen.'

Louve was tired of defending his childhood. It was happy, but that didn't mean it fit. Only one of the reasons he'd left it behind…and was now sitting next to a murderer, wishing he could have at least one restful night. The irony was not lost on him.

'So here I am and the parchment isn't,' Louve said.

'You believe me so easily?'

'It's not as if I have permission to inspect your rooms. What is the alternative?'

Ian stared at Louve for more than a few heartbeats, more than a few breaths. He felt the flickering torches tap out the time as Ian thought out the ramifications to Louve's impulsive request.

The easy answer should have been a refusal. That's what he believed Ian would say. Instead, he said, 'Do you think a sister's love is stronger than a brother's?'

Louve's heart stopped. 'I haven't any siblings, so I couldn't compare.'

'Ah, perhaps that is why you form such loyal friendships.' Ian shifted. 'Tomorrow I am gone. It is as simple as that. So I'll let my guards know you have my permission to enter my quarters. I'll even let you take anything from there.'

'Anything?'

'If it wants to go, yes,' Ian said.

'Parchments rarely speak about desires,' Louve said carefully.

Ian gave a low chuckle. 'But women rarely speak of anything else. Mine talks when I watch her. The... entertainment is almost enough for me to forget.'

More than once, Ian had mentioned watching his mistress. Now...only now, Louve understood why Ian kept her. Not because he feared he'd spoken in his sleep as Balthus surmised, but because Ian didn't lie with Margery, someone else did. For Bied's sake, for her sister's, he needed to feign more interest in the parchment.

'It doesn't sound as though you need anything from your room, but one travels easier than another, and that one I find more enticing. I accept that proposal.'

Ian flashed a smile that did not reach his pale eyes. 'There will be consequences.'

Louve knew there would be. Ian might be going on a hunt, but not all of his guards would be gone. Everyone he cared for was at risk. All he wanted to do was rescue Bied and Margery and be done with it all.

But he wasn't here for them. He was here because he gave his oath to his friends and, while Ian sat before him, while it was still the dead of night and there were no interruptions, the game had to continue.

'Room or no room, permission or not, since you report the parchment is elsewhere,' Louve said, 'will you, to keep my dull life interesting, fill my mind with useless information and reveal where it is?'

Ian pointed at Louve with the hand holding the wine cup. 'Safe with my wife and children whom I haven't seen for years.'

Louve felt his world spin and, despite wishing otherwise, he believed the eldest brother. The parchment wasn't here and everything they'd done for the last few weeks was for naught.

All that could be obtained was more information if Ian was in a divulging mood.

'With your wife? What is to stop me from—'

'You won't find them,' Ian said. 'I secured them in a home and they aren't there any longer. I did well marrying that woman. She's good, you know. Innocent. I thought her biddable and for a time she was. Then she learnt and learnt too well.

'When I knew my mind was malleable, I tucked her away far in the north. Not so far that I couldn't kill her and the children in the middle of the night, but it would take some time. I'd have to think of it and all the while it would be inconvenient.'

There was only one way Ian knew she wasn't in the home any more. 'You decided to do it, though.'

'Oh, yes. Not so long in the recent past. I was quite perturbed that they weren't there, came home and immediately tried to kill Balthus. Merely to…move matters along a bit. But even that was ruined. Mistakes!'

'What happened when you went up there?'

'Cobwebs, dust, spiders, creatures living in every corner. I left her there and I don't think she unpacked because it was empty. Probably left the day after I did. Which meant years have passed. Even if I could find her now… no. My time is over. They have the parchment, but nothing else.'

Ian leaned his head back; his expression was well worn. 'You are a good friend to the Warstones.'

'I am not your friend.'

'You warn me away, like someone who still has his soul intact, though it's clear you like the games. Still, I've enjoyed this conversation. Did I give you what you wanted?'

'You came to my room. Did you get yours?'

'The wine is decent,' Ian said. 'I can enjoy it though I am but a reed to a disloyal breeze. I like that I could talk to you in all my many forms. I liked that you played along.'

'What is it you want, Ian? I think we're both tired and need to rest.' Whatever this was, the game would continue, but the night would end. He didn't have enough wine to prolong this amicably and he never wanted to reach for the dagger. It would be preferable if they both lived one more day.

'I cannot face my wife or children and apologise to them. They're…good, other than the Warstone blood, they're good. My wife thinks I'm good…or she did once a long time ago.' Ian sighed. 'I'd like to face my brother and apologise for what I did, too.'

'He is here, as are you, you don't need my help to tell him of your remorse.'

'With my parents here and my Steward gone, it will be up to me, won't it? That will prove to be enlightening, tomorrow.' Ian closed his eyes, his expression dark and yet untroubled. 'How is your sword arm?'

Louve was fast losing the threads of this conversation. 'Do you wish to train together tomorrow in the lists?'

Ian blinked and his pale eyes sought out Louve again. 'You're my friend, aren't you? I've never had one before and you've been one to so many. You're good at being a friend to a Warstone. Do you know how rare that is?'

'Friendship requires trust and trust takes years to earn.'

'Years might not be a possibility. I don't want to throw daggers any more, but I can't keep up with my actions any more. And even if I stay my hand, it doesn't mean others won't throw theirs.' Ian stood and set his cup on the table. 'Make me a promise.'

'No.'

Ian laughed, but it sounded weary. 'Don't you want to hear it first?'

'No.'

'You would make a good Warstone,' Ian said. 'I'll tell you anyway. When it comes to the end of me, because it's soon, take care of my wife and sons.'

If his wife and sons were in hiding, then they were already safe. 'You don't intend to kill me?' Louve asked.

'In the whole world, you are as inconsequential as your happy childhood home. For me, I am extremely tired. So incredibly...' Ian opened and closed the door as quietly as he came in.

Louve wasn't certain he had the strength to rise and return to his bed. There would only be a few more hours before the dawn. Before a hunt occurred where 'years might not be a possibility.'

For whom? Balthus? Ian? The Warstones? Any number of the servants? Himself?

Bied.

Louve had a thousand words he wanted to say to her,

but there was too much and not enough time. If they got through this, he vowed that whatever trust she'd lost, he would earn it. That one shared moment on a kitchen floor wouldn't be all they had together. They'd talk, he'd compromise, anything, until only the Warstone intrigues separated them, and when the game was done, that would be gone as well.

In the meantime, the Warstones were on the hunt and for more than just deer. No parchment; Balthus at risk. If Ian didn't order the guards to slaughter him, there was nothing stopping his parents from ordering their guards to do so.

On the hunt, would they even bother to make it look like an accident? No. Reynold would know the truth and come for his brother and forfeit his own life.

At least Bied would have her sister and they could escape before the day played out. He wondered, if he told her everything, if she'd give him a chance? Or would he yet again not be accepted and left to fate?

Chapter Eighteen

'Why aren't you in the kitchens?'

Bied jumped at the loud whisper behind her.

Louve's presence in the Hall was as surprising as waking this morning and realising everything Tess had reported was true. The family were off on a hunt. She'd watched guards, even that big brute, leave with Lord Warstone and his family. They'd be gone for hours and Margery was upstairs…waiting for her, or so Bied liked to believe.

She hurried her steps towards the stairwell leading to the private chambers. Louve hurried his until he was alongside her. 'What are you doing?'

She was doing what she needed to do. What he said he'd help her with and yet hadn't. She wasn't being fair, but surely he knew of the hunt and the opportunity? She was doing what must be done.

Lifting the tray she held, she said, 'I'm delivering food for the mistress upstairs, sir.'

He pivoted to stand in front of her. The tray she carried wasn't large enough to keep a distance that would make seeing him again any less potent.

This man… She might have been inebriated when she first saw him, when her impression was that he couldn't be real. No man had his colouring, his build. His smile was enough to make her forget her next thought. He wasn't perfect. What he was, was temptation.

What they'd done last night in the kitchens where anyone could walk in, she couldn't forget. Everything he said and did, the warmth they shared, was unexpected. The pieces of their past bewildering to her heart.

That man, however, was gone. This man who barred the way to her sister was the man who had commanded the kitchen upon his arrival. Who had followed her to the ale cellars and demanded what she did there. This man, this mercenary, expected to be obeyed. But she wasn't a woman who would.

She stepped to the side to get around him, but Louve moved with her. 'Please sir, the bread will dry out if it's exposed too long.'

'Don't.' Louve peered over her shoulder.

Facing Louve, she couldn't see anyone else. The fortress was large, but no room was ever empty for long. When all he did was wait, she did, too, but only because a confrontation where she slammed the tray in his face and ran up the stairs would cause more attention than she needed.

His eyes flicked back to hers. 'What did you think you would do upstairs? Walk past the guards?'

Carrying a tray of bread and cheese, that was exactly what she expected. Jeanne, Margery's servant, had even helped her prepare the food so it would look exactly like hers did every day. There was no reason the guards would starve her sister and one servant or another delivering it shouldn't matter.

She didn't want to listen to anything Louve said, but he was Usher and there were too many eyes. If the guards suspected her, if there was any suspicion she was related to Margery, she didn't know what the consequences would

be. She couldn't risk her sister, who flinched from a man with a cold pale gaze, and Louve was delaying her!

'You know what I'm doing,' she breathed.

He took a step closer, whispered, 'I told you—'

She didn't have to explain her actions to any man. She'd done that all her life until she got wise to them taking advantage of a woman raising children alone. 'You changed your mind. Can you move, please?'

'I *changed* my mind?'

A scrape of a bench behind them made her flinch. Louve just caught the roll that slid off and put it back on the tray.

Gaze imperious, he said, 'Follow me.'

The Usher giving an order. Since he turned to face the staircase leading to her sister, she obeyed.

Up the staircase she followed the man whom she'd kissed, touched, whom she'd told her failings to. He played at being an usher, but there wasn't anything about his demeanour that said he was servant. He played games with Ian of Warstone, but last night felt nothing like a game between them.

How could they have been so close…and not want the same things? He said he wanted a home and a wife, but everything he did was the opposite of that. No matter, now wasn't the time to contemplate any future with him. Soon she'd escape with her sister.

At the top and along the hallway, guards were on rotations. Many were talking low and heatedly. Preparing for something she knew nothing about, but Louve did not change his pace and she kept to the same. When they approached a door with one guard, Louve stopped. 'You know why I am here.'

'But not why she is here.'

'She is a servant,' Louve said. 'You don't expect me to carry a tray of food.'

The guard didn't move. Sounds behind them indicated several guards had followed them up the staircase and she could see two more farther down the hall.

'Is her presence such a threat you think to hesitate?' Louve taunted.

The guard's eyes narrowed. 'Lord Warstone does not hire idiots. It's not the threat, but the deviation from the agreement that I question.'

A cry, tiny, almost unrecognisable. Her sister was on the other side. Oh, to shove everyone away and fling it open! The guard's gaze pivoted to her and she knew she made that sound. If they denied her now, she'd never forgive herself for showing emotion, so she actively didn't look his way.

'What do you think will happen with Lord Warstone,' Louve said, 'if I am denied access?'

The guard's blank gaze stayed with her, but she kept her eyes straight towards the door. She knew it was dangerous, Margery had written a message and Louve had warned her, but while in the kitchens and under the Steward's care, then Louve's, she didn't feel it. But that dead stare from the guard wound caution tight through her veins.

Without a sign of capitulation, without a turn of his stare, the guard simply opened the door and stepped aside. Louve entered first; a sound inside of surprise. Bied followed next though the guard's position forced her to take in his size, his stench.

She hurried past him and dared a look over her shoulder as the door slammed shut. She hadn't even turned around when her sister's arms clasped the side of her. 'Biedeluue! How did you get here?'

They were in an antechamber, several narrow windows providing light. Sumptuous chairs and little tables along the walls, ready for...whatever happened in rooms

like these. A couple of weeks here in this fortress and the luxury continued to surprise her.

Aware that Louve went to one of the windows and looked down below, Bied dropped into her sister's hug. 'I brought a tray of food up. Jeanne's slicing vegetables in the kitchens today.'

'Who is he?' Margery indicated with her chin.

Her heart swelling with relief, Bied pulled away to simply look at her sister. It was Margery. Safe. Alive. Not looking nearly as uneasy as she had in the Hall. There was still some light in her eyes.

'This is Louve,' she said. 'He's Usher here.'

Her sister eyed Louve and Bied. Feeling suddenly awkward at her sister's beautiful assessing gaze, she set the tray down.

'He's here because...because...' Bied started. What was he doing? Louve was riffling through the contents on a table where there were papers and a quill, opening up a large flat box and then another.

'Which one is his chest?' Louve said.

Louve had gone mad. Margery just answered, 'They're all his chests. Except for the two gowns, everything is his.'

'Where does he keep paperwork?' Louve said. 'Messages?'

Margery pointed. 'He writes everything there.'

Louve shook his head. 'When he receives messages, where do those go?'

'You're not an usher.'

'Tell me.'

'The messenger makes this odd knock on that door,' Margery said. 'A guard opens it—I have to turn my back and face that window until he tells me I can turn again.'

'Except you've watched it.'

'A bit when I didn't turn fast enough. He doesn't like that.'

Margery's voice wasn't like anything Bied had ever heard before. Assured. Matter of fact and, most puzzling of all, not surprised by Louve's line of questioning. Bied didn't understand any of it.

'Where else can I look for a piece of parchment about this size with drawings? Something beautiful and colourful.'

Margery shook her head. 'There's nothing like that here. Trust me, I've searched. He doesn't leave the messages here. I don't even know what he writes and, as for anything else, I've upturned this place every single day looking for anything to get me out.'

'Does Lord Warstone talk in his sleep?'

'Not about papers.'

Louve's expression darkened. 'What, then, and be quick about it.'

'It's none of your concern.'

'Nothing about papers, nothing about…gems?' Louve asked.

Margery glowered. 'Nothing that should concern an usher, only wives.'

Bied didn't understand the rapid questions Louve asked her sister, but more so, she couldn't believe how quickly Margery answered. Her younger sister had changed since she'd been here. The younger Margery would have collapsed when they entered and waited to be whisked away. This one had her hands fisted at her side and answered only because she wanted to.

Giving one last measured gaze at Margery, Louve strode back to the window, peered one way and then the other, cursed, but then gave out a huff of amusement.

Bied exchanged a look with Margery, but her sister only shrugged. 'Why are you here?'

'Aren't you going to ask him what he wanted with those questions?' Bied said.

'I've been in this room for far too long and am certain it's safer not to ask.'

'I brought her here—I'll keep you both safe,' Louve announced.

Margery rolled her wide eyes. 'Why are you in the fortress?'

Her sister might not want to ask questions of Louve, but Bied did and she fully intended to later.

'You sent me the message,' Bied said. 'You said you were in danger.'

'That message was for our brothers, not for you.'

Bied swallowed back the hurt those words caused. 'Who else has helped you in the past?'

Margery's sparkling eyes softened. 'With bumps and bruises. How can you be so reckless to come here?'

Louve made a suspicious sound behind her, which Bied ignored. She needed to ignore everything to do with him.

'Me, reckless!' Bied said. 'I warned you of Lord Warstone. Nothing you said eased any of my concerns. All you talked about was how handsome he was, how charming.'

Margery gasped. 'Is that why you're here? I only said that for your sake.'

'What?' Bied said.

'If I had told you I was only involved with a man for the coin, for connections—which all exist, mind you—would you have let me go?'

No, she wouldn't have. Margery's words were sinking in. 'So…you're not broken-hearted.'

Margery grimaced. 'Absolutely not.'

'You put yourself in this danger for nothing?'

'You aren't nothing. Our family isn't nothing,' Margery said. 'You work and give coin to Mother and to the others. Yet you save nothing for yourself and what Lord Warstone promised me, well…'

'You did this for me?'

'I knew he was different than the others. I heard rumours he was dangerous, but his offer would have been enough to truly make a difference. Especially with Mabile, who wrote to me and—'

'Mabile!' Bied said. 'Why didn't anyone tell me?'

'I don't know why she sent it to me instead of you, but in truth, we never know where you go until you write to us and I've been here for so long.' Margery eyed the door and sighed.

'What is happening to Mabile?'

'She's pregnant again and she did so poorly before, and won't be able—'

'You have only moments,' Louve interrupted.

Bied shook her head. For days, her thoughts and deeds had been interrupted with Louve. Now Margery painfully reminded her of her responsibilities at home. Bied relied on Mabile helping their mother, who needed help simply relieving herself. If Mabile was pregnant again, she couldn't do her duties.

'He truly is protecting us,' Margery said, a note of awe in her voice. 'I'm curious now, who is he?'

Louve's back turned to her, Margery whispering—did they think there was someone eavesdropping?

'I don't know,' Bied said. 'He's lying.'

Louve cleared his throat and eyed Margery from her toes up. 'Are you poisoning the ale?'

'What?' Margery said.

Bied immediately stood in front of her sister. 'She wouldn't do that.'

'There are casks that are poisoned—are you, or someone you know, putting poison in the ale?'

'Was that what was wrong with it?' Margery said.

Bied turned to her sister. 'You didn't drink any more of it, did you?'

Margery shook her head. 'It was vile. I've been drinking wine ever since.'

'And your hand?' Bied asked.

Margery raised it. 'Wrapped, but it was only a shallow cut.'

Relieved, Bied squeezed her sister and Margery stiffened. Flinging herself away, Bied said, 'You *are* hurt! Let's get you out of here, you need to rest, to heal.'

'It's not what you think.'

'You wrote that letter. You have a swollen lip and goodness knows what else, and you tell me it's not what I think? What is it that you think I think?'

Margery's face screwed up, then she shrugged. 'Just that.'

Bied felt the familiar spike of annoyance. Margery had always been contrary and dramatic. 'I came here to rescue you.'

'I can see that. Though you were supposed to send someone else.'

'When it comes to the family, I've always come to your aid.'

'Except this time, we needed someone who could use a weapon against trained men,' Margery said. 'You can't fight any of these warriors.'

'If you needed a sword, you should have said that. I would have found one, or some weapon or...' She was being foolish, she wasn't trained to fight, which was why she had intended to work her way towards her sister.

'I thought that the words *truly dangerous* would have been enough. I found that tiny scrap of paper and I had to take the chance. Ian's wealthy, but he doesn't leave blank parchment around.'

'I can see them through the woods,' Louve announced. 'The party could be on a chase, or on the way back.'

'He's no usher,' Margery said, eyeing Louve. No, he

wasn't. His strength, his cunning, the way he assessed situations… The way he commanded those around him.

Feeling as though she should keep some of his secrets, she said, 'He *can* organise a household.'

'That's good for you, then, since you're so terrible,' Margery said.

'You need to pack,' Louve said.

Margery stepped back. 'I'm not going anywhere.'

Louve peered over his shoulder. 'Say that again.'

'I'm not going anywhere without Evrart.'

'Evrart!' Bied said over the roaring beginning in her ears. She couldn't have heard her sister correctly. 'Lord Warstone is the one who has kept you trapped.'

'He did—he is!' Margery said. 'He was terribly charming at first, but for the time we've been here, he's been distracted. And he's never asked for…which I'm grateful for, but it was all very frightening. I had to send that note.'

'They are returning,' Louve said. 'Balthus is alive.'

The relief in Louve's voice sent chills across her neck. 'Alive?'

Louve's jaw tightened before he flashed her a look. 'I meant Balthus is riding with them. The first of the guard has cleared the woods and there's someone travelling with them I don't recognise. Lord Warstone can't be far behind now. We have to go, there's no time to pack.'

'I'm not leaving,' Margery said.

Bied looked to Louve, who was at the door. 'Help me.'

Louve kept his gaze on Margery. 'I don't think your sister is understanding.'

'And you do?' Bied said. 'What is this?'

'Your sister wants away from Ian, but not this man,' Louve said.

'Evrart,' said Margery.

'Where's Evrart now?' Bied said.

'With Ian.'

'Why does he matter?' Bied cried.

'He doesn't,' Louve said. 'We've got to go.'

'No!' Bied said. 'None of this makes sense.'

Margery's eyes narrowed on Louve. 'What deal did Ian make with you, *Usher*? He negotiates like the devil.'

'He said I could have you if you left the room,' Louve said. 'Since I had Bied, since she had this message from you, since I knew you loved your sister, it seemed as though I couldn't lose.'

'Who is Evrart?' Bied said.

'He's Ian's personal guard,' Louve announced.

'That brute?' Bied gasped.

'Don't!' Margery slashed out her arm. 'Don't say anything bad about him. He's a good man and has had a trying time with his appearance.'

Louve went back to the window. 'They're coming through the gates now, but it looks as though they want to attend their horses. Odd, but we'll take it. Explain, Margery, and fast. Your sister won't leave this room otherwise.'

'I beg to differ! I'll leave within half a heartbeat if she explains herself!'

Margery cried out, 'I'm in love.'

Bied had heard this all too often. 'Are you jesting?'

'Truly this time,' Margery said. 'We tried to fight it. Ian wouldn't approve and the danger is to us both! Then, it seemed he turned a blind eye and it…happened.'

'Ian didn't turn a blind eye,' Louve said.

Margery paled. 'What do you mean?'

Louve glanced to Bied, shook his head once, then gazed at her sister. His expression was grave. 'He likes to watch.'

Margery's bandaged hand fluttered to her chest. 'You don't mean it.'

Bied couldn't understand what they meant until Louve dipped his chin and looked away.

Margery held her hand to her mouth. 'Oh, Evrart can't ever know. I think I'm going to be sick.'

'Your sister said that to me once.' Louve glanced to Bied.

'This is not the time for jests,' Bied uttered. 'Where are you getting this humour and would you please choose a disposition?' Bied pulled Margery's hand in hers. 'Margery, we have to go. Your lip is cut, and you flinched at dinner. Lord Warstone is hurting you.'

Margery grimaced. 'It's not Lord Warstone. His personal guard…he's big…and I don't exactly… Must I explain this in front of him?'

'No, you don't,' Louve said. 'I understand.'

'Yes, *she* does,' Bied said. 'Because I see her with a swollen lip. My youngest sister has been hurt by some guard of Lord Warstone!'

Margery made an uncomfortable sound. 'Bied, it's not what you're thinking. He's large, I jumped, and we crashed. Please know that Evrart feels all the worse for it, but… I don't. You saw him act like an idiot trying to cheer me.'

Bied felt the flush against her cheeks as understanding dawned. 'No more.'

'It seems your sister likes more,' Louve said. Margery giggled.

Bied rounded on him. 'Enough from you!'

'Lord Warstone cut you in front of everyone.' Bied pointed at Margery's hand. 'If you stay, how can you guarantee he won't do it again?'

'She can't. That's the Warstone training. Has it been happening more often?' Louve said.

'I don't know him well enough, but Evrart says he's been slipping,' Margery said.

Bied gasped, seeing the concern on her sister's face. 'You can't feel for him?'

'If you heard him late at night, when he's sleeping—' Margery stopped.

Louve darted a glance at her on the way to the window, his frown deepening as if he, too, wanted to know what Margery refused to say.

'They've left the stables.' Louve peered out in different directions. 'It's time. I can't guarantee what will happen if Ian sees us here. If we get trapped on that stairwell, we'll have trouble.'

'What do we do?' she asked.

'We leave her.' Louve's voice was absolutely dead with certainty.

Bied's heart stopped. 'We'll all go. This... Evrart will follow.'

'He can't,' Margery and Louve said at the same time.

Bied pointed at Louve. 'What are you not telling me?'

'He owes Lord Warstone a debt,' Margery said. 'Ian knows where Evrart's family is.'

When the words sank in, Bied's heart panicked against her ribcage. 'I didn't come here for nothing.'

'You have no weaponry, no training,' Margery said, her voice firm. 'I told you to bring our brothers who at least can fight. How are you supposed to get us past the guards? I'd hoped that with a few, and Evrart's training, we could have a chance.'

'You've been here for months,' Louve said. 'Unless they were trained by a demon himself for years, nothing would give your brothers a chance.'

Margery looked away.

'You knew that. Evrart told you not to send the message and you did it anyway,' Louve hissed.

'I didn't tell him until after I'd sent the message. When I told him it was my sister in the Hall, he flew into a—' Margery turned to Louve. 'Oh, if Lord Warstone watches, does he hear?'

Louve gave one nod and locked his eyes with Bied. 'That means he knows who you are. We're leaving.'

'You truly care for him, don't you?' Bied said.

'I do. Swear to me that—'

'No!' Bied cried out. Louve grabbed her hands. 'Stop grabbing my hands!'

He didn't let go. 'Not this time. Your sister is safe as long as Ian wants her to be. If we're here when he enters the room, we're dead. He's been listening and knows you are sisters. That's why he wanted this game with me.'

'Game? How many games can there be?'

'Go. Go. Go.' Margery pushed against her back. 'I'll find you. Ian can't last for ever. He'll make a mistake.'

Bied yanked her hand and Louve grabbed her wrist.

Chapter Nineteen

'What are you doing? Where are we going?' Bied demanded.

Louve only clasped her wrist tighter. It was more than the difference of their size in the strides he took that hurried them along. It was his urgent pace, the insistent pull on her arm. It should have hurt, it should have been a warning to her, but he ensured she was too engaged in keeping up with him to notice the desperation in his actions.

He was certain she could hear it, though, in his uneven breath from biting back all the words he struggled to contain. Until they slammed into the linen closet, the shelves replenished, the space somehow smaller.

'Louve—'

Louve caged her against the back wall, until everything about her was pressed against him and the wall and there was nowhere for her to go. He wanted her...*needed* her like this.

'Quiet,' he whispered against the top of her head, breathing her scent in, snagging her fine hair through the stubble along his chin.

Louve couldn't get his heart, his breath, his body under control. He half wanted to spin this woman around and laugh with her just from the sheer relief they were alive. His other half wanted to shake her, yell curses before he kissed her because she took risks.

Instead he held her, not to contain her, but to contain himself. They were safe for now, but it wouldn't last. 'Reckless, foolish, what were you thinking? What were you doing?'

She squirmed, but he followed her along, kept her trapped. He leaned even more, the feel of her against him, the warmth, the heat. 'You knew what I was doing.'

'I told you I would help,' he said. 'I told you.'

'Then you—then we talked and—'

'And what? Because you wouldn't be with me, so therefore I'd abandon my vow, abandon you?'

He couldn't do it. He wanted a home, a wife. In the past, just the thought of both got him through the worst of times. Now that he'd met Bied, he wanted no wife but her, one who was courageous and trouble. With much work to be done with the Jewell of Kings, it'd be years until they could settle, though...

Would she accept him in return? She said she didn't want a husband, but maybe she just needed more time to trust him. He cupped her head between his palms, kept her pressed against him. 'Bied, I will never aba—'

Quick jagged pain to his chest, his body spasmed, and she shoved him away before he realised that she'd bitten him.

With a murderous expression, she pushed past him, but he stood before the door.

'Let me out of here,' she said.

If she'd had a goblet in her hand, she would have used it on him. Instead, he had her ire. He deserved her hatred for not telling her everything, but that didn't stop him wanting her, especially now, in this brief moment. In this room.

Full breasts, flushed cheeks accentuating plump red

lips. Her hands were on those hips he'd dreamt about since the kitchens when she'd gained balance from the floor to the chair. Just that image shot anticipation through him, tightening everything inside him, pooling any thoughts towards only one direction: her.

Something of his thoughts must have registered for her eyes flared, one hand slipped off her hip. But she didn't say anything and he was suddenly incapable of it.

Their eyes locked, his fear facing her hot anger. Anger morphing to something else. Something just as feral, wild…just as uncontained as the insistence in him. To take. To give. To claim.

'I can't let you leave here,' he said. 'It's dangerous, they'd kill you as soon as greet you.' Louve's entire body shuddered. 'Back down, Bied.'

Eyes narrowing, she snatched a linen and chucked it at his face. It hit him. The next one she threw, he batted away.

'What do you think that will do?' he scoffed.

'Move you!' she shouted.

He shoved her body against the wall. Now he felt the heat of her breath, the pounding of her heartbeat. 'This is the only direction I want to go.'

Her arms were trapped, but she still tried to shove him away. Did she know what that did to him? The snap of his hips against hers stopped her.

She gasped. He growled, 'If you had gone up there alone, carrying that little tray, they would have made you taste the food to see if it was poisoned.'

'It wasn't!'

She gaped at him as though he was possessed, and he was right now. It was why he held her closer, his hips seemingly unable to release from the cradle of hers, reminding him that she was alive. They were alive and alone.

'We know that, but they wouldn't,' Louve said. Her eyes were mesmerising with only a flared darkness he was fast losing himself in. 'When they found that it wasn't poisoned, they'd start questioning you.'

'I wouldn't tell them anything and there would be no need to. I am a servant here and am simply delivering food.'

She didn't understand and he was loath to tell her. He'd been that innocent of the Warstone malevolence once as well. 'You were not assigned to that room. They would have questioned you with cuts from their daggers, with broken fingers, with whatever means they were given.'

She shook her head. 'But Ian isn't up there, it was just her. There would be no need for such measures.'

'It's his private chambers and he'll invoke whatever protective measures he wants. This is ours.'

'Ours? What are you—'

His hands slipped down, his fingers dug into the side of her hips, her flesh gave way under his rough touch. He groaned. 'Ours. In this fortress, I claim this storage room for us.'

'I'm angry at you. You're angry at me and you…jest?'

He was, he did, but that wasn't what he thought of now. 'The softness of your skin. The way your body yields to mine. It drives me mad. You drive me to madness. I almost lost you, after the night we spent on that unforgiving kitchen floor. Without a chance to rectify what we could be.'

'Now you're protective? I don't understand. There's nothing we can be. You say you want—oh! I am not talking of this here. Move, I need to get to my—'

He leaned in, suckled the skin along her neck, revelled in her gasp. 'They've returned, are spreading around the courtyard and soon will be in this fortress. If we leave right now, you'll put your sister in more danger.'

She jolted. 'Damn you.'

He stilled at the sound of anguish in her tone. He

wanted this room, this moment, but if it brought her pain...
he'd stop.

'We shouldn't leave just yet, but I'll move if you need
me to.' He pulled up, reverently cupped her cheeks, took
her mouth, once, twice. 'You can leave if it's what you
want.'

'I want answers,' she said against his lips.

She stayed and he was incapable of withdrawing from
her. He pulled in her lower lip and nipped it gently between his teeth. 'Answers. Those are what you want?' Just
a bit longer, if she'd allow it. Just a... His kiss deepened
as he lashed his tongue against hers, pressed a little more
into her before pulling away.

'Tell me.'

'Yes!'

Could he give words to her now? His body rejecting the
answer before it could be formed, he clamped his hands on
the shelf far above their heads, pushing away until nothing between them touched except their breaths. Hers were
short pants. His had gone ragged. It might kill him, but
she deserved answers. If she wanted them now, he'd try.

Her eyes widened, but her shock was all he dared reg-
ister. If he contemplated her lips glistening from their
kisses, to the flush of her cheeks that was part anger, part
need, he'd never make it through. He'd stutter, become
that madman she thought he was.

Her brows drew in, her eyes roaming his features, already looking for answers, and he knew he'd choose the
right path for them. He kept his expression open, allowing her to see everything he couldn't say just yet. What he
would tell her later, when his body caught up to the fact
they'd survived. She was alive and he needed to kiss her
and never stop. Ever. For years.

She fisted her fingers into his tunic and yanked him to

her. 'Who are you, truly?' she said, the words battering against the most vulnerable part of his throat.

His arms were shuddering. 'Louve. I am, truly. Am simply…'

She kissed the arc of his neck, right where he was silently begging for her to touch. Over and over, soothing caresses of her tongue, feverish nips of her teeth until he was shaking with his lust.

'Bied,' he said, attempting to keep some reasoning, just for this moment, nothing else. But it was lost before it began. Right now, Bied was his. If nothing else, they could have this time, in this room. He had to make certain that was what she wanted because…because… 'Do you want this?'

She stroked her long fingers up his chest and sank her nails into his shoulders. Words gone, his lips latched on to hers.

Louve's kisses were heady sips of wine. His low growl deep in his chest was her surrender.

Inside beat the questions she needed to ask—what they were doing, where were they going?—but Bied needed more of this man who had gained her trust the moment he pushed himself away from her. His ravenous gaze was fierce because he was fighting against himself and he allowed her to be witness to it all.

The battle was there in the flush across his cheekbones, the wet seam of his lips, in the bulging of his forearms as he clenched the shelf above her. It was there in the pulse throbbing at the centre of his throat, its uneven pace telling her more than any words he might have said.

He held himself away, so she'd trust him. And she answered that frantic pulse by pressing her kiss, her own need, against the battle he fought.

And he answered. Slick slides of his tongue before they broke apart and he latched his lips on to her throat, down her collarbone to her gown that loosened enough to allow a few of his kisses there, too. She wanted more.

Thrusting her hands through his hair, the scent, the coarse feel of it through her fingers as heady as the weight of him against her. She couldn't stop there and slid her hands down his sides. Traced just under his tunic and above his breeches, feeling the shiver of sinew under his heated skin.

He clutched her hand against his stomach. 'Bied.'

A warning that had her eyes raising to his. 'You're always grabbing my hands.'

'Because they undo me.'

She smiled. 'I was trying to undo you.'

His eyes lit up, a curve to his lips. He released his other hand from the shelf, ripped off the ties on his breeches and shoved down his braies enough to free him. He still clutched her hand, but her other was free.

His eyes widened when he guessed her intent. 'No, you don't.'

Wrapping his arm around her waist, he fisted her gown and chemise up to her waist. The voluminous folds barred her sight, but she felt his hair-roughened thighs between hers, his hand cupping under her knee. The gentle pressure to lift her up.

Her hands went to his shoulders for balance. His thumb caressed the tender crease on the back of her knee, as he lowered his head to capture her lips.

More rasping kisses, more welcoming weight, but he was holding back. 'Louve, please.'

When he didn't move she grasped his hips, yanking herself towards him, and she felt the smooth slide between her thighs, but not where she needed it.

'Now you decide not to hunch,' she huffed. 'You're too tall.'

His smile was smug. 'Maybe I wanted to feel you climbing on me. Do you know what your curves do to me?'

Now it was her turn to give him a knowing look. 'Yes.'

'Tilt your hips,' he ordered, his gaze promising to meet her challenge. She did.

He lifted her leg that bit more. 'Do you want me, Bied? Is this what you want? You know—'

'You're repeating. You do that, you know, and I, yes—' She couldn't finish that sentence. 'And I—'

He chuckled, groaned and slid his palm up the back of her thigh and, with a strength she didn't want to ever end, he shunted forward.

Pleasure. Desire. Her hands grasping one point of him, then another. Never finding purchase, her thoughts lost to reason, to anything but Louve and what was happening between them. Her entire body trembling.

His harsh breath against her neck, he pulled away, his head going back, his eyes clenching. 'Maddening,' he whispered as he moved. 'Wild. Reckless. Brave. Cour—'

She pressed her lips, her body, her very heart against any part of him she could reach, until they surrendered to the place where words were unnecessary. Until it was only them.

It was moments with both their heartbeats easing before she realised where they were again.

'Are you…?' he said. She felt him swallow. 'Are you well?'

More than she could say. 'I need answers.'

Chuckling, he kissed her temple. 'You do.'

Straightening, he arranged her clothing, folding and binding the poorly woven cloth as if it was the finest of linens. When he raised his eyes to hers, he caught her bewildered gaze.

He brushed his thumb against her chin. 'Later. I want to

spend time with you that doesn't involve walls or floors. When there's time I could properly undress and explore all of you.'

'There's a lot of me to explore.'

He clenched his eyes. 'Don't tempt me, I'm barely restraining myself now.'

'That was restraint?' she teased.

'If I have a chance to kiss and touch all the parts of you I desire, what lies after that will show you that, yes, what we just shared was restrained.'

More humour from this man, more smiles. Did he know what those dimples of his—a dull thump, and the sound of footsteps outside the door, made her jump.

Louve whispered in her ear, 'Do they not know this is our room?'

She wanted to laugh, but there was a sadness in his eyes that stopped her. It was just there along the edges of the humour and she wanted to soothe it. It was easy to believe in this man even before she should have, but she needed to know what they faced outside their room. Their room.

Ridiculous man. She wanted his teasing, his jokes, she wanted to share whatever burden he bore because she could see it was a heavy one.

Which was frightening given her own mistrust, her own experience with men, with families. But her concern was lessened by the warmth of his touch along her arms, by the joy of what they shared. That would be enough to get them through whatever it was outside this room.

'Now tell me,' she demanded. 'What were those questions you asked my sister? Why did we truly leave her there?'

Louve rubbed the outside of her arms, waiting. There were no other sounds, no other moments he could comfort and hold this remarkable woman.

After he told her what she needed to hear, she might

not even allow this touch. Maybe the Warstone conflicts would keep them apart. Those guards. He'd seen that look before. If anything had been just a bit different than what Ian had allowed, both he and Bied would be dead.

He didn't want to give her up. Didn't know how he could. But…she didn't want a husband, might never want one. Might not even want a man by her side. He'd told her he was a mercenary, but did she know what that truly meant? Probably not and he was no simple hired sword.

And that came all the more crashing down when he walked into Ian's private chambers and realised he'd been manipulated. Warstones and their games which might never end. Ian talked about how he liked the games, but the truth was…he simply understood them. That's all; he could give them up. If she wanted him to, he would.

After eyeing those guards, knowing that more flanked them, he knew he couldn't risk her like that again. He didn't want to give her up, but the realisation was he might have to. Everyone was back from the hunt and, once they left this room, nothing would be the same. Still, he'd try to get the sisters to safety if she'd let him.

Giving her the truth at least gave her a choice. He released her arms and stepped back. Was grateful she remained and that her expression was only curious. No, there was more there, it was in the sheen of her pale skin, her reddened cheeks and lips because of the roughness of his jaw, the pressure of their kisses. What they had just shared.

In the past it was easier to avoid such questions of who he was, what he did. He'd flash a grin, make some sort of comment to distract. Perhaps he would ask questions instead, anything to avoid talking about himself.

Except this was Biedeluue and, for him, she was the distraction. And one he wanted to keep.

'You wouldn't have made it up those stairs and to her room.' The thought of what would have happened if she'd gone up there alone shook through him again. How close he came to losing her before they'd had this stolen moment. He wanted more of them.

'What are you doing?' she said.

'Reaching for your hand.'

'Every time you hold my hand…something happens.'

He lowered his chin. 'I promise you it will be only answers this time.'

'Answers are good, but I want my sister,' she said.

'I know you do, but we can't get her now. We couldn't be up there one more moment.'

If she was frightened, he'd let her out of here and forget the consequences of getting caught. But she hadn't been frightened, not so far, and her determination he could negotiate with.

He just needed to make her understand something that he was only beginning to. That he needed her more than this mission, but now might be all they had. Even if the sisters escaped and he did, too, he couldn't go after them without jeopardising their safety. All this before they could get through their own desires in life.

'What's going on?' she said.

'You were there. She won't leave without Evrart.'

'Margery loves her family. I am her family and she asked for me.'

'She asked for a sword arm.'

Bied looked away.

'I'm sorry,' he said immediately. 'I'm going about this wrong.'

Her eyes wandered from the crown of his head to the tips of his fingers and back again. He'd have to explain. He enclosed her hand between both of his. Feeling the warmth, the tiny slide of her fingers against his. She was alive, she was alive and he could tell her.

'I was an usher at one point in my life,' Louve said.

'You already spoke of this, then you became a mercenary. Now you're here playing some game with Ian of Warstone,' Bied said. 'I don't want to talk about what happened between us or my demanding to know you, I need to understand why you dragged me away from my sister, why we can't get to her!'

He couldn't help but feel lightened by her impatience. It was her. 'This is important, though. After I left that life as an usher, I became a mercenary…for Reynold, one of the four brothers of Warstone.'

'No.' She snatched her hand and he let it go. 'No. We just escaped—'

'I'm still me,' Louve said, knowing what she meant. They had just touched, shared themselves, and he was friends with a Warstone. 'I haven't changed.'

'Only you have been paid by *these* monsters.'

'He's good, Bied. Out of all of them, he's good. And the youngest, Balthus, might be as well. Ian…is complicated.'

'Ian needs to be killed.'

Fierce. Courageous. What other woman would have charged into this Warstone fortress to help break a sister free? 'Most likely true, but Reynold sent Balthus and me—'

'Stop,' she interrupted. Bied's expression was one of confusion, of doubt and then understanding. None of it took her long, he didn't expect it to. 'You're here for that parchment. One brother sent you here to steal from the other. How does this affect my sister and why is this dangerous?'

'For what that parchment represents—even I don't completely understand it. Do you believe in legends?'

'Stories, if they're true.'

'This one is,' he said. 'It's not a French story. It's not entirely an English one, but this one is told there frequently. There's this gem. It's ugly, but through the ages a story was attached to it. That whoever holds it holds power. The story has changed over the centuries. Most recently because of the conflict in Scotland, it has changed to whoever holds the gem holds the power of Scotland.

'You can imagine why the King of England or any driven family like the Warstones would want it.'

Her brows drew in. 'This sounds familiar. It's a jewel, isn't it? The Jewell of Kings.'

Feeling as though Fate hurried their parting, he nodded. 'The Jewell of Kings, like Excalibur, is a legend, but it's based in some truth. It's been hidden inside a dagger's handle for years and has recently resurfaced. Reynold...' he shook his head '... Reynold loves to read—you wouldn't believe how he lugs books around from one place to the other. He's left daggers and swords behind in his haste to travel from one location to another, but his books, those always were wrapped first.'

'What has this to do with the parchment?'

Impatient. Demanding. Still staying with him though he had befriended a Warstone.

'The legend might also contain a treasure, but all the bits of information are spread about,' Louve said. 'One part is on the dagger's hilt, the others are words written on parchment. It could have been an entire book, but I don't know. All Reynold knows is that Ian has a complete piece and he wants that.'

'Thus, he can rule over others. Have power and wealth and—'

'No, so he can hide the whole lot and be done with it. He wants nothing else than to settle down with his wife in their home and have peace.'

Something flitted behind her eyes, something which made him uneasy, but it was quickly gone. 'But the parchment's not here,' she said.

'It appears not,' he said.

'Ian knows who you are, doesn't he?' At his nod, she continued, 'What of Balthus? How can he be good if he's hunting with his family, if he's a Warstone?'

How to explain Balthus when he'd spent so little time with him as well? 'I pretended I was an usher. Here, he's also pretending to be someone he's not.'

She snorted. 'With any hope, he's better at it than you are.'

'He is, or else he'd already be dead. I'm here to protect him.'

'From his brother or his parents?'

'Most would not guess Balthus needed protection from his parents.'

She frowned. 'I've known adults, parents and otherwise, who are dishonourable...who don't deserve to be in the presence of children. Tess also told me they were never here under the same roof, which is a hint that their relations are torn. That stuck with me because if my family could be safe, fed, I'd give anything to be with them under one roof.'

Louve wanted to ask questions. Biedeluue's expression when she talked of children and parents—there was something there...something personal. 'I can't rule out that they wouldn't kill him.'

'That's what you meant when you said Balthus was alive. You thought his own parents would kill him on the hunt?' She gasped. 'Could they have poisoned the ale?'

He couldn't see how that was possible, but anything was probable when it came to them. That wasn't what concerned him, however. 'You're taking this too... You're understanding too readily and now you're helping me solve one of the mysteries?'

'I have siblings whom I have had to protect from numerous situations.' She flapped her hand. 'Margery the most of all. At some point, I'm going to grab every last goblet in this house and smash it against a wall, after I drink wine from every cup first. But right now, I need to get my sister free of this.'

He waited, fascinated by the numerous thoughts behind her troubled eyes. He had thought it would be difficult to tell her. He had thought she'd lean away from him when she fully understood not only that he was a hired sword, but who he worked for. He had thought—

She poked him in the chest. 'If I understand correctly, we've got a murdering family who want to kill each other, all to get some gem that the King of England is after.'

Unfortunately, Bied understood all too completely. 'It's not just them. Everywhere they spread their poison, they spread danger. They could not have got this far without allies and support. Without others undermining other families and countries.'

'All this is happening in this fortress while my sister is trapped in that room,' she said, pointing in the general direction of the private chambers.

Margery had a strength that had surprised him. The night of the feast, she'd appeared as though a cruel word could fell her, but the Margery he'd questioned was nothing like Bied had described her. Bied seemed equally bewildered and impressed by her younger sister.

'I think we can safely say Margery's being trapped in that room isn't entirely Ian's doing,' Louve said. 'You might have a lot more in common with her. You're both stubborn, both fierce.'

'Fierce!' Bied said, then stopped. 'Was it this place that changed her or—'

'She would not have survived long in Ian's presence if she didn't have the strength already.'

'Battles over legends and kingdoms,' she breathed. 'It's almost incomprehensible.'

'All of that is happening while we were in our own private storage room.'

'Now you jest. I cannot honestly tell if there is humour in you, or tragedy.'

Both. 'I'd jest more. I'd tell you more of the Warstone intrigues if you'd trust me some.'

'Trust you? There's no point to that now. I'm leaving.'

Her words! Once they left this room all of it would change. Ian would know he'd failed to bring anything out of his room. Balthus, no doubt, would have done something to tip his hand, and there was no parchment for Reynold. This was all before the elder Lord and Lady Warstone played their part.

'There's a point because you need to know the truth,' he said. 'I wanted this time with you, to tell you, show you my feelings.'

She snorted. 'You haven't shown me your feelings. You've been telling me, *repeating* to me, of danger, danger, danger, which doesn't seem as though it will ever end. I already knew about your concerns here because I can see it with my own eyes. That guard outside my sister's door, he would have harmed us, wouldn't he?

Louve nodded. That guard would have killed her. How could he be contemplating trying to keep her? He couldn't. It was…simply the time they had, the way she felt in his arms. He needed her and he needed her safe. Some trust was necessary for that.

'Knowing the details,' she said, 'explains what is happening, but doesn't earn my confidence.'

'Bied, I—' He stopped himself. 'Can we have a bit of understanding between us? Maybe let me…borrow that as well.'

'You can't.' She shook her head, sighed. 'You have a little of it—how can you not after this room?—but what you told me is too much danger for my sister, my family!

Moreover, I'm not certain it's my trust you need to earn, but your own. You say you want peace, but when has your life not been like this? I think…this is the life you want.' She brushed her gown. 'There's no time for this now. I hear everyone and so can you.'

This was the life he wanted? The danger, the plots, and subterfuge? He knew how to play the games, but he wanted what his friend Nicholas had, what Reynold was just now building. A family. Something, someone of his own.

The voices in the hall were getting louder and he needed to warn her.

'I'll do what I can to get you and your sister out of here. When we leave here, it will be different. I might need to do some acts, but know—'

She placed her hand on his mouth. 'I know. You need to keep Balthus safe, might be cruel or order me about as an usher would. Or something else that you're not telling me that I can almost guess at in those blue eyes of yours. But know that I need to protect Evrart.'

Tragedy. Humour. One of them won.

The merest thought of Biedeluue protecting Evrart burst a situation far too unfathomable through his heart which ached. The warrior was larger than an oak and weighed twice as much as all the guards put together. 'Protect… Evrart.'

She nodded in earnest, her expression brooking no argument. 'Because if something happens to him my sister won't forgive me. That's what she wanted me to promise if you hadn't yanked me out of there. So move.'

She was serious. Louve looked at her. Looked again, but he couldn't stop his eyes from watering, or ease the instant tightness in his chest. The ache. He wanted to laugh and mourn. This woman! He imagined her as he saw her that first day. Shuffling from side to side, her arms outstretched. But instead of shouting to protect the children, she'd shout—

'We'll need to stop,' he choked. 'By the kitchens.'

'Why?'

'To get some goblets.' Louve laughed.

Her eyes crinkling at the corners, Bied threw a dozen linens at him, before she marched out of the room ahead of him.

She didn't see him take one last look at their room.

Chapter Twenty

Flying past the guards and servants who gave them room, Louve hurried behind Bied, ready to block anyone who stopped her. The moment the linen door was open, all laughter was gone. Now he needed to protect her, knowing full well their time together was over. He shouldn't even try to keep her. She needed to be as far away from the danger as possible.

Whatever game Ian wanted to play, he won. *They know. They always know.* Duped in this, but he could see no other angle when he negotiated to gain access to the private chambers.

How could there be any other interpretation? Her lip was cut, she pulled away from Ian's touch and sent a message to Bied to rescue her.

Ah, but he hadn't taken in the entirety of the situation. He hadn't registered the giant of a warrior, Evrart, attempting to cheer her. He thought he was only making a fool of himself for Lord Warstone. Maybe if he had bothered to look at the warrior, he would have noticed a look of concern, but he kept his eyes on the enemy. Which, of course, Ian would have been aware of.

Down the stairs, Bied in front, her height all the more

noticeable, the efficient way her hips swung at each step a beacon for his eyes. Even now.

Was he trying to get them killed with distractions? Was she, because she was a distraction? They weren't done. Not nearly done enough and he burned for her. How was he to let her go? If he had his way, she would be a distraction for ever and they only had heartbeats of moments left.

He'd seen the Warstones emerge from the forests. Balthus was safe, but he felt as though time was not in their favour. That events had changed and he just didn't know what they were. No more time to deliberate on whether he could trust Balthus or Reynold. For better or worse, he had to play the game before him.

When they hit the bottom of the stairwell, he grabbed Bied's wrist to hurry their steps to the kitchen. There was a possibility he could hide her there until…the Hall was teeming with people, guards and Warstones.

Near the dais, Balthus and Ian were conversing, their heads close together. From this angle they appeared more like brothers than enemies. The shock of it stopped him, which yanked Bied against him and brought attention their way.

Ian's eyes locked on him holding her wrist. His expression turned quickly to a victorious knowing while Balthus rolled his eyes. One brother discovering his weakness. The other disappointed he'd displayed it.

Why had he grabbed Bied's wrist? Nothing for it now. Keeping his hold, he positioned himself in front of her.

Bied hadn't meant to cry out and slam into Louve when he suddenly stopped, but the man had legs as long as countries and it took everything in her to keep up and gawk at the Hall which seethed something menacing. Most of the people she didn't recognise; many of the guards had weaponry at their waists or in their hands.

'Why is there no food on the tables?'

Bied swung her gaze towards the haughty voice. Lady Warstone strode across the Hall as if she owned it. Her green gown with enormous sleeves was so fine the weave shimmered as it flowed behind her.

'I agree!' Lord Warstone was as tall as his sons, his frame thicker, but no less formidable. 'Are we to starve here?'

Ian must have given some sort of signal because three guards strode to the kitchens, their feet thudding against rushes roaring in her ears.

Louve didn't make a sound, but his stance blocking her told enough, as did his protectively holding her wrist, his finger tapping gently at her pulse as if to let her know what he could not say.

He didn't need to say anything, she knew they were trapped between predators. He said it would be different when they left the linen room, but she wasn't prepared for it to happen so fast.

She thought there would be moments to prepare, but the Hall was flooding with people as if there was a gathering or announcement. Had Louve known such a sight would greet them and was he to be an usher or a mercenary? His back was to her, but the tension in his shoulders told her perhaps he didn't know either.

If so, who did that make her when he continued to hold her wrist?

'Oh, there's Usher standing there,' Lady Warstone drawled. 'What are you doing with your household if he is so lazy? It appears he's clasping a servant while your guards are fetching, how odd.'

'There's plenty of guards to spare, Mother, and they were closest to the doors.' Ian's voice perfectly mimicked his parent. 'Usher and the cook are new, let them stay to celebrate our successful hunt and the return of a most faithful servant. Come, isn't it happy news we could meet him on the road? There's a feast to be had tonight!'

Lady Warstone waved her hand. 'As if that much game will be prepared properly by tonight. Do you have any of that venison from yesterday? If so, get your cook to do something. I am terribly hungry.'

'Don't be obtuse, dear,' her husband said, eyeing Bied and Louve. 'This is our son. There's more afoot here. See how protective this Usher is of his cook. Are they married? Is there a bond we're about to break?'

Elder Warstone eyed them both as if they were a feast. Louve's finger swept across her inner wrist once again and she took what comfort she could from it.

She was ready to run or fight and all they'd done was enter a Hall where people were talking. Talking! But it was the way they conversed, a flow between them that was tangible the more words were said. It was that feeling the words made that raised the hairs on the back of her neck, made her wish for a weapon so she could end them.

Whatever it was the Warstones created, she'd never experienced it before, not in all her travels. If she had to put a name to the feeling that permeated the Great Hall, she'd call it malice. But even that fell far short.

The doors behind them opened and many heads turned to watch servants including Tess, Galen and Henry carrying trays with multiple goblets. Too many.

Bied gasped. Louve clasped her wrist that bit tighter as he, too, realised the implication at the same time she did. The faithful servant whom Ian had met on the road had to be Steward.

More guards coming down the staircase behind them, but no Margery. In front more guards poured in from outside, including Evrart, whose eyes stayed a moment with Louve's, then Bied's. For some reason, that, too, brought her comfort as she recognised the person at his side. Stew-

ard, with a rigid smile slashing across his face, had returned.

He didn't look at all well. His thin frame was gaunt,
his pale skin sallow with drips of sweat beading under his
nose. The sweat must have been profuse for her to see it
a distance. He'd brought back the favoured goblets, but it
seemed as though it had taken a toll on him. Or perhaps
he didn't like being in this Hall any more than she did.

'Here are the refreshments, Mother,' Ian said, his voice
booming from wall to wall. 'Wine for you all.'

Ian's mother wasn't looking at the servants carrying
wine. Her pinched gaze was focused on the Steward and
his wide, almost frantic, gaze was solely towards Lady
Warstone. His father, however, appeared delighted and
grabbed the first goblet, drinking it down and placing it
on the next tray where he snatched another.

It was an odd way of serving refreshments. Customar-
ily, the goblets would be empty and there would be someone carrying a pitcher of wine behind, or the wine would
be on a table in the Hall to serve from. Perhaps it was another English way of serving she was unaware of, but it
was little wonder Henry and Galen were there because
the trays would be heavy.

As Bied tried to catch the gaze of any of her friends,
she watched Ian stand by the dais with his family, while
Balthus, conversing with one guard, shifted away. Evrart
and the Steward remained side by side like matched sen-
tinels, though Steward seemed on the edge of collapse.

Why she was noting everyone's positions in the room
she couldn't say. Or, perhaps, the fact she couldn't see
Louve's expression made her desperate to determine from
others what was occurring.

As people drank, as servants with pitchers refilled
those whose goblets were already empty, the smell of food
began wafting from the kitchens. Her stomach growled

even though she was hardly hungry, could at any moment be sick. Her lips were dry, however, and she eyed the goblets of liquid, but as tray after tray passed them, it became clear she and Louve were ignored...as was Steward.

With shaking knees, she stepped forward to see some of Louve's profile to determine his thoughts on their being overlooked and was surprised to see the same bored expression on his face as the Warstones' held. If he hadn't continued to hold her wrist, she would have collapsed. Who...was this man? Who were any of them? How was it just moments before she'd told him she'd protect Evrart for Margery? Now, she absorbed Louve's slight touch to remain standing.

Another slam of the kitchen door and Tess carried a tray with three goblets. She walked steadily towards them, her eyes conveying a meaning Bied was desperate to understand.

As Louve turned to her friend, his expression never changed. He released her wrist to grasp two of the goblets and Tess's eyes widened as he lessened the burden she carried.

'Refreshments for the servants, my boy,' the elder Lord Warstone declared. 'Something different, I presume?'

'Ale!' Ian said. 'They might celebrate with us, but I won't waste our wine on them.'

'Rightly so, dear. Some servants can be such a disappointment.' Ian's mother held out her goblet for a server with a pitcher to refill it, but the lady's arm was shaking and some of the wine hit the floor.

Louve handed a goblet to Bied. He, too, was trying to tell her something. But there was so much in that blue gaze of his, so much that had nothing to do with any of the malevolence surrounding them, and everything to do with something softer. True. What—

'I love you,' he mouthed before he turned away and his expression was once again void of emotion.

Overflowing with emotion, Bied's heart thumped hard in her chest. Right on the back of the utter joy of seeing those words from Louve was the realisation that she didn't silently say them back. That she couldn't say them back because he'd purposefully turned away. And the realisation, too, of if she could, would it be true for her?

How could he say such words to her? If they got through this chilling celebration, she'd throw linen-wrapped goblets at him.

If, because they were served ale. She didn't need to question whether it was from the poisoned cask. It had to be, though she couldn't decipher the colour, and the scents of onion and roasting meat wafting from the kitchens masked anything unusual in the smell.

With an almost macabre fascination, she watched Tess traverse between the tables and men, to stand before Evrart and the Steward and raise the tray for one of them to take the remaining goblet.

'No!'

'Careful, Bied,' Louve whispered.

No one looked their way—whatever she had said or done, only Louve noticed. But Margery's Evrart was at risk. He might be taller than the sky and as wide as the earth, but poison could fell any man. She'd vowed, she'd *promised* she'd take care of him. Louve had made fun of her, but she meant it and—

Steward grasped the goblet with the weakest of holds.

'Come, come, Steward,' Ian said. 'Take care of the ale and goblet. They were both made with the utmost care as you well know.'

Bied exhaled, noticing that Evrart had a goblet already, one with wine, and that Tess, with a glance her way, was returning to the kitchens along with Henry and Galen.

She might be stuck in the perilous Hall, but her friends were safe.

Ian raised his goblet. 'Now before we partake of a feast to end all feasts, I'd like us to give thanks for the War-stone bounty that never ceases.' He turned to his parents. 'To give thanks for generous parents whose journeys can never be restful, but still they come to visit their children.'

Ian surveyed the room, the eerie silence of the Hall sending a roar in Bied's ears. 'Are all goblets filled?'

Seemingly satisfied, he lifted his goblet up again. 'And finally, I'd like to thank my brother for returning home, for the time we shared on the hunt. It meant far more than I could ever say.'

Balthus straightened; Bied felt Louve tense. She clenched her goblet, prepared to use it if she had to. Balthus raised his goblet, eyed the Hall as a whole, his gaze snagging on her and Louve before he returned to staring at his family.

'To your good health, dear brother,' Balthus cheered.

Ian's smile was broad and wide, and with another re-sounding cry that was echoed by all he drank deep of his cup.

As did Evrart, as did Louve. And with a look behind her, filled with a tinge of remorse and relief that Margery wasn't there, so did she.

Chapter Twenty-One

Louve silently cursed the whole lot of them for causing the woman, who courageously and stubbornly remained at his side, to fear.

At any moment she could have wrenched her hand free and walked away. He didn't know what would happen if she did. He felt that this gathering wasn't for them, but it could have been. However, when the kitchen doors opened and servants carrying goblets entered, he knew with certainty it was not.

It had been the Steward he'd spied in the woods. The Steward who was too relieved when he'd first arrived at the fortress and much too eager to get away. The same Steward standing next to Evrart as goblets were dispensed. What was in the goblets? They would soon discover.

Warstones and their games.

Maybe he liked to play games, too, because he enjoyed telling Bied he loved her. Revelled in the widening of her eyes and the parting of her lips. Adored that moment when his words registered. Despite the ache in his heart that their time was drawing near, it was everything he could do not to laugh at her reaction.

Though he was served ale, he wasn't worried at all when Ian toasted to his family. He didn't like that he couldn't tell Bied his thoughts as he drank it, hoping Bied would do the same. Keeping appearances of strength was sometimes more important than having any.

'Is there something wrong with the ale, Steward?' Ian's voice shot across the happy echoes of cheers which immediately died.

The Steward startled. 'No, my lord, it is quite satisfactory as would be expected at any Warstone fortress.'

'Then why didn't you drink?' Ian said.

There were over a hundred people in the Hall and all of the exits were blocked.

'I did, my lord,' Steward said in his reedy tone. 'I, who have been a part of your life since you were a child, am humbled to celebrate with your family.'

The smile Ian gave then was one of a man who risked everything against an enemy and won. 'Then celebrate, please, have a drink.'

'Come, son,' Lady Warstone said. 'He has been a loyal servant for our family for many years. Perhaps serving him ale was a poor choice.'

Ian stared at his mother. His eyes did not blink, he did not flinch. He did not acknowledge her existence. Then he whipped his head, that same pale predatory focus on the lean servant who was visibly shaking.

'You are correct, Mother, Steward is too loyal for me to treat him as such. Therefore, I insist he drink what's in that cup and, after that, I will give him wine.'

'I would like some wine,' his father boomed, and a servant with a pitcher skittered over.

The room was riveted to the Steward. With Balthus remaining the requisite space apart from the next warrior, Louve's only concern was Bied, who was visibly trembling. He wanted to warn her, to comfort her. She'd have guessed what would happen when the Steward drank.

There would be something within her wanting to prevent it and also to escape witnessing it.

She could do neither and he willed her to understand. If she even closed her eyes, it might be used against them. Still, he stepped closer to her, a brush of his arm against hers, an opportunity for her to lean on him if needed. She might not trust him at all after this, but while she was close, he'd be there.

It was all he could do, as the Steward drank, his height and frailty revealing to all the rhythmic movements in his throat as he gulped every drop.

When he was done, he turned to set the goblet down on the table behind him. He didn't make it. His body jerked and he gave a harsh sound as his breath was cut off. A moment more until his body slammed on to the table with a dull thud. An arm flung out and Evrart stepped to the side to avoid it. The goblet, however, hit the rushes at their feet, rolled and remained perfectly intact.

A quiet hush and Louve, hating her every tremble, pressed his arm against Bied. Silently willing her to take comfort because it wasn't over yet and all heightened attention needed to remain away from them.

Ian strode over to the Steward and upturned his goblet of wine over the dead body. With a glare at Evrart, he said, 'Get rid of this, it's in an inconvenient spot for when we dine.'

Bied's trembles stopped. If she used her reckless courage, it wouldn't bode well for any of them. He leaned over. 'Hold, Bied, there's more to come.'

'How much?' she whispered back. 'Margery?'

'Is safe—Evrart will soon be. They might not be looking at us, but we are noticed.'

She looked at him, understanding in her eyes. 'Balthus,' she whispered.

Balthus was in danger and knew it for he had been

moving around the room, each step he took bringing him closer to Bied's side.

Evrart disappeared with the Steward's body and Ian turned to the crowd. 'Now shall we eat? Everybody, eat!'

Servants streamed through with trays laden with food and the crowd released sound, voices, scraped benches as all of Ian's guards sat at tables nearest the high table and far from where they stood in the back. The senior Lord Warstone eagerly walked to his position on the dais, but Lady Warstone stopped her son as he strode to do the same. Their guards remained standing.

Louve should not have heard all that was said between mother and son, except Ian never lowered his voice.

'But the food is prepared... Stay... It is too costly to move about so often... Yes, I understand... Take some repast with you?'

'We need to sit at the empty table near Balthus and away from the parents.' At her wide eyes on him, he leaned down and whispered, 'The Steward altered the ale we tasted. It was always his fate.'

'But he—'

Shaking his head, Louve threaded his fingers through Bied's and squeezed. She clasped back just as hard. No more trembles. If they got through this day, he vowed he'd get her to safety.

Bied wanted to crumple to the floor or storm the Hall. It was the violence of the conversation, the swiftness of the murder. It was the utter discount of both of those by the audience that drained everything from her. When Louve released her hand, she almost protested, until he pressed an arm against hers and she drew from his warmth and strength. Days ago, she couldn't imagine leaning on any man and even this man she shouldn't. If they left this room alive, there was still so much separating them. But her heart... It hurt for her, for Louve, and she needed to stay strong for her sister, who had to be alive. Bied couldn't think any other way.

'I'm a mere kitchen servant, shouldn't I leave—'

'I won't let you out of my sight, and there are women here.'

Those women were for the men and they weren't exactly sitting. 'My gown isn't like theirs.'

His eyes narrowed. 'Your gown will stay as it is.'

She didn't question why they didn't simply leave. Not as the rest of it all unfolded. Evrart disappearing, Ian's guards sitting down despite their lord not sitting, other guards leaving the Hall to the outside or up to their quarters. Were they leaving?

Positioning them on the corner of a bench, Louve kept his body turned outwards; she, however, being on the inside, was restricted by the bench and the table.

The conversation between Lady Warstone and Ian was barely audible, but Lady Warstone's skin was flushed, her eyes resembling grey daggers. The rest of her, however, was serene. Her hands simply clasped in front of her in that eerie way she had. Bied was certain at any moment she would strike.

No. Bied's mind spun, taking all that she had seen, all that Louve had told her, but her thoughts were too terrible. Had Lady Warstone already struck…and lost? The Steward was a servant whom Ian had inherited from his family. Steward couldn't look away from Ian's mother as if begging her to save him. Biedeluue had experienced and seen much harm in her village, but this… How could she order a servant to poison, to kill, her son?

And Louve called these games? As for Ian, his pale eyes were manic, a grin on his face that wouldn't ease even as his voice was overly soothing.

He was proud of killing the Steward; however, the elder Warstone didn't appear pleased. He sat, demanded food and repeatedly lifted his knife to his mouth while never taking his eyes from his wife's back. Balthus, who was now on their side of the room, also kept his eyes on his father.

'Bied, I would get you out of here if it was safe.' Louve's gaze was on Warstone's guards, who were flowing throughout the room, their movements efficient as if they were prepared for this precise departure. 'When we rushed down here, I had hoped we'd make it to the kitchens.'

She didn't doubt Louve's words. 'If I could grab my sister, I would get you out of here, too.'

His chin dipped and for a moment she thought he'd look at her, but she liked that his mouth lifted enough for one of his dimples to appear. 'At least I know my importance.'

Oh. Bied coughed before her sudden laugh could be heard. But her laughter couldn't ease and Louve patted her back as if she truly was choking. Was this panic? She needed to stay strong for her family.

'There can't be a guard up there, so Margery's purposefully remaining in the rooms,' Louve said, seemingly knowing the direction of her thoughts.

She didn't know if that was any comfort because what had Margery experienced to know it was safer to be in that room versus the Hall?

'How long is it safe?'

Louve's gaze was now on Balthus. His free hand was making some sort of gesture. 'We're about to find out.'

Balthus's relaxed mien belied the fact that at the side of his leg, he, too, was rapidly moving his fingers. Counting? Or some signal?

'Do I need to know?' she said.

Louve's eyes were still that blue that was unfair for any man, but his grave expression chilled her. 'I hope you never know.'

Whatever it was, it was soon. Ian was striding towards his father, while Lady Warstone swept down the aisle towards Balthus, who straightened and reciprocated his mother's kisses and touch. Who mimicked the same regretful tone as she said her farewells.

Her words were of a loving mother, promising she'd visit him soon as she clasped Balthus's wrapped hand and snapped a finger.

If they hadn't been sitting so close, and heard the break, Bied wouldn't have known. Other than a flare from his nostrils, Balthus gave no indication of the agony she caused him.

Pivoting, Lady Warstone stopped in front of Louve, who immediately stood and bowed his head.

'You're very odd for a servant and are all too familiar with my sons,' Lady Warstone said. 'Shouldn't you be somewhere else?'

The hairs on Bied's arms rose. She hated being wedged between the bench and table, and slowly slid to the end. She didn't know what she would do, but if it came down to it, she'd do...something.

Balthus remained stoic, his injured hand at his side. He wasn't trying to fix his broken finger and his expression remained neutral. However, if his mother tried that with Louve...

'As Usher for this fortress, here is the best place for me to be of service now that the Steward is indisposed, my lady,' Louve said. 'I am sorry you could not stay.'

Lady Warstone's eyes turned calculating. 'Having met you, I can see how our time here could have been interesting. Alas, I'm afraid, I've overstayed my welcome.'

'There will always be a next time for family to share a good drink together,' Louve said.

One brow rose and her mouth curved. None of the humour reached her eyes, though, and Bied tensed.

'Ah, yes, family. Please do tell that…man who is no longer our son he will not win this.'

Lady Warstone joined Ian and her husband and a few words were exchanged.

'Pretend to eat,' Louve whispered in her ear. He grabbed a trencher and loaded it with meat, vegetables, fish and almonds, and set it before her. He, however, did not sit.

Even if she was starving, Bied couldn't get the fish with parsley on top of the lamb with hot rosemary sauce down her closed throat. Let alone the fact there was no knife, which might have come in use. Had he done it on purpose?

Over the voices of people eating, Bied could hear the mounting of horses. A household that large could not have been packed to leave this quickly unless it was anticipated that the Steward would get killed in front of everyone. Lady Warstone had purposefully ordered the Steward to poison her son, and then…knew that her son would prevail? Or that she'd need to make a quick escape? Just as she thought before: it was incomprehensible.

To think her sister had been witness to these types of events! Despite the Warstones leaving there was no ease to the room. And as Ian strode towards Balthus and Louve, her own caution tightened once again.

Clapping his hands loudly, his stride sure, Ian declared, 'And that's another day they tried to kill me and failed.'

Louve's laugh chilled Bied's heart. She'd never heard that sound from him before.

'They were trying to kill you, but you killed the Steward,' Louve said.

'He was following Mother's orders. Apparently, his loyalty to her trumped mine. Foolish man, as if I couldn't taste that foul tisane as many times as she made us drink it. He should have tried something else.'

'Maybe it was another test,' Balthus said. 'Unlike your attempts.'

Ian's grin faded. 'I thought we resolved all that on the hunt.'

'Trust takes years, Ian,' Louve said. 'Remember?'

Ian's gaze drew blank before he blinked. 'Ah, yes, but trust was for friendship, correct? Something brothers surely do not need. Thus, a dagger thrown here or there doesn't matter.'

Louve widened his stance and something flitted across his eyes that pierced fear through her caution. Bied eased more of her body from the table. Whatever Ian just said made Louve wary, so she would be as well.

Balthus cleared his throat. 'There will be an argument for the ages between our parents tonight.'

Ian's lips curved. 'I was certain Father would throw his dining knife at her back.'

'He'd want to make it personal.' Balthus grinned.

'How much more personal than her not telling him her plans to kill you, his favoured son?' Ian said.

'As personal as our father not telling our mother about attempts to kill you, *her* favourite,' Balthus said. 'You are fortunate not to have siblings, Louve.'

'I believe I'm fortunate not to have parents such as yours,' Louve quipped.

Balthus and Ian both laughed. Bied ran her hands down her skirt and glanced again at the stairwell for her sister and the exit for Evrart. She also eyed the spare knives on the table next to hers. The wealth to have knives simply left around, but nowhere near her!

These men talked of family and friendships, but their stances spoke of battlefields and death. Bied glanced around the hall for any hidden dangers and saw none. Most of the guards were already tearing parts of their trenchers. None looked as if they were interested in the conversation happening between these three.

What was happening? Why were family and friendships words that tensed Louve's shoulders and flexed Balthus's good hand?

'Our parents...' Balthus shook his head as if imagining a recalcitrant child. 'Can you imagine the chaos they'd cause if they conversed their schemes with each other?'

'I believe they talked the King into that massacre at Berwick.' Ian frowned. 'Oh, yes, and they shared in the other massacre of that village in Scotland.'

'I thought you did that,' Louve said.

Massacres! Bied wished with all her heart she wasn't sitting. The way Louve held himself, the way he talked, it broke her to see him so. All of them, smiling, but so cold. She desperately ached to make it stop.

'Do you like it there? I despise Scotland and can't imagine any place worse.' Ian gave a fake shudder. 'What made you think I did that?'

'Because of that Englishman you hired,' Louve pointed out.

'Sir Richard Howe's loyalty seems to be along the lines of my former Steward's. Who knows what side he's truly on?' Ian's gaze whipped to Balthus. 'What was that look?'

'What look?' Balthus said.

'You just shared a look with my Usher.'

'I'm looking everywhere, Brother. Your Usher, you... your men.'

'But he is *my* friend, aren't you, Louve?' Ian turned to Louve, the smile returning to his face, but it appeared... fixed. 'You said you'd be my—'

Bied watched it all in horror. The tenor of the conversation tense, but awkward. Ian's voice faded in and out. The movement of his hand hidden in the folds of his tunic revealing one of the dining knives…and its sudden lethal trajectory.

Roaring, Louve vaulted and released a dagger towards Ian. Guards rushed towards them.

And Balthus with a bandaged hand reacting too slowly. Her eyes on Louve, on Ian, Bied bounded from the table and shoved Balthus away from Ian's thrown blade.

Not enough.

The blade cut across the top of her palm as it struck Balthus. Louve's own blade's flight arcing towards Ian. A fierce light in his pale eyes, Ian wrenched his body—

No!

Balthus falling, Bied clasped to him, tumbling over, pressing into the blade!

Circled by gaping guards, Bied scrambled away from Balthus. The blade struck his arm. Relief until she registered his closed eyes, his fast breath and fevered skin. Something was wrong.

She turned. Louve knelt on rushes, cradling Ian. Guards on their side as well, casting shadows across their bent forms.

'Curse you and your ancestors,' Louve choked. 'You didn't have to go this way.'

'I always was,' Ian gasped, blood trailing from his mouth. 'Don't forget…you made a promise.'

Then a sound from Ian that Bied never wanted to hear. And a vision she never wanted to see: Louve clutching Ian's lifeless body.

There was no anger in Louve's voice, no disdain, only anguish. Only one word repeated over and over: *no.*

'Louve!' Bied cried out. 'Balthus lives!'

Chapter Twenty-Two

'You need to rest,' Louve said, coming up to Bied in the winding hallway that connected the private chambers.

It was late—most of the household had gone to bed after a day he never wanted to repeat. Balthus's hand and Ian's death had scoured Louve's heart all day. Regret battered his every deed until he second-guessed even the most basic of directions he gave.

They'd whisked Balthus to a room where a healer could help him recover. The guards had carried Ian's body to the chapel. For reasons that he couldn't address, the priest laid his body near that of the Steward's. Their funerals would have to be discussed tomorrow, decisions he'd have to make. He hoped this time, they were the right ones.

When he wanted only to stay at Balthus's side, he'd been plagued with immediate emergencies. The first was to get his own mercenaries out of the forest and into the fortress. Something which made Louve feel more secure for the safety of Balthus, Bied and Margery, but which caused more unrest with Ian's men. Ordering Ian's men to follow him was no easy feat. Twice he had had to prove his worth via sword, a sword he wanted never to see again, it being the same one he had to use to sever Balthus's hand.

It'd only taken moments after the healer unwrapped

Balthus's hand to know it could not be saved. It was swollen and almost all black. Bied had wept at his side, asking all the questions he should have, but his throat had closed.

When she turned her broken gaze to his, he knew what had to be done and done swiftly while Balthus remained unconscious. But…the agony of Balthus's scream before he succumbed back into that darkness still echoed in Louve's mind.

The only good, if there could be any, was that Balthus had a chance to live and the guards, ever loyal to a Warstone, kept their duties which he increased in case Ian's parents came charging back. He'd also sent a messenger out to Troyes, to tell Reynold that his brother was dead and Balthus gravely injured. When Reynold arrived, he'd let him know both were his fault.

There were times when he tried to bring up his desires of a wife, a home, peace, just to get him through, but the words only pained him more and he knew why. None would ever actualise for him. He could imagine no wife other than Bied, though too much separated them and, after what happened in the Hall, what should always separate them.

He loved her. Even if she could accept him as a mercenary, as a man with no home, would he allow it knowing that with the Warstones, and Ian's last words, there was so much more to do and it was up to him to do it? No. He couldn't.

That brought him to the other truth. The one Bied mentioned when they talked of trust and trusting himself. The conversation with Ian about him liking the games.

He said he wanted a wife, a plot of land, peace, but Bied was right, he never chose that for himself. He fooled himself, thinking it was because the right woman wasn't at Mei Solis, but had he ever pursued anyone else other than the widow Mary, who was unavailable?

And he wasn't just good at the games, of the thoughts and intrigue, he was fascinated by them. He'd pursued a friendship with Reynold of Warstone because he wanted more late-night conversations.

He wanted Bied with every breath he would ever take, but she didn't want a husband. Even if she did, she loved her family, and the life he led, the one that spilled blood and wine in a Hall, would never be good or safe for her and the ones she loved.

So he went about his duties, knowing that, soon, he'd say goodbye. But not now.

Most of the torches were unlit, but the one flickering behind her in the hall was enough to see her swaying on her feet. She'd changed clothes since this morning, her hair was unbound and damp. Refreshed, but there was a slump to her shoulders, her walk uneven. A hollowness around her eyes that likely mimicked his own.

All day, she'd overseen the cleaning of the Hall, the comforting of the servants, the multitude of questions. He'd watched her all day, stolen moments to talk with her about the fortress care, to enquire about her hand, which was only scraped. But it'd been hours since he'd seen her this close. It felt like centuries since it was just them in the linen room.

'I'll rest now,' she said. 'I was visiting with my sister again. Evrart's been with her since this morning. Did you know there's a tunnel to the private chambers? When he left the Hall, he just came back in and up the stairs, and…' She stopped. 'Don't mind me. I'm relieved that she was never alone today.'

'Will they stay—'

'No, they moved to Evrart's room which is a door down. That bed is enormous.' She yawned. 'There were men outside his door I didn't recognise.'

'Balthus and I came with mercenaries—they've been paid to wait in the forest this whole time.'

'And they did?'

'They've been promised more coin.'

'To wait in halls?'

He heard the humour in her voice, but it didn't carry given her eyes kept closing.

'To guard your sister. We'll have some of our own outside my room. Come,' he said, clasping her wrist and escorting her to his room.

Bied didn't protest when Louve brought her to his room. The bed was large, the room thankfully private. Needing quiet, she'd been reluctant to return to the quarters where she slept with Tess and everyone.

Louve stayed silent as he dipped a linen in a basin and wrung out the water. Walking carefully over to her, he gently washed her face and neck. He gave her no words, simply a cool gentle touch. Then he did the same to himself with more brisk efficiency.

She didn't know how he liked to sleep, but she hadn't any spare strength to ask or to wait so she crawled into his bed and pulled the quilt over her.

Only a moment later it was lifted and Louve adjusted himself beside her. Less than that when his arm wrapped around her and pulled her close. She settled further in his arms, further into the soothing silence he created. It was as if he knew just how to care for her. She was exhausted, but her mind could not rest.

'I thought it was for us,' Bied said.

'What was for us?'

'The ale. When three goblets were handed out. You, me, Evrart and, somewhere upstairs, I imagined Margery was handed one as well.'

'You drank it anyway.'

'If Margery was drinking it, if you—' She didn't want to finish those thoughts. 'I was relieved it wasn't handed to Evrart—at least I kept my promise to my sister.'

She felt him rubbing his chin against the top of her head. Felt the pull of her hairs caught in his dark whiskers that were never completely gone no matter if he shaved. She loved that part of him. She loved… She was scared she loved him.

'I don't know what to say,' he said.

'I know.' She closed her eyes. 'This is the life you chose.'

'I might not have known the extent of this dark world, but, yes, I did volunteer.'

She adjusted herself to see a bit more of him. 'You told me of the danger, but a man was poisoned in front of so many and then…carried out like filthy rushes.'

'It is difficult to explain danger and I wish I could have protected you from all of it.'

'You're awfully good at it,' she said. 'Louve, I'm only here because my sister wrote me a rescue message. Even with this Evrart, I will continue to beg her to return home. To be done with it all. He can come, too.'

'I know.'

'Are you certain you only want a wife, peace and small plot of land?'

'I thought about the words you said. About the choices I've made and what I truly want.'

When it got quiet, she wondered if he'd fallen asleep. She knew he was as tired as she, that they only spoke because there was so much to say.

'You're right to have doubts. What I say I want and what I do are contradictory. But I still want those things… just differently than I thought.' He touched the small scar under her chin. 'A hot turnip, huh?'

Part of her wanted to keep talking, but the warmth and

security of the room was already lulling her. Words and thoughts were harder to form and there would be time to talk before she left. It seemed with Louve's abrupt subject change he felt the same.

'A turnip popped out of the boiling pot and landed all over me. It hurt.'

She felt him trace the small, thin scar there. Felt him wondering about her words and what he saw on her skin. 'Then I scrambled all over the place to get away from the offending vegetable and hit my chin on a table or chair or…something.'

His low chuckle vibrated through her as his finger continued to trace along her jawline. It felt…soothing, as did his body against hers. She was grateful she wasn't alone today; she was grateful it was him beside her.

Yawning, she adjusted the quilt some more. 'I think we need to talk about you and me.'

His finger stopped its caress. 'Is there an us?'

A warm bed, long legs for her icy feet. Her body begged for sleep. 'Did you mean those words you said to me in the Hall? The ones you said without sound?'

Long moments as he no doubt shifted throughout the entire day and she regretted her choice of words. She was so tired.

But when he eased against her back, when he gathered her more securely in his arms and brushed his jaw against her head in that caress she was beginning to crave, she knew he remembered the right words.

'Very much,' he said.

She knew what his answer would be. She did. It was in the way he gathered her in his arms now, the way he protected her as best he could. But even if she had feelings for him, where did that leave her or her family? They needed her to work. Margery's coin would stop now and, with Mabile's pregnancy, there would be difficult days ahead, especially since she needed to find work elsewhere.

Louve said his pursuits hadn't changed, only became different. How different could they be when he, too, had to work for coin? And Louve…he would be chasing after danger for ever, not peace.

Even if he managed a home, she could never stay in kitchens or till fields. It would be reliving her worst nightmare. Yet, Louve had been good to her and he deserved some answer. Even if the words were slurred and barely audible.

'I don't see how we can be together,' Bied replied, barely getting the words out before succumbing to sleep.

Chapter Twenty-Three

Bied woke, saw two slumberous eyes softly looking at her, yelled like a banshee and recoiled…violently.

Louve yelped, the quilt was flung into the air and she banged her arm into the wall so roughly it throbbed.

'What kind of perverse pleasure do you get sneaking up on me!' She was cradling her arm while Louve was laughing so hard, tears sprang from the corners of his eyes.

'I was sleeping next to you all night, at what point could I have sneaked up?'

She'd never slept with anyone overnight before. Oh, she'd had men and a night in various locations. A linen closet wasn't so odd given the multitude of occupations she'd had over the years, but laying in someone's arms for comfort…that was something entirely different.

'I don't know, you just did.'

'You're beautiful when you sleep,' he said, lying back on his side, his head propped up on one arm.

'There! I knew you were being devious,' she huffed. 'Watching me sleep.'

'Your lips look softer and the way they part makes a man wish you were awake.'

'If you say I snore, you will soon be finding a new room in which to sleep.'

He grabbed her calf and rubbed it. 'Threatening to take over my room, are you?'

Not if he kept doing that. His thumb was digging in a bit, making her leg and other bits feel altogether better. He gave her a knowing smile. Sly!

He wore a tunic covering the expanse of his chest which didn't seem entirely fair, so she tugged on the quilt some more to cover more of her and— 'You're naked.'

He smirked. 'I compromised since I usually don't sleep with anything.'

That image made her just want to stay in bed all day. With that thought alone, the world outside their room crashed within her again. He must have seen it on her expression because he stilled his hands on her calf.

'We should go,' she said.

He closed his eyes. When he opened them the humour was gone and a bit of that tragedy circled about.

'I know you came here to rescue Margery, but what if she doesn't want to go?'

'Where else can she stay? Evrart has no other home than here, and this place isn't safe. No matter how…big… he is, he can't protect her here when Balthus recovers. And who is to say Balthus will want her here, or the other Warstones? This isn't their home. And… I'm sorry.'

'No, I understand. I do. It's something I know all too much of. You remember my telling you how I managed another's estate?'

When she nodded, he continued, 'I was good at it, but… I always knew it wasn't mine and it didn't fit. It wasn't the home that I dreamed of sharing with a wife.'

'With Mary,' she said.

His hands on her leg jerked. 'Until you brought her up that day in the cellars, I hadn't thought of her in years, not in any true sense. It was…what she represented more than her that I wanted. I know that now.

'She wasn't you, Bied,' he said. 'I never told her I loved her, never asked her to marry me. In the end, she wasn't reckless enough for me. She'd…find a way to season my food.'

How could he make her want to laugh and cry at the same time? He started running his hand up and down her leg, the pressure gentle, possessive. Like an offering. If she wanted more, he'd give it, or he'd stay like this and take away the little aches and pains of the day.

His words both scared and warmed her. She already knew he didn't love Mary. Louve was too…he stayed with the people he loved. Cared for them until he was sacrificing his own soul to do so. She saw that when he threw the knife towards Ian to save Balthus, then when he cradled Ian afterwards.

No. When this man loved, he truly loved, and that's what frightened her because where did that leave them?

Even forgetting her own family responsibilities. He had great ones as well. Louve wasn't a Warstone, family, or in any sense an usher, and yet he had his own battles to fight. All this… Warstone intrigue, lies, murder. It seemed he'd been embroiled in it for years. And he was good at it. If she knew nothing else about him other than how he was yesterday in the Hall, she'd be terrified of him. But just that same day, she'd thrown linens at him. They'd *laughed*.

A man that adept at what he did didn't act like a man who wanted a land somewhere, a wife, peace.

'I don't want the kitchens, or seasoned food, or a plot of land that we have to work for every day.'

He laid her leg back on the bed. 'I kept that thought of a house, a home, a wife because I wanted something…that was mine. I've been that selfish and that naive.'

Not naive or selfish… Lonely. How could this man be alone?

'You have no family or siblings?'

He shook his head.

Her heart wanted to tell him she wanted him, that she'd be by his side, that... 'We should go,' she repeated.

'We have so many obstacles—I know there can be no... us, but why do I feel there's more separating you and me than what you're telling me?' he said. 'If there is any urgency, Evrart or Henry know to knock on our door. The healer and her two apprentices are with Balthus at all times. If he stirs, they'll notify me immediately. We've got time.'

She needed a bit more time to tell him about her family, her mother and father. He deserved to know, but she wasn't ready. After yesterday, everything felt too exposed within her.

'What happens now?' she asked. 'With everyone else?'

He exhaled. 'I'll need to talk to the priest about the burials. When Balthus wakes, he might want something different, but we don't know when that will be.'

She liked it that he talked as if Balthus waking was a certainty. 'What do you want?'

'Ian needs to be remembered for the good he's done. With no confession, the priest might fight me, but he will be buried on sacred ground here. I refuse to have him interned at his familial ancestral home. Those monsters do not deserve him.

'As for the Steward, he endangered this family. Loyalty or not, I'll leave his soul up to God.'

He lifted his eyes to hers. 'The guards and I have come to an understanding—as long as Balthus lives, I'll give the orders. None of them wants to do it and Evrart and the other men we paid have my back when tempers rise. Which is often since their work has almost doubled.

'In the meantime, the fortress and the protection of it will be...challenging, especially if the Warstones attack. And as you have already guessed, I like those challenges.'

'Those challenges aren't safe for my family.'

'I don't want any of you near them. At the end of the day, I am simply a mercenary who can't protect you from them. I know you want to leave with your sister, but right now, I can't promise safe passage.'

'I'll stay for a time, Louve, until Balthus wakes. I'll help with what you cannot do. That'll give some time to—'

The pounding on the door made them both jump. 'Louve,' Evrart called out. 'There's a message.'

Torment. The conversation with Evrart was rushed and quiet in the hallway revealed the message he'd sent to Reynold never made it.

Foolish of him to order it sent in daylight, the rider having no experience with subterfuge. Whoever Ian used as messengers didn't announce themselves either out of loyalty to the man he'd killed or knowing a messenger from this fortress wouldn't be welcome in Troyes.

Then he checked on Balthus, whose fever continued, then on to the chapel and Ian's rites, then to another fight, this one between his own men and Ian's. There were few glimpses of Bied. The entire day nothing but loss. He carried an ache in his chest that was all his fault. Too many regrets, too many choices he should have made. When he couldn't stand one more moment, when he couldn't wait until night fell, he sought out Bied, clasped her wrist, and pulled her into the linen room.

With the toes of their feet touching and nothing else, he said, 'Biedeluue.'

Her breath hitched. 'Louve.'

Her eyes, her hair, her words, everything about her a temptation. He didn't know what impulse it was to yank her in here, but the fact she stayed, the fact…he needed her.

So he kissed those lips like he should have done this

morning, kissed them again until they had to take a breath. He wanted more. He'd always want more.

'Hmm,' she said, brushing away a lock of his hair. 'You're all dusty.'

Because he had to strike down a perfectly good guard and now he had one less man for tonight's shift. He didn't want to talk of that.

'How is your sister?' he asked.

'You pulled me in here to talk?' she said.

All his thoughts scattered as his blood pooled low. He shouldn't, it would be all the harder to let her go when this was over. Bied's open expression and her words, though... Fisting the gown at her waist, he tugged her hips back and forth until she laughed.

'Are you sure?' he said, already a rasp to his voice as his thoughts turned to hearing more of that laugh. To claiming her.

'You can borrow me some more,' she teased.

'I do like the way these hips move, but... I want a bed under you.' He brushed her neck with multiple soft kisses. 'I want your gown off, your chemise off.' He leaned to the other side and grazed the column with his teeth. 'Then I want my clothes off.'

She laughed. 'Men always want their clothes off, and how are you so certain I'll give you a next time?'

This wasn't permanent. He knew she'd talked to her sister. They couldn't stay here. Even if Balthus had the best intentions and allowed them to stay, his focus wouldn't be on Bied or Margery. He couldn't want her to stay here and he didn't know where he'd be sent to next. There was no future with them together.

But they could have tonight. 'Because I know how to woo with words.'

'Perhaps you do.' Giving him a pointed look, she patted his chest. 'My sister is well, thank you. No guards, no Jeanne since she's returned to the kitchen. Thus, Margery's been exploring this fortress. She enjoys the gardens. I don't think she ever paid attention to the gardens at our village. Yesterday, she was in the kitchens moving items around, until Tess brandished a pot at her and ordered her out. Maybe she was imprisoned too long, because today she was giving instructions to the pantler on provisions.'

'How about you, with her?'

'She's…reluctant to go. Or at least to return home. Evrart has family that he's hoping are no longer under threat.' Bied frowned. 'She's different than the last time I saw her. Yet I can't help but think about what happened yesterday. She didn't witness it and maybe doesn't fully understand.'

How to tell her? 'I don't think your sister is as you remember. She didn't faint when we entered the room and she kept up with my odd questions.'

'I think you're right.' Bied rubbed her eyes. 'She wrote that message, but it wasn't so I'd rescue her, it was so she'd have help to rescue herself. She's stronger, isn't she? That first feast, she diverted Ian's attention away from me. *She* protected me.'

'Everyone needs help. I think she gained strength just by your troublesome, reckless self being here,' Louve said. 'And there's no doubting Evrart's regard for her.'

'I'm hardly trouble.' She flashed a smile. 'No, any man who is as large as he is attempting some foolish tale to cheer her far surpasses what I could hope for my sister.'

Bied's smile wobbled, her thoughts seemingly as plagued as his. He kept one hand anchored on her hip, another he trailed along the fascinating strained folds of her gown. It would be so easy to kiss her until they were both distracted. But he wanted to know her thoughts, to hear her burdens.

'Tess yelling would be a fearsome sight,' Louve said.

'I've never seen her lose her patience,' Bied said. 'Formidable, yes, but…she was terrified when she served us that ale. She knew it was poisoned. Ian's instructions to her were very specific, but when you grabbed both goblets instead of one, she didn't know what to do. She was no longer certain which goblets you took.'

Releasing his hold on Bied, he said, 'There were many deeds that day I'd change. Actions I'd take differently.'

So many times over the last few days, he could have changed the path they were on. Ian had warned him that years weren't a possibility. Told him that with his parents here, it would be up to him. Ian had practically announced he would do this. Louve had saved one brother, but sacrificed another—where was the justice?

'What is it?' she said, her eyes searching his. 'Has Balthus worsened? I haven't seen him since midday.'

She laid her palm on his cheek, he leaned into that warmth. He wanted her to share her burdens and, instead, he was giving her his. 'Yesterday, I sent a message to Reynold in Troyes. To tell of Ian's death and Balthus's accident. The messenger didn't arrive at Troyes, and didn't return here, but his horse did.'

Bied dropped her arm. All in a matter of a fortnight she was living in a nightmare, yet Louve had been living in it for years and he seemed torn telling her. This wasn't the life for her, or her family, but while she was here, while she could give support for Louve, she would.

'Tell me,' she said.

'I reported too much in the message,' Louve said, his voice bitter. 'I knew better. I didn't even code it. Thus, the elder Warstones know Ian is dead and Balthus is in grave condition. This entire day has been nothing but waiting for their attack.'

'But the guards will—'

'I only have a few men in our pay, the other guards are

loyal to Warstones—where do you think I've got these
new bruises from? They know I have no worth. When
Balthus wakes, I'll be no more or less than they are. And
I might be less when Reynold arrives and sees what I
have done.'

'Reynold? You saved Balthus's life!'

'By chopping off his hand and killing his other brother,'
he said. 'I had to send another missive to Reynold this
morning to tell him that. Those words were difficult to
write knowing I could be sending another messenger to
his death. And he knew it, too.'

Now it was her turn to not know what to say, or how
to comfort. Instead of being in bed where she could put
her arms around him, she could only stand and face him.

'They were brothers!' A choked sound escaped his lips.
'Family. Despite how much they hated each other, I don't
think any of them wished to kill each other and I was
standing there the entire time. I should have... I have
no family, no wife, no children, no parents or siblings. I
should have put myself between them.'

Bied slumped against the linen shelves. They bit into
her back, but it was nothing to the agony she witnessed
in front of her. How did they get here? From kisses, to
regrets. She wished they could be somewhere else and
not this linen room where at any moment someone could
interrupt them, yet when else were they to talk about it?

'You can't take responsibility over everything.'

'Reports the woman who came to rescue her sister.'

She deserved that. 'In my talks with Margery, it appears
I'm a bit overprotective of my grown siblings.'

'Not just your siblings, you launched yourself at Balthus. Ian's knife could have lodged itself in you!' He let
out some sound, then a curse. 'And you've been defending me, too.'

She might be willing to let her siblings free, but there

wasn't a chance she wouldn't protect this man. 'Louve, there's something I need to tell you about yesterday in the Hall.'

He slumped against the opposite wall and slid until his feet touched hers. 'Don't tell me more. I already have nightmares with your brave recklessness!'

She thought to tease him some more, but she needed to be brave a bit longer. 'When I...shoved Balthus, my gaze was towards Ian, so I watched the knife you threw.'

He bowed his head as if the effort was just too much. 'Why?'

'I was watching Ian because I didn't know what he would do and Ian moved.'

He raised his head. 'What are you saying?'

'He angled his body,' she said as clearly as she could, knowing she couldn't repeat it. 'At the last moment, he threw himself towards the dagger.'

Blue eyes dark with anguish. 'He said he was but a reed to a disloyal breeze.'

'What?'

'Ian's reason was slipping and he knew it. He also knew his mother was trying to kill him. All he had at the end was betrayal and I was the man who ensured it.'

'No! At the end, he said something about your promise.'

'He wanted me find his wife and sons, to apologise for him.' Louve rubbed his face. 'I lied to the priest about those words. I told him that Ian made a dying confession so he could be buried in sacred ground.'

Shoving away from the shelf, she cupped his jaw and rubbed away the few tears that had escaped. Strong arms wrapped around her and she rested her cheek against his chest.

'I didn't want to kill him,' Louve said, rubbing his chin along her head.

'I know. He was your...very odd friend with some good

in him. You were right to lie to the priest to bury him here. Ian was right to put his trust in you.'

Some of the tension in Louve's body eased. 'I kept thinking there was good in him and then he threw that dagger. It was instinct to throw mine.'

'There was good,' she said, looking back up at him. 'Margery told me what Ian said in his sleep. They were words about his wife and children. You said his reason was slipping, but he still loved them. Maybe he was worried about losing that last bit of good in him. Maybe he trusted you to help him.'

'I'm trying to comprehend what you're telling me,' he said. 'You believe he threw that dagger on purpose, knowing that I'd throw mine, so he could die?'

She paused, needing to tell Louve more while she could. Balthus could wake or die, but either way everything would change for them.

'Complicated, I know—maybe you're not the only one who is good at second-guessing Warstones and their games. And, yesterday can't all be about you. I'm not too certain I didn't make it worse for Balthus's hand when we crashed to the floor.'

His gaze softened. 'So that's what we've been doing the last few days, living with second-guesses and regret.'

'It appears so.'

'Bied, there's one thing I haven't regretted or second-guessed, and that's those words I said.'

That he loved her and her heart knew she loved him as well. Why else had she wanted to trust him when he told her he'd rescue her sister? Why else stand next to him in the Hall, and worry about Balthus? Why else did she lie with him in the vilest of kitchens? And when he pulled her into this foolish room, why did she want to just stare until her heart was full of the sight of him?

There was love between them, but there were also burdens. Legends and gems, and parchment. They were both homeless and needed to earn their coin.

And even if they could scrape enough up to have some little place somewhere, she was certain she couldn't go down the path of her mother. Of just waiting to be abandoned or…

No, in that Louve would be different. She hardly remembered her father, but if they had a house and home, Louve wouldn't leave. He wasn't weak. But…a home where they'd till land and bake bread would just bring back all the memories of leering, pawing men, and…she'd have to tell him what she'd done to secure their home. It would break her.

No, she loved him, and as such she had to let him go.

'I have to provide for my family and you have to play those games and where will that take you?'

His eyes! One moment of pain, of vulnerability, but something she said…hurt him.

Then with a growl and a predatory gleam, he said. 'The games take me nowhere tonight and I'm still thinking about that bed.'

Going to sleep with his arms around her, of seizing any last moments together? She grabbed his wrist. 'Let's go.'

Chapter Twenty-Four

'You're awake.' Rubbing the sleep from his eyes, Louve entered Balthus's room. It was dark outside, but morning was coming. He'd barely heard the healer's soft knock on their door and Bied hadn't heard it at all so he left her to her rest. She'd gone to bed mere hours ago.

'I wish I wasn't,' Balthus said, his words groggy.

'We'll disagree for ever on that one.' Louve sat at the chair nearby. 'I'll be returning that missive you wrote before the hunt. The one that tells Reynold the regrettable years as brothers you lost and the sincere regard you have for him.'

A corner of Balthus's lip curved. 'You didn't read it.'

'Because it was sealed? That only encouraged me.'

More of a smile. 'No, because that isn't what I told my brother.'

Games! Louve cursed.

Balthus laughed, choked, and Louve grabbed the cup on the table, filled it with watered wine and brought it to Balthus's lips until he eased his head on the pillow.

'I understand the healers have been giving you all they can for pain,' Louve said. 'I'd hoped you would have slept longer.'

'The pain is just a bit more...' Balthus faded. 'This

cursed strap and quilt won't let me see. My hand is gone, isn't it?'

'Don't force it,' Louve said. 'Your arm's been secured to the post so you wouldn't accidentally damage it in your sleep.'

'Well, now that you're here—' Balthus pointed his chin to the strap '—release me.'

'You didn't tell me how bad it was,' Louve said. 'We didn't get to it in time.'

'We've been hiding lots of deeds from each other,' Balthus said, fighting the bindings that held his arm to the bed.

'Stop trying to move your arm, and this is different!' Louve said. 'You should have seen a healer.'

'It sounds…' Balthus said. 'You care?'

Louve took two breaths; he'd had enough of Warstones.

'I had seen a healer,' Balthus said, his voice gruff. 'At my family home. I continued to apply the clean linens and poultice given to me. There wasn't any one in Troyes.'

Because they'd barely arrived in Troyes when Balthus and he had been sent out again. 'Ian has one.'

'You know I couldn't see Ian's healer, at least not while Ian…' Balthus swallowed. 'It was bad when mother first burned it, and it seemed to heal. I must have damaged it again between Troyes and now, and her breaking the—I need to see it.'

Louve wanted to fight the order, but if he had been in Balthus's position, he would have demanded the same. He unlashed the arm and cradled it in both his hands. 'It'll look worse than… Ian's dagger hit the same arm, which is why the wrapping is excessive. But though you fainted, that cut was superficial.'

'I do not faint,' Balthus bit out.

Louve attempted to jest, but his words were flat. He

knew why—there was one point he wanted Balthus to understand.

'It was my sword.' Louve faced Balthus and waited for the accusations and hatred he deserved. He had taken moments to sharpen and clean his weapon of any fragments. The strike cut clean and the healer immediately responded. Still, he was the one who did the deed.

Balthus's expression didn't change. 'Stop being a coward and lift it.'

Huffing out a breath, Louve brought the left arm into Balthus's field of vision. It was wrapped in fresh linens to his shoulder. Blood seeped in places and the poultice caused brown stains, but there was no mistaking that his limb ended too abruptly. That—

'You, too?' Balthus said.

Balthus was looking over his shoulder. Louve turned and saw Bied leaning against the door, tears streaming down her face.

'I'm so sorry,' she said, moving into the room, and wiping her cheeks. Her hair was unbound, her gown hastily pulled over her chemise…her feet were bare. She'd gotten little sleep since Ian was buried, but she was more beautiful now than ever.

Louve held his arm as Balthus slowly lowered his gaze. The youngest Warstone's body shuddered as if with a blow. There were no words of comfort. He could tell Balthus how fortunate he'd only lost the hand above the wrist, and not the entire arm, but it didn't matter.

'I shouldn't have hit you that way,' Bied said.

'What?' Balthus said, his breaths mere pants as he rotated the amputated limb in Louve's hold.

'I shoved you and, when you fell, your hand slammed, and the impact made it worse.'

Balthus lowered his arm, his gaze taking in Louve, then Bied.

'Are you both blaming yourselves for this?' Balthus's eyes threaded with bewilderment. 'I knew I was going to lose it, though I stubbornly attempted to take care. My mother broke that finger just before Ian's attack. I could feel something then... I was standing there conversing with my brother, knowing our mother's action had completed the damage. I couldn't react quickly enough.'

'Still—' she said.

'You couldn't have pushed me more gently out of harm's way.'

Bied's brows rose. 'I wish I could have done *something*.'

'You did,' Balthus said. 'Both of you saved my life.'

'When you're well, I expect your rage,' Louve said.

'Why? Because of my hand, or because you threw the dagger that killed my brother? I saw you throw—I saw what Ian did. This fighting begins and ends with my parents. And that is all.' Balthus's eyes shone for just a moment before he blinked. 'When I am well, I expect to best you in training and gloat.'

Balthus's words eased some of the tightness in Louve's chest. So many factors, but he never meant it to end the way it did. 'For that coward comment, I'll race you on horseback.'

Balthus eyed him. 'Since I've known you, no one has beaten you in a race. You'd purposefully set up a one-handed man?'

Louve merely raised one brow. 'Afraid?'

Balthus laughed, coughed and Louve grabbed the cup for him to take a drink.

Bied took a step and laid her palm on Balthus's forehead. 'You still have a fever. I'll send the healer in to tend to your needs before you rest.'

'I feel as though I have been resting—how long?'

'Eight days. Sometimes you'd wake, but wouldn't stay that way for long,' Louve said.

Days where he and Bied had reached some compromise where they touched more and talked less. She hadn't told him she loved him, though he swore he felt caring in her touch, in their soft words. But what did he know? No woman had ever loved him and perhaps this one never would as well.

Could he blame her? He had coin, but no home. He had ways of making more coin, of obtaining a home, but the life of a mercenary would take him far away from any family life. She had a family she needed to care for and…there was just too much danger with no certainty to protect her. He might tell her he loved her, because he did, and after what he'd witnessed in that Hall he wanted to tell her every day for all the days they had left, but he could never demand she do the same.

Why would he want her to suffer the pain he did?

'You need to know we've had all the guards on shorter rotations to stay alert and I sent a message to Reynold—he'll be here soon,' Louve said.

'He can't…' Balthus said. 'He can't come here.'

Louve scoffed. 'Reynold will do what he wants, as you well know.'

'But our parents are travelling—there will be traps everywhere.' Balthus inhaled sharply. 'Do they know Ian is gone?'

'The first messenger I sent out with the missive didn't arrive. His horse wandered back.' Louve bared his teeth. 'They know. I have sent out many of your men since then to track your family. They won't surprise me like that again.'

'My men?' Balthus said.

'This fortress is no longer Ian's.'

Balthus clenched his eyes.

'Do you need some tisane?' Bied said.

'Two brothers gone,' Balthus whispered.

Bied looked to Louve. 'He had to, to protect you. If Louve hadn't released that blade, I would have.'

Balthus whipped his gaze to hers. 'Again, you think I'd blame you? I don't understand either one of you. Is this what ordinary families are like?'

'Where we worry about feelings and showing loyalty and caring?' Louve laughed low, his heart full of Bied's fierce protectiveness of him. 'Welcome to our side.'

'I don't know if I'd want it, it's too complicated.' Balthus closed his eyes.

'You should rest,' Bied said.

'Eight days of rest, just a bit more,' Balthus said, but at Bied's expression Balthus softened his stance. 'If I may.'

'Make it quick,' she agreed.

Balthus cocked his head as though Bied was someone he couldn't comprehend; Louve was very familiar with that feeling.

'You didn't, by chance, find the parchment?' Balthus said.

'I have turned every stone, pried open floorboards and opened every box. Your brother had some good hiding places, and beautiful trinkets, but no parchment. It is likely true it is with Ian's wife and children.'

'Who are probably no longer in France,' Balthus said.

'I'll need to find them,' Louve said. 'I told Ian I would.'

Balthus's laugh was thin. 'If my dear sister-in-law has hidden, do you think she'll want to be found?'

'There's no one else to—'

'When I'm healed, I'll leave,' Balthus said. 'Remember, I still need to prove my deeds. Lying here and healing is hardly a test of my loyalty.'

'Your brother wanted to apologise to them. He had wanted to be a better husband.'

Balthus eyes dimmed. 'Then that's a message best coming from a Warstone since there's much we have to apologise for. It's been years, but she might recognise me. It's settled, then?'

All Louve had to do was wonder if Ian would have accepted Balthus finding his wife and sons. In his heart Louve knew he would, because it would mean a brother hadn't betrayed him.

Louve gave a curt nod, and Balthus closed his eyes, drawing in a shaky breath.

'Do you need anything?' Louve whispered low.

Balthus gave a shake to his head. 'I'm relieved to be handing this monstrosity over to you. In truth, I hate this place, but if we don't keep control my parents will seize this fortress before you expel your last breath.'

'Wait—' Louve said.

Bied gasped.

Balthus's eyes sharpened on her.

'You can't grant me this,' Louve said.

'True, missives will need to be sent to both Kings and recordings will have to be archived, but after that it's yours.'

'It's a Warstone fortress,' Louve said. There were numerous reasons why he didn't want this—it being a Warstone holding and prone to attacks was only one of the reasons. The other was Bied. Although...

Balthus's eyes grew heavy. 'Wasn't it you who bantered about a property and peace and all that? Who will protest? Reynold? Not likely.'

'What am I to do with this?' Louve said.

Balthus blinked, his eyes taking on a look Louve didn't expect. Softer. *Regretful.* 'You must. Unless they can be appeased, and they will never be appeased, you have made terrible enemies of my parents. I will tell them what has occurred, that you saved one life for another, but...one parent will demand retribution.'

Beside him, Bied choked back a cry. 'Balthus, of course he'll—'

'I need to think about this,' Louve interrupted. He would not be swayed until he conversed with Bied. 'Give me time.'

Bied waved her arm around. 'For what?'

'I think you two need to converse.' Balthus snorted, then purposefully closed his eyes. 'I can't believe I just suggested a discussion. This side truly is fraught with peril.'

Chapter Twenty-Five

'Where did you come from?' Bied said. 'You're drenched!'

Louve closed the door behind him, his eyes greedy for this woman sitting on the edge of the bed. One of her legs dangled over and she was dressed in a generous chemise, with her hair unbound and a comb in hand. He was so grateful it was the end of another day, the demands were put to rest, and he could be in the modest room with her again.

After they had left Balthus's room that morning, Evrart and Tess were waiting for them in the hallway. Louve didn't want to part from Bied. Not after Balthus's proposition, not after that spike of fear he saw in her eyes. He wasn't done with her yet.

'I went to the tanners who wanted new tools. I was only there for one conversation, but couldn't bear to go anywhere else except the lake afterwards.'

'The lake! That's outside the walls and it must have been horribly cold.' She canted her head to the side and ran the comb through her hair. 'I hope you took someone with you.'

She was always beautiful to him, but especially when she was protective. It warmed him that she gave some of her fierceness to him.

'Henry.' He pulled off his tunic and threw it in the corner where it splattered. 'But he stank far worse than I since I made him enter the building for inspection.'

'Henry wouldn't know which end of the sword to hold.' She pointed the comb at the far wall. 'One of those chests has some linens. I can't remember which one. If you can't find it, I'll have to check supplies tomorrow.'

Tasks. Duties. It'd been this way for days since the Warstones' visit. This day, however, was different. Balthus said the fortress could be his. Separated from Bied, he'd spent the day thinking about it. The benefits and the dangers. The burdens and... Bied.

Curious. Louve had looked into the ledgers, only to find them abysmal. It appeared the Steward had been stealing for years from the Warstones, but there was no information on where the coin had gone.

If he had to guess, it went to the paid knight, the Englishman, Sir Richard Howe, to support his campaigns to secure the Jewell of Kings for the Warstones. But Ian had seemed genuinely surprised he had brought him up. Where Howe received his coin from then would need to be investigated. Was it possible Ian's wife had taken it from Ian?

Too many threads to follow up on in the games played. Too many messengers and enquiries to send out. There was enough to do in this fortress alone. Mei Solis, the estate he'd taken care of for years, was large, but this hold was enormous. The tenants would take him months to know. But now that he'd met the Warstones he understood full well why Reynold fought his parents. Those two could never gain more power and wealth.

This fortress, if he could bring it under control, would set back their plans. It would be difficult, though. Some of the guards continued their undisciplined behaviour. There were a few who'd changed their ways and who'd stopped treating the servers like part of the feast, but many still defied his orders.

The possibilities…but only if Bied stayed. Did she like it here?

Over the last few days, he'd never found her in the kitchens with her head over a pot. Instead she was encouraging an apprentice cook and rearranging others with their roles throughout the house. Cook, or rather he should be called Mathew, was often in the winter garden with Margery and the priest who was agitated over their plans for spring planting. There were more disputes, more learning and fewer accomplishments, but he could see why Bied repositioned people. It would just take time. Would she stay? He would not force her. Her heart was so generous, and already Margery might be persuaded to stay. She could sway Bied and yet…he wanted it to be her decision.

One he wondered about, for she still did not voice her feelings over him. This time with her felt easy, natural could she love him some day?

He rolled down his breeches along with his braies and threw them in the same direction. Knowing he was fully naked and that she'd be watching, he strolled slowly to the far wall to begin the search for linens to dry off. He heard her exhale before she got off the bed, grabbed one of his dry tunics and tossed it to him.

'We need to talk and I can't do that if you're all…' She swirled her comb at him.

Clutching the tunic to his side so as not to impede her view, he said, 'Bending and stretching over locked—'

'Don't say it. Don't!' she said. 'I know you're not the dark growly type and light and humour are more you, but truly you can be too much.'

'If you despise it, why are you laughing?' He pulled the tunic over his head, just for her sensibilities, and since he knew where the linens were, he flipped open the chest and grabbed a small cloth.

'If tomorrow you can't find your things, just remember this conversation.'

'I'm simply pleased you believe I'm appealing.' He smirked. 'As for my clothing... I'll merely do what you did and wear someone else's which is too tight for me.'

'That was not me! Tess grabbed Bess's gown. Oh, I can't even say that sentence!' she said. 'I'll figure out something to do with your clothing and you're only giving me ideas.'

'What will you do with it?' He dragged the linen through his hair. 'Tie my tunics to the rafters? Hide my shoes in the kitchen's cast-iron pots?'

At her gaping, he laughed. 'You'll have to be devious when it comes to me.'

Pointing the comb at him, she said, 'Oh, you truly should not have said that.'

'Why is it me you seek retribution from when I was the injured party? You wearing that tight gown all day caused my breeches to be too ti—'

'Out!' Wiping eyes sheening with laughter, she declared, 'Take all those wet things out, you!'

Chuckling, he scooped up his clothes and wrapped them in the damp linens and opened the door. A few quick words with the guards and the door was closed again.

When Louve turned, the mirth from Bied's face was gone, her expression one he'd hoped to delay. 'What are those thoughts in that mind of yours?'

'Balthus is awake.' She set the comb in her lap.

At her simple words, the dancing light in his eyes dimmed and Louve took a step back to lean against the wall opposite the bed.

She knew why he did it. The chairs were off near the chests and to converse with her he'd have to sit on the bed next to her. A part of her was relieved he didn't. This conversation would be difficult enough.

'I thank you for staying until he was. I could not have accomplished as much if you had not been here.' He gave a slight smile. 'I was right about you.'

'You're never right about me.'

'In this I was. When I first saw you with that foolish goblet game and all the servants rallied behind you, playing along in the middle of the day in flagrant abuse of supplies and duties, I said to myself that I would use you if I could.'

'Well, that was a nice thought,' she said as drily as she could, though she knew she couldn't quite keep a stern expression.

'It was one of my more cunning thoughts to ally myself with such a clever woman.'

'You do like to woo with words,' she said, knowing her cheeks were now flushed with the compliment.

He frowned. 'What we share here had nothing to do with the games.'

She stretched and tossed the comb onto the table. 'Oh, I know. I think if we could have avoided the entanglement in a linen room we would have.'

He looked sharply to the side, and exhaled roughly as if she…as if she gutted him. Did he think she didn't want him? No, he was so confident in everything, and absolutely glorious, any woman would want him. Except that foolish Mary and… Why was she even contemplating this?

'Why did you tell him you'd think about the fortress?' she said. 'Hadn't you told me that all you ever wanted was a home? Well, this is quite the shelter.'

He looked down at his feet, swallowed and looked up at her. What was in his eyes…

'What do you want, Bied? I've said what I wanted

enough, though the finer bits are different as I said, but ultimately, it's the same.'

'What do I want?' she said.

'I know you wanted to rescue your sister, but now what? Why do I get the impression that, even if I handed you everything—coin for your family, a place for them all to live, why does my soul tell me you'd still say no?'

He looked down, then back up. 'I love you, Bied, and at this point I'll do anything you want if it would just make the difference between having you in my life and not, but even if I did, I still feel you won't accept me.'

How was any woman to resist him? Biedeluue knew she couldn't and hadn't been since the moment she looked into his eyes. 'Accept you? I love you. How could I not?'

Two steps and he was before her. 'Those words, yet still you hesitate. Why?'

'It's my family,' she said. How could her heart pound this hard and not escape?

Was it him because he stood as still as any man, yet she could feel his body vibrate with the need to sweep her off the bed…or keep her very firmly on it?

Was it her? Could it be her heart trying to escape the pain in her past, or did it fear telling him would change his opinion of her?

Or…was her heart trying to reach him because it knew it would be safe?

How she wished she knew the answer to that before she had to go through voicing her agony. But he needed to know, and it was time to tell him.

Slowly he took a step, another, and gently sat on the bed, so close she could be wrapped in his arms. She knew he wanted her there, could see the wary joy in his eyes at her telling him that she cared for him, but he was also far enough away not to scare her.

How could this man know the inner workings of her heart?

'Margery's here with Evrart,' he said, his voice calm, soothing almost. 'Your mother, your brothers and sister, with all her daughters, are welcome. You'd never have to work in the kitchens or the fields. You could rearrange everyone's positions until I'm the garderobe cleaner. Anything. Is it the games?'

She shook her head. 'This is a fortress, Louve, how could we not be safe?'

'You know the answer to that. There will always be plots and danger here. I'll always have to—'

'No,' she interrupted. 'Remember how you said I took it all so easily? That I'm able to contribute and make suggestions? I might like the games as well. I may not always like the results, however, but I understand why they must be played.'

'Then what?'

'It's difficult for me to have… How could all my worries for them be solved so easily?' It was unfathomable.

'Oh, we have conflicts to overcome, Bied.' He gave her a look. 'But I won't be distracted again. Tell me.'

'My hesitations on any of this begin with Margery. Her birth was difficult, and my mother's health was never the same. She tilled what she could, fed us if there was anything more after tenancy fees, but it wasn't possible for her to do it all, so when we could, we helped.

'Matters became harder and my father… I was angry at him for so long and consequently every man I've met since. I harshly judged your entire gender for his weakness of leaving a wife and five children who needed him.'

'Bied, I would never—'

She laid a hand on his arm. 'You're different. You stay. You…grab my wrist to keep me by you.'

'If I could keep you permanently at my side, I would,'

he said, then he dipped his chin in that way he had. 'And I like grabbing your wrists and also your—'

She hit his arm. 'Don't say it. Just don't.'

'Hand! I was going to say your hand.'

As if she was fooled.

'Bied, tell me of you, please.'

'It's difficult.' She took her hand off his arm and clasped both hands in her lap.

'I'm beginning to understand that,' he said.

'I am the eldest, so I helped with everything that needed it. Nothing of this is anything unusual in any home. Servet and Isnard helped with the fields, Mabile with Margery, but what was unusual was Margery.'

Louve adjusted on the bed. Bied felt a moment where she wanted to start kissing him right on the scar under his left eye and never stop, never say a word more of her ugly past. His eyes dropped to her lips and back up as if he, too, knew the directions of her thoughts. She had to do this.

'There we were, my father left us, my mother weak, becoming more broken as the years went on, Margery becoming more beautiful. We worked well together, though. Then the rains came late, or winter arrived early, I can't remember how the true difficulty began.

'That's when the neighbours came by to offer help, but what they truly wanted was Margery.'

'How old was she, then?'

'Eight, perhaps. I feared some of them wouldn't wait until she came of age. Thus, for their generosity to use an ox, or to help in the fields some afternoon…they had me.'

He clasped her hands then, waited a heartbeat, two. She was grateful for those beats, the fact he just sat with her and didn't move her hands to his lap, but kept them in hers.

She'd seen so much of this man, his patience, his determination, but the quiet strength he gave her when the world was just too much…that was another reason why she loved him.

'Did you not have any other family, or some leniency from taxes, or villagers? I ask not because of the choice you made, Bied, but because I hate to think you were alone.'

She released one of her hands and covered his. 'I know no other family and I told you how the other neighbours stole her when she was an infant just to hold her for a while. I think they all hated and coveted her.'

'She's the youngest,' he said. 'How old were you when she was eight?'

'Thirteen or fourteen when the neighbour approached me about using his ox and the price.'

His hand flinched. 'Does he still live?'

'Louve,' she said. What did he think he would do? 'I don't often return to the village and, when I do, I don't stay long.'

'I don't want you there ever again. There's no making this…right. My first feeling is to—' Louve shook his head. 'Even what I want to do in my thoughts isn't enough.'

'Don't,' she said. 'I hated that time. My father leaving broke my mother and the work did the rest. Since then I have done everything I can to avoid it, but I wouldn't change what I did. What happened to me, I did for my family and I haven't had to make those choices since.'

'I'm beginning to understand why you avoid the outside…and the inside,' he said.

'I worked and worked and worked…and it still wasn't enough. Still they came for me, then they came for her. I was gone from the village when a nobleman rode through and saw her. I knew we couldn't keep her, that eventually she would have a husband and children. My brother said that the man was older, kind, and my sister has never spoken of it. I'd always assumed she did it for herself, though. But knowing she's been helping, I now wonder if she didn't…if she didn't sacrifice for us, like I did.

'Mother broken by a man was enough, I don't want anyone else I love to—'

He upturned her hands and began to trace along the curves of her palms.

'No kitchens, no fields, no husband…and here we are.'

'I knew no other men other than my father and our neighbours. Only those who shirked their responsibility or took advantage. And after travelling from one village to the other, I saw the same.'

'That's why you asked me about taxes.'

She blushed, glanced away. 'I would never ask that of you now. But I wasn't certain at first. You told me Mary was a widow and men…'

He wouldn't, couldn't, take her words to heart, but he did. Patience, he reminded himself; she'd been through so much. 'Nicholas's request for taxes was so lenient his estate fell apart and he left to become a mercenary to earn the coin himself. There are some men who are different.'

'Like the Warstones,' she said.

He blinked. 'That's not the direction I thought this conversation would go.'

'I know, but I think we need to talk of them now.'

'I don't want them anywhere in this room.'

'I think I understand why you stay with them. There's good in them, isn't there? I saw it in Balthus's eyes when you got so angry at him for not telling you of the extent of his injury. They don't know love or family, do they?' When he shook his head, she continued, 'I can see why you care for them now. His parents, though…'

'Bied, are you saying you'll stay here? Is that why you're bringing them up? If you want me to, I will accept this fortress, but that means we could be under siege tomorrow, or your family would be at risk or… I can't let them win. Not after that woman broke his finger or damaged Ian so—'

She placed her hand on his mouth. 'I think we both might share in that overprotectiveness. I know you told me of the danger. What I witnessed in that Hall was far beyond anything I could imagine or that I could ever want for me or my family, but it's you, isn't it?'

'I thought I wanted peace, but you're right,' he said. 'I kept pursuing danger and gained skills navigating it, and there's too much at stake for me to walk away. I can't, I won't leave it.'

'I don't want you to walk away. I understand it, I'll just…throw more linens and shove people out of danger in the future,' she said. 'It will be nothing new—I always came to the rescue of my family and I couldn't stay in one position for very long before I caused trouble. I don't think I was meant for much peace.

'Moreover, you've already given up on everything else you wanted. Living with danger and ridding the world of those parents would be worth it.'

'Giving up on what I want? Ried, you are all—'

'This fortress and land aren't some small plot somewhere. And that biddable wife?'

He dipped his chin. 'That certainly isn't you. I have no idea who will cook my food, or till my fields.'

'Not me, never…that is, if it's me you still want,' she said.

'You think anything you told me changed how I feel for you?'

She smiled, knowing her heart was wise to choose him. 'For the briefest, tiniest of moments. I never…shared what happened with me with anyone. But now that I have—'

'Feel better?'

Blinking back the tears that threatened to mar the sight of her seeing this glorious man, she nodded. 'I know you are not my father, or like those men in the village. I never wanted a husband, but if I did, he'd be you.'

He grabbed her wrist and her smile became a grin.

'So you get everything you ever wanted, but I don't, yet how could I be so happy?' he said. 'My life will be full of trouble, recklessness—'

'Don't forget how I'll torture you with Bess's gowns that are entirely too small.'

He groaned. 'I can't believe your friend thought that was a good choice.'

'Just wait until I get Tess to help me. You'll wish I would only put thistles in your braies.'

When that light hit his eyes, the one he got when he was about to kiss her, she laid a hand on his chest. 'I…may be pregnant.' she blurted. 'I've been careful before. Not that that is any certainty, but we haven't been careful at all.'

His eyes held no disquiet, just more of that calmness and strength. Around her wrist, she felt that little tug that told her he was about to pull her onto his lap. 'This worries you?'

'In the past, I was relieved when I wasn't, but, no, it doesn't worry me with you,' she said. 'Would it worry you, if I couldn't?'

'There's children here with no parents because Ian had no regard for the lives of his guards. That little red-haired boy…'

'Thomas,' she said.

'Could be part of our family.' He flashed a grin. 'I am not worried whether we have children of our own or we have to permanently borrow ten children or more.'

'Ten!'

'I can't see us with any fewer…given we're both overly protective.'

'So,' she said, 'we live in this fortress with my family and at least ten children. All while we're under siege, se-

curing legends and battling between kingdoms. Sounds…
complicated. We could simply pack our bags and sneak
out of here. You haven't given Balthus your agreement.
Maybe we could live in inns the rest of our lives and have
other people bring us food.'

Her trying to hold back a grin and look serious was
what broke Louve's laughter and he gathered her close,
holding her as he wanted to the moment she'd nervously
told him she loved him.

If it was difficult for her to tell him, it was thrice as
hard for him to hear the words he'd ached for from her.

'Leave all this danger behind us?' he said. 'How could
you give up dodging arrows…or turnips?'

'Don't! I know, there will be hardship ahead, but there
can be laughter now.'

Balthus would recover. Ian was dead and his parents
would want revenge. Somewhere a legend needed to be
captured and hidden again. In the meantime, he'd protect
this woman and her family, and the large family they'd
grow.

He rubbed her back. 'There can be laughter. For in-
stance, your travelling idea was humorous.'

She eyed him, already guessing he was jesting, already
thinking of how to best him. 'No, it wasn't.'

'When you travel, you have to rest. And there won't be
an inn for miles who would take us.'

Bied grabbed a pillow. 'Because of our laughter, because we'll talk too much with words that make no sense?'

Eyeing that pillow which she held like a weapon, Louve
pretended to give merit to her argument. 'Perhaps, but I
think it'll be for something else.'

'Because we'll have ten children and be far too bois-
terous.'

'There could be ten of us, or…twenty,' he said, loving
how her eyes widened, 'but that still won't be the reason.'

She narrowed her eyes. Partly in play, partly because she was becoming full of that ire he liked. 'Because you don't have enough coin to pay for rooms?'

'You know better than that.'

'Why, then?' She raised the pillow a bit higher, all the more ready to throw it at him. 'Why would no inn take us?'

'Because they'll fear for their goblets!' He laughed.

Bied threw the pillow over her shoulder and kissed him instead.

* * * * *

If you enjoyed this story, be sure to read
the previous books in Nicole Locke's
Lovers and Legends miniseries

The Knight's Broken Promise
Her Enemy Highlander
The Highland Laird's Bride
In Debt to the Enemy Lord
The Knight's Scarred Maiden
Her Christmas Knight
Reclaimed by the Knight
Her Dark Knight's Redemption
Captured by Her Enemy Knight